Pride & PROTECTION

K.C. WELLS

Chapter One

Late October 2017

"That's the last one," Jon said, wiping his brow with his hand as he dumped a large box just inside the front door. "Do I get my beer now?"

Del Walters snorted. "Seeing as I carried most of 'em, I think *I'm* the one who deserves the beer." His back ached like a son of a bitch, but that was nothing a long soak in the tub wouldn't cure. And he knew just the tub for the job, snuggled into a corner with windows on both sides, and nothing but green beyond them.

Maybe this won't be so bad. Except Del knew he was kidding himself. Sure, it was a great house, the only one he'd viewed that had made him want to put in an offer *right then and there,* so no one else got their hands on it. But the house was just somewhere to rest his head, somewhere he'd have to sell pretty swiftly if this venture went tits up.

And let's be honest here. That's a distinct possibility.

"You okay, bro?" Jon was regarding him intently, his eyes full of concern. "I mean, you're not regrettin'—"

"You hush," Del admonished him. "We talked about this, remember? And you didn't have to twist my arm all that much, right?"

Jon's furrowed brow told Del he wasn't buying it. "I know, but—"

"But nothing." Del wiped his forehead with his bandanna. "If we're gonna make a go of this, then we have to think positively. There's no room for doubts. Right?" He waited until Jon's shoulders relaxed. "Besides, think of all that fog I won't be missing." He smiled.

Jon's returning smile was faint, but definitely there. "Sure. Although I don't think the gay bar in Knoxville will hold a candle to any bar in the Castro. Not to mention all those restaurants you loved, the clubs, the—"

"Jon." Del kept his tone low and even. "It was my decision to move here, right?" Christ, he *knew* this would happen. Jon was a born worrier. "Knoxville will do just fine. And if it doesn't, there's always Atlanta." He grinned. "Who knows? LaFollette might prove to be a seething hotbed of closeted guys forming a line to get in my bed."

Jon stared at him for a moment, his eyes wide, then promptly erupted into raucous laughter. He wiped his eyes. "Jesus, Del, *warn* me next time you wanna say something like that. I almost barfed up a lung."

Del cackled. "I take it I'm deluding myself?" Not that he didn't already know what to expect. Jon had been honest on that front. It didn't matter anyway. Del wasn't thinking about hooking up with anyone, not when he was still raw from—

You said you weren't gonna think about him, remember? Not that he was surprised. Lane was slippery enough to worm his way into Del's thoughts in a heartbeat. Del gave himself a quick mental smack upside the head. There were more important things to think about, like the new business. Jon had done all the groundwork, and the market was there. All they had to do was hook their new clients and reel 'em in.

In theory.

"I think you're crazy. Certifiable." Jon huffed. "Not that I didn't *know* that already. One look at that sign you had made for the shop was all the proof I needed."

"What's wrong with it?" Del asked, feigning innocence. "I didn't hear you saying, 'no no no' when I came up with it."

"That's 'cause I didn't realize you were serious!" Jon rolled his eyes. "I mean, come *on*, Del. 'Rainbow Racers'? Here?" He snorted, sounding uncannily like Del. "Why not go the whole hog and just put up a sign that says 'Hey y'all! I'm gay. Now come on down an' bring your pitchforks an' brandin' irons.'"

Del winced. "Ouch." He peered at Jon. "What worries me is that I can't tell if you mean all that. D'you *really* think the sign will be bad for business? Because now's the time to tell me. We don't open for a week or two. I can always change it." He tensed a little, awaiting Jon's response.

Jon rolled out a heavy sigh. "There wouldn't even *be* a business without you, bro. And a deal's a deal. Your money, your say on how we run it." He gave a half-smile. "Besides, everywhere you look these days, there are rainbows, right? The sign doesn't *have* to mean that, right? Doesn't mean they're gonna take one look at you and scream 'Homo', now does it? Because hell, you sure don't *look* gay."

Del snickered. "Not sure if that was a compliment or an insult."

Jon blinked. "Oh puh-*lease*. Look at you. You're built like a fucking mountain. You got that full-on gray beard going for you. You got a belly on ya." He gestured toward Del. "There is *nothing* about this picture that says 'gay'."

Del let out a chuckle. "Lord, I can tell *you've* never set foot in San Francisco during the Folsom Street Fair." When Jon frowned, Del waved his hand. "Just a few thousand guys who look like me, and all of them as queer as a three-dollar bill."

"There are gonna be two of us working in the shop," Jon said quietly. "So as long as you don't…" He clammed up.

"Don't what?" Del was intrigued.

Jon rolled his eyes again. "As long as you don't go acting all *gay*, we'll be fine."

Del stared at him. "And what, may I ask, constitutes 'acting all gay'?"

"Do I have to spell it out? Flirting with the guys, for one thing. Getting all LGBTQ activist for another. I know what you're like, and LaFollette is *not* the town for that shit, believe me."

Del speared him with a look. "Fine. I won't flirt. I'll keep the conversations away from politics." He tensed his shoulders. "But I will *not* go back into the closet. Not for you. Not for anyone. You hear me?"

Jon swallowed. "I wouldn't ask you to. You have *no* idea how fucking proud I am of you, of how you've never hidden who you are, not even when we were kids. I'm just… concerned, is all. You've been living in California. LaFollette is *nothing* like California, and I don't want to see you get hurt."

Del flung his bandanna onto a nearby box, took three strides across the room, and enveloped his brother in a firm hug. "I know," he whispered. "Love you, bro."

Jon wrapped his arms around Del, his cheek pressed against Del's. "Love you too." He released him, took a step back and smiled. "You're helping make my dream come true."

Del patted him on the shoulder. "How about that beer?"

Jon's eyes lit up. "*Now* you're talking." He tilted his head to one side. "It *is* cold, right?"

"Does the Pope shit in the woods?" Del asked with a grin. "Dude, it was the first thing I did this morning when we got here. I made sure the refrigerator was switched on and working, then I filled it with brewskis. Gotta get your priorities right."

"Amen to that." Jon headed for the kitchen.

Del stood in the middle of the wide space, gazing at the chaos surrounding him. It would take him a week to get the place how he wanted it, but at least the bed was put together, there was beer in the refrigerator, and pizza at the other end of a phone call. Anything else was gravy.

"Wanna go up to the observation deck?" he called out to Jon. "It's pleasant outside this evening." The temperature had reached seventy-five degrees by midday, and the air was still warm.

"Sure." Jon walked over to him, a beer in each hand. "This really is a great house. Reminds me of a lighthouse."

Del laughed. "Funny. That was why I bought it. It reminded me of a lighthouse I'd seen up the coast from Provincetown." The house by the lake was spread over three levels, but it wasn't huge: the second level loft only had room for two futon chairs and two ottomans. And the spiral staircase up the middle of the house was surely a space-saving device. The two bedrooms and bathrooms were on the main floor, but there was a queen-sized futon up on the observation deck. Del could already imagine sleeping up there on summer evenings, the windows open, the sheets thrown back to let the night air cool his naked body.

Maybe two naked bodies? He could dream, right?

Then Del pushed aside such thoughts. Sex would have to wait.

They had a business to launch.

"Right. Time I was outta here." Jon tossed the cans into the recycling bin, then peered at the boxes. "You gonna make a start on this lot?"

Del snickered. "I think getting everything into the house was quite enough for one day." He'd return the U-Haul in the morning.

Jon chuckled. "Yeah, right. I know you. I give it ten minutes before you're opening a box and unpacking it." He grabbed his jacket from the rack beside the double front doors.

Del opened them for him. "Well, that's where you're wrong. I'm going to take a stroll down to the lake."

"You mean, Big Creek, don'tcha?" Jon laughed. "Why not? It's a lovely night. I, on the other hand, am gonna go back to my house and my cat."

Del laid a hand on Jon's shoulder. "No regrets about moving here?"

"Nope. I wanted someplace small and rural. LaFollette has that in spades. It's taken me a while to get used to living here though. Maybe a year to realize the folks around here aren't rednecks—they just talk that way." He bit his lip. "Well, most of 'em aren't rednecks. There *are* some exceptions."

"Aren't there always?" Del grinned. "Besides, I hate to tell ya, but folks around here sound just like the folks back home in South Carolina. At least to my ear."

Jon gave him an inquiring glance. "What about you? Sure you got no regrets?"

Del let out a low growl. "Dude, I just drove over two and a half thousand miles to be here. You don't do that on a whim, okay?" He'd taken four days to drive across the country, straight through Nevada, the north of Utah, the south of Wyoming, right through the middle of Nebraska and Missouri, heading down to Tennessee. Then one day of nothing but sleep to recover from it, before he'd even considered moving his shit into the house.

Finally, it was done. He was in.

He patted Jon on the back. "Go home to your cat. She'll be yowling for her supper."

Jon huffed. "That cat has plenty of food. And if she gets hungry, she can always catch herself a hot mouse for supper. That's why I keep her, right?"

Del said nothing. He'd watched Delilah from across the living room the previous night. She didn't look like she could catch a thing, she was so fat.

He waved Jon off as he backed out of the driveway and onto the dirt track that called itself Lake Drive Lane. *Lane, my ass. The damn road has delusions of grandeur.* When the sound of Jon's truck faded into the distance, Del pulled his own jacket from its hook, locked the front door after him, and walked around the side of the house toward the trees at the rear of the property. It was only a short stroll before he reached the water's edge, and he stood there for a moment, gazing out over the still surface. It was six-thirty, and the sun had almost set. The expanse of sky above his head was a collision of reds and golds, the clouds seeming like they were on fire. The light was reflected in the water, giving it the appearance of molten metal.

God, this is beautiful.

Del took a moment to breathe. After a week of upheaval, he

was more than ready to get his life back on an even keel. Except he knew that wouldn't be for a while yet. They had the premises to sort out, ready for the grand opening. That meant a couple of weeks of making sure all the stock was there: the bikes; the accessories; and the information on local trails…

I hope to God this works.

When Jon had first approached him with the idea, Del had reacted with an initial fit of laughter. When he'd gotten more under control, Del saw the idea with more enthusiasm. He'd only just sold his company, and was thinking about a new challenge, so the timing was perfect. What was less than perfect was the location.

Del didn't doubt for a second that they could make a go of this venture. At forty-six, he'd built up and sold off enough enterprises that he knew what he was doing, and Jon was more than happy to follow his lead. And he was more than ready for a move. As much as he loved San Francisco, lately it had begun to lose its luster. Gentrification, rising rents, politics…. It had all added to the push Del needed to say yes when Jon asked him to help realize his dream. It was only the location that gave him pause.

Of all the places to choose, why the hell did he choose Tennessee?

Del's initial visit hadn't put him off. Jon had taken him on the trails and there were enough of them to convince Del that this might work really well. Competition was non-existent, and they had enough capital between them to cater for all tastes, from basic trail bikes to top-of-the-line trikes. The premises had a workshop attached, which was perfect, and Del certainly had the skills to fix anything that came through those doors. Sure, they might need an extra pair of hands to keep the sales area and workshop clean, but that was fine: they planned to hire someone young and local, and train him or her.

Still…. Fucking Tennessee. *Not* the most LGBT-friendly of places. Thank God Atlanta wasn't that far away. Del could already hear the siren call of its gay bars and restaurants. He planned to escape there once a month and decompress.

That whole 'don't act all gay' part of the conversation still irritated him, however. *As if I'd do anything to jeopardize the business*. Del was no fool. Even if he could find things that fit, he wasn't about to mince along Central Avenue in heels and a pair of tight silver shorts, waving a rainbow flag. He might as well paint a red target on his back with a sign saying Shoot Me.

Besides, who'd want to see *his* hairy ass sticking out of a pair of booty shorts?

Del bid a silent good night to the lake, turned his back on it, and walked slowly back to his new home. He knew what would happen when he got there. In spite of his protestations to Jon, the tug of those boxes demanding to be unpacked would prove too strong to ignore.

Sleep is for the weak anyway.

Chapter Two

"Christ, are you out of your fucking *mind*?"

Well, I thought he'd be quicker than this. Del had figured it would take Jon all of five minutes to notice the new sign. As it was, it had been there a whole day. Not that Del had any intention of leaving it in the window. He was just messing with Jon's head, sort of payback for the 'don't act too gay' comment that still rankled.

"Is there a problem?" he asked in as innocent a tone as he could muster.

"Problem?" Jon marched into the shop and pointed in the direction of the offending sign. "Hell, this business will be dead in the water before we even open the doors." He gaped at Del. "I thought we talked about this."

Sighing, Del went over to the window and removed the hand-painted sign he'd seen in a store on Castro Street before he left San Francisco. "I guess 'Love is Love' is a little more in your face than you had in mind?" He bit his lip.

Jon narrowed his gaze. "This was a joke, wasn't it? 'Specially after I mentioned the shop sign."

Del snorted. "Course it was a joke. I was never gonna leave it there. Mind you, it did take you a damn sight longer to see it than I'd anticipated." Judging from Jon's grave expression, however, his brother didn't share his sense of humor. "Come on, bro. It's down now."

Jon folded his arms across his chest. "Sure. Great. And in the meantime, how many people do you think saw it? Hmm? The damage could already have been done." He shook his head. "You had to do it, right? Lord, why did I ever think this would work?

You are gonna drive me crazy."

Del put down the sign and went over to him, laying his hand on Jon's arm. "Now, you listen to me. You asked me in on this because of the two of us, I'm the one with a head for business. We'll be nice and not mention your past efforts."

"Yeah, thanks for that," Jon muttered.

"So this is what's going to happen. I will do as you ask. I will tone down 'the gay'," he air-quoted. "And we will give this business everything we've got. When we've made it a success, you can buy me out. It'll be all yours." And Del would be outta there.

Jon blinked. "Seriously?"

Del nodded. "By then, I figure, this business will be so successful that you couldn't kill it even if you tried. Not to mention, I'll have trained someone up to work alongside you."

There was that narrowed gaze again. "You mean, someone to babysit me?"

Del patted his arm. "You came up with this plan. You did all the groundwork. But we both know that part has never been a problem for you. It's what you do once the sign says 'Open' that—"

"Yeah, yeah, all right, I get the point," Jon grumbled. "Seriously though? You'd sell me your share?"

Del knew exactly what was going through Jon's mind. Jon would always have Del's back, Del knew that, but he also knew that the probability of them working peacefully together was pretty slim: they were simply so different. At least this way, Jon could almost glimpse the light at the end of the tunnel.

Del too, for that matter.

He cupped Jon's nape. "You watch. We'll have this business turnin' a profit in no time, then you can stop worryin' about what I'm gonna say or do next." Jon's startled blink told Del he'd nailed it. He reached over to the counter and handed Jon the plastic-covered sheet of paper. "Here. Stick this in the window."

Jon perused it. "Are you running the same ad in the papers?"

Del shook his head. "I figure anyone with an interest in bikes is gonna be up here at some point, checking us out. I'll take the guy—or gal—who gets off their butt and makes the effort to see what we've got, over the one who sees an ad in the paper, any day."

"And what are you gonna do with that sign?" Jon glared at it.

Del laughed. "Relax. It's coming home with me. Anyone who gets past *my* front door isn't likely to be offended by it."

Jon snorted. "Hell, the way *you* talk, anyone who gets invited to your house won't be there to look at the decoration." He grinned. "Unless you put it on your bedroom ceiling. You know, along with the mirrors?" He snickered.

Del stroked his beard. "Now *there's* an idea." He laughed. "Come on, you. We've got work to do. We have a grand opening next week. Tuesday. Remember?"

And Del intended for it to be a big deal in LaFollette.

If there was a positive side to living in LaFollette, this was it.

Del took off his crash helmet, placed it on the trike's seat, and looked out over the town. He was on the Tank Springs trail, and the view from up there was breathtaking. The fall colors were magnificent, a canopy of oranges, reds and browns, as far as he could see. Beyond them lay the town, spread out in a thin line.

This was the right thing to do. He'd had enough of arranging bikes, getting the workshop ready, and putting up posters on every flat surface available to him to announce the opening. He'd needed some fresh air, and taking one of the trikes for a trial run had seemed the best plan. The cloud cover could have been less, but even so, the sun continued to peep through. He estimated the temperature at a very pleasant sixty degrees, not bad for the tail end of October. Of course, the rains got heavier, right around the corner in December, so he was making the most of it.

"You're the first person I've ever met up here."

Del gave a start, and turned to see who was intruding on his solitude. Any thoughts of blasting them for giving him such a fright, died the second he laid eyes on the guy with the dark blond buzz cut, standing beside a bicycle. *Yum.* The younger man was maybe in his mid-twenties, lean and just the right height for Del. Right age, too.

What made it even better? Del had been around the block enough times to know he was being checked out. Yup, there was definite interest in those pale brown eyes.

Things were looking up.

Del gave a laid-back smile. "And it's my first visit up here too. I was just admiring the view." Which had improved about a thousand percent. The guy wore a cycling top that swelled in all the right places over his chest and biceps, clinging to his abs, and as for those shorts… Black fabric hugged his toned thighs, molding itself around the guy's not-so-subtle package.

Better and better.

The guy's eyes gleamed. "Me too." When Del widened his smile, he pointed to Del's trike. "That's some set of wheels."

"Sure is. He's a Harley Davidson Tri Glide Ultra."

The guy smiled. "I'd heard bikes are usually female."

Del grinned. "Not when I'm riding."

Oh Lord. The guy swallowed, and that bob of his Adam's apple drew Del's attention to his neck. The skin there was the same golden tan as his face, which was covered with blond stubble. Inside, Del was grinning. *Come to Daddy. You* know *you wanna.* The guy couldn't have made it more obvious, short of rubbing his crotch.

Maybe he's shy. Maybe he needs a hint.

Del didn't go in for subtlety.

He patted the trike's seat. "Speaking of which, wanna come for a ride?"

The guy blinked. "Excuse me?"

"I rent out these babies—well, I *will* be, once the business is officially open. I can't let you take it out on your own, but… there's a passenger seat if you wanna hop on and see what it can do." Del crossed his heart. "I promise not to go too fast."

Fuck, the way the guy worried his lip with his teeth... *Hoo boy, do I wanna take you for a ride.* Inside his leathers, Del's cock was granite.

The guy laughed. "Do you always offer complete strangers a ride?"

Grinning, Del strode over to him, his hand outstretched. "Del Walters. Always happy to meet a fellow rider." He resisted the urge to lick his lips.

The guy bent over to drop his helmet to the ground next to the cycle, and Del took a good, hard look. *This day can't get any better.* Then the guy straightened, his own hand extended. "Taylor Cox. Not that there's any comparison between my mountain bike and that beast *you're* ridin'." They shook, before Taylor took a step back. "How long have you been in Tennessee?"

Del snorted. "Long enough that 'y'all' is starting to sound like everybody says it."

Taylor snickered. "Well, duh. That's because everybody does." Both of them laughed at that.

"I suppose it *is* pretty obvious I'm not a native to these parts."

Taylor bit his lip again, and Del groaned internally. "Just a little." Taylor cocked his head to one side. "I'd hazard a guess at... the west coast?"

"Give that man a cee-gar." What Del wouldn't give for one, right at that moment.

"So, how are you finding us so far?" That gleam in Taylor's eyes? Hell no, Del was not imagining *that.*

"Let's just say I'm taking my time. Getting to know a few locals would be a bonus." *Starting with you, sweetheart.*

Taylor stilled. "You have a bike shop? Whereabouts?"

"Up on Central Avenue. You might have seen the fliers. The grand opening is next week." Del upped the wattage on that smile. "Why don't you come along? It's gonna be fun. Then maybe we can arrange an official test drive." Except he wasn't thinking about bikes.

Del wanted to test drive Taylor's tight ass. All. Night. Long.

"Central Avenue? The shop's in LaFollette?"

Del got the impression he'd just said the wrong thing. "Yeah. You can't miss the sign."

Taylor nodded slowly. "Rainbow Racers."

Yeah, Del had said the wrong thing all right. *Well, fuck.* Except something didn't add up. There had been no mistaking the way Taylor had looked at him. *Like he wanted to lick the leathers right off of me.*

Before he could utter a word, Taylor reached down for his helmet. "Sorry, but I've gotta run. Just remembered something I was s'pposed to do."

"Sure." Del pasted on a bright smile, but inside he was gutted. *You can't get away fast enough, can you?* "Maybe I'll see you around town?"

"Maybe." Taylor's tone was noncommittal. "Good to meet ya. And welcome to LaFollette." With that, he put on his helmet, fastened it securely, then swung his leg over the bar and pedaled away.

Del stared after him, trying to analyze the brief conversation. It had started heading downhill when he'd mentioned working in LaFollette. Obviously not some random guy passing through then. The real dip had been the mention of the shop by name.

So either he's a hater who's seen the sign, put two and two together, and whose little brain is currently screaming 'There be a Homo in LaFollette!' or...

The *or* was more interesting.

He's gay or bi, and right now his little brain is screaming at him that he might just possibly have outed himself, and he's diving back into his closet.

Del knew which notion he was leaning toward, which presented all kinds of possibilities. There was only one way to deal with haters, and that was ignore them until they overstepped the mark, then hit them with the full force of the law—or whatever that amounted to in a small town in the south.

But a closeted guy?

That could prove to be very entertaining.

Not to mention, a challenge.

Chapter Three

"You got any plans for tonight?" Officer Mark Teagle leered at Taylor as they signed out. Friday night loomed, not that Taylor had much to get excited about. At least he was off duty.

Behind Mark, Ethan Dyer snorted. "Yeah, Mark, an' we all know what *you* mean by plans." He gave Taylor a friendly wink. "Wanna bet Mark's bedpost is just a mess of notches? That *is* where you keep score, ain't it, Mark? Of all your 'conquests'?" he air-quoted. Ethan was on duty that night, along with Dale Abernathy and three or four other officers.

Mark gave him a withering glance in the mirror as he combed his hair, taking his time as usual. "An' how would you know? As if I'd let you within two feet of *my* bed."

"What's that supposed to mean?" Ethan asked good-naturedly.

Taylor knew what was coming. It wasn't the first time Ethan had ended up in Mark's firing line.

Mark turned slowly to face him, his eyes gleaming. "I *mean*, a guy your age, with no steady girlfriend to speak of, who don't date? In *my* book, that all adds up to one type of guy—"

"Like any of us are interested in what's in *your* book, Teagle," Lieutenant Larry Purdy said with a smirk as he entered the squad room. "And for the record, there is *nothing* wrong with being single and not dating." He leveled a hard stare at Mark, who paled.

"Wasn't talkin' 'bout *you*, Lieutenant."

"Course not. You wouldn't badmouth a fellow officer, would you, Teagle?" Larry's face was a picture of innocence.

Taylor silently cheered him on. Mark was a toxic little pus-bag at times, usually when neither the Chief, the Captain, or the Lieutenant were in earshot. It didn't take much effort to figure out Mark thought Ethan was gay, not that hearing him voice such a thing would've come as a surprise: Mark was an easy hater to spot.

What concerned Taylor were the ones who kept such thoughts to themselves.

"And don't you go worrying about Cox's plans for this evening." Larry grinned. "He's not going to be getting up to anything he shouldn't—not if he likes his balls where they are."

Aw crap. He had to go an' say that, didn't he?

That was all it took to have the guys grinning at him.

"Woo hoo. Dinner with the Chief *again*?" Ethan waggled his eyebrows. "Remember now, no playin' footsie with the chief's little girl."

"An' if you do, wait till he's watchin' TV or somethin'," Mark suggested. There was that leer again. "But I guess you've gotten past first base by now." He sniffed the air. "Can you guys smell something? It's… it's…" He beamed. "I got it. It's that brown shit on Taylor's nose. Gee, wonder where that came from?"

Taylor took it all with good grace, smiling and laughing right along with them. It was common knowledge he'd been over for dinner on several occasions, and no one asked why: they didn't need to. The chief had a daughter, and in a town like LaFollette, female, twenty-two, and single added up to only one thing—a daddy desperate not to have an old maid on his hands.

"I'm sure Taylor will be the perfect gentleman," Larry said, flashing his white teeth. Then he speared Mark with a look. "It's not as if *you'll* ever get your feet under the Chief's table."

"Only if the Chief's got a real hankerin' to be a grandpa," Ethan said with a snicker. He gave Mark a sideways glance. "How many kids you got so far? You aimin' to have yourself a football team by the time you're thirty?" More snickers from Taylor, Larry, and Dale Abernathy who'd just entered the room and was standing by the counter, smirking.

Mark drew himself up to his full height of five feet seven and aimed a frosty glare at Ethan. "So what if I've got a few kids? Just goes to prove I'm a real man." He cupped his package.

Ethan rolled his eyes. "Puh-lease. It just goes to prove you ain't got the sense to cover up, you moron."

"And if you're a real man, what does that make the rest of us?" Dale asked, clearly amused. "In my book, a *real* man doesn't parade his inability to use protection like it was a virtue. What makes it worse is you're a serving police officer who denies paternity and doesn't pay a cent in child support."

"Just 'cause they *say* I'm the father, don't make it so," Mark retorted.

"We all done for the day or what?" Chief of Police Frank Tillerson stood in the doorway, arms folded across his broad chest. "Last time I looked, there were thirteen officers working in this department, and five officers standing around chewing the fat." He arched his eyebrows. "In *my* book, that's five guys who need to quit their jawing and do some work." He aimed a look at Taylor. "And some of you have places to be, right?"

"Yes, sir." Taylor gave a nod to his co-workers, picked up his bag, and headed to his car. He had an hour or so before he was expected for dinner. Just enough time to get home, shower off the day, and change into something casual. He'd already picked up a bunch of flowers to give to Mrs. Tillerson—his momma would pitch a fit if she learned he'd turned up with empty hands—and they were in the trunk.

He drove automatically through the streets toward his small house, his mind not on his driving, but on the evening to come. Another evening of chicken and mashed potatoes, or fish pie, or whatever else was on the menu. Another meal where he'd be polite, laugh at the chief's stories, answer Mrs. Tillerson's questions, and exchange brief conversations with Denise. Not that he didn't like her—they just didn't seem to have that much in common. But during every meal, Taylor was conscious of the glances between the chief and his wife, not to mention the thoughtful, kinda hopeful way the chief regarded him, and it always filled his heart with dread.

Sorry, Chief, but this is not *gonna go the way you think it is.*

What he hoped more than anything, was that Denise wasn't getting the wrong idea too. Taylor was always careful not to be overly friendly, or to say anything that might be construed as an invitation to… more. So far, he felt he'd pulled it off, but despite the apparent lack of progress between him and Denise, the chief showed no signs of letting up on the dinner invitations.

Of course, Taylor knew how to put a stop to those. He just wasn't about to do it. So that meant more weekend trips to Atlanta, where at least he was safe from prying eyes.

Yeah, right. And who had he run into, his last visit to Atlanta? Only his friend, Jake Greenwood, and a bunch of Jake's friends. What were the odds? Never mind the irony—Taylor's first crush had been on Jake's brother Caleb, who was dead, God rest his soul. But that weekend had been pretty momentous for one reason—he'd come out to Jake and his friend Liam.

Okay, so it wasn't as horrendous as he'd thought it would be. Then again, Jake was a friend—a gay friend. Easy to come out when you know you're not gonna get your head bashed in for it. It didn't mean he had any intention of letting anyone *else* in LaFollette into his secret. And it wasn't as if anyone in town had turned his head, even slightly.

Only that wasn't true, was it?

There he was again, at the forefront of Taylor's mind. That hunk of a guy in leathers, up on the trail. Just thinking about the way he filled those leathers sent shivers down Taylor's spine, his blood pumping in a certain direction, and his heart doing a happy dance. This wasn't a case of mild attraction. Hell no. This was insta-lust, pure and simple.

Pure? Not so much.

Fuck, he ticked all of Taylor's boxes, some of which he never knew he had until that moment. An honest-to-goodness bear, with a broad chest, thick, muscled upper arms, a beard that was mostly gray, with a smattering of brown, and blue eyes that seemed to see *everything,* right down to Taylor's bones.

Right through those tight-as-fuck cycling shorts to his thickening dick, *that* was for sure.

It was great when Taylor had this… feeling that not only might the guy—Del, *that* was his name—be gay, but that the attraction might be mutual.

It had gone to hell when he realized Del was no stranger passing through, but an inhabitant of LaFollette. That changed everything.

Once Taylor had returned home from his ride that day, he'd slipped into a paralyzing spiral of analysis. *What did I say to him? Was I obvious? It wasn't as if I came on to him or anything. Did I?* Then he reconsidered. He'd known *exactly* what he was doing when he bent down to drop his helmet to the ground, presenting Del with the picture of his ass in tight cycling shorts. It had to be the most flirtatious thing Taylor had ever done in his life, and it was probably going to backfire on him spectacularly.

Because Del was an unknown quantity.

It didn't matter if Del was gay, straight, bi… Del could out him in a heartbeat.

This is what I get for letting my dick do the thinking.

Taylor pulled into his driveway and switched off the engine, staring morosely at his front door. *And* this *is why I'm having dinner with the Chief.* The ribbing and snickering from his co-workers didn't matter. He could put up with all of that crap, if it meant he gave everyone the impression of being a nice, straight boy.

The only thing was, how long would he have to keep on doing it?

"We'll clear the table, Mama," Denise informed her mom. "You an' Daddy go watch that movie you were talkin' about."

The chief cocked his head to one side. "You gonna stay and watch it with us, Taylor? You're welcome to."

Shit. That was a new one.

Before Taylor could answer, Denise laughed. "I don't think that's Taylor's kind of movie, Daddy. I'll make you some of your favorite popcorn, how 'bout that? Taylor an' me, we'll talk in the kitchen." She inclined her head toward the table, and Taylor got the hint. Together, they cleared away the dishes, silverware and glasses, carrying them into the kitchen. Once inside, Denise deposited them beside the sink, went back to the door, pulled it to almost shut, and listened.

Taylor didn't know what to make of her. This was *not* how dinners generally went in the Tillerson household. Usually, it was a case of sitting around the dining table, enduring the agony of what felt like an interrogation—or an interview.

"Okay," she announced with a smile. "The TV's on. That's *them* taken care of for a while." Gently, she closed the door.

Taylor's heartbeat sped up. *What the hell?* He did *not* like the way things were going.

Denise arched her eyebrows, so like her daddy. "Well? What are you waitin' for? There's soap in the cabinet under the sink. Those dishes won't wash themselves." She narrowed her gaze. "You *can* wash dishes, right?"

In spite of his apprehension, Taylor snorted. "Well, duh." He got on with his task, running hot water into the sink. Denise joined him. It was then that he noticed the dishwasher.

"Never mind that," she said with a wave of her hand. "If they walk in here for something, we're doin' something useful." Denise leaned against the sink cabinet. "In the meantime, we're gonna have a little talk."

Taylor *definitely* didn't like how this evening was progressing. "You got a topic in mind?" he asked, doing his best to keep his voice even.

"Oh yeah." Denise brushed her long brown hair away from her face and gazed at him intently. "You've been comin' here for dinner for several months now, and I am *still* tryin' to work you out."

"What's to work out?" Taylor said lightly. "Your daddy is my boss. He says come have dinner, I come. Simple as that."

"Oh, that part I get. What I want to know is *why* you keep comin'." That intense gaze didn't waver.

For one awful moment, Taylor felt naked, like she could see right through to the heart of him—the decidedly *gay* heart of him. His stomach clenched, and sweat popped out on his brow.

And through it all, that scrutiny did not falter.

"So I guess it comes down to two things. Are you doing this to suck up to my daddy—or do you just not want to hurt his feelings? Because I get the distinct impression you do *not* wanna be here."

Damn. I guess I overdid it. Taylor cleared his throat. "What gives you that idea?"

She opened her eyes wide. "You are obviously *not* here due to any interest in me. That much I can tell." Her eyes glittered. "Besides, you haven't once made a move on me. Not even so much as a slap on my ass."

He blinked. "As if I'd do that!"

Denise laughed. "No, you wouldn't. Others would, however. An' before we go any further, I feel it only fair to let you off the hook."

"Excuse me?" This conversation was taking a bewildering turn.

She grinned. "I'm not interested in you either. But as long as my daddy keeps invitin' you, it gets him off my back. I am *so* sick of the 'when are you gonna find yourself a husb—boyfriend?' routine."

Relief washed through him in a surging tide. "I see." Taylor thrust his clammy hands into the hot water and got on with his task.

"Now, I'm not stupid," Denise continued. "I see how things work in this town if you happen to be female. If you're not married and pregnant by the time you're twenty, that's pretty much it.

You're done." She sighed. "And if you're not remotely interested in havin' a husband or kids, there must be something wrong with you."

Taylor paused. "What do *you* want out of life?"

Her smile had a sad quality to it that made his heart ache. "I want to study. To go to college. But… my mama and daddy think that's for boys. Girls get to stay at home, keep house, and bring up kids."

Which only reinforced Taylor's fears about the Chief. This was *not* a man who would be happy to have an openly gay officer in his department. So what if there was in Knoxville? That was Knoxville, not LaFollette.

"It's just occurred to me that there's a third reason why you keep on comin' here." Denise regarded him thoughtfully. "What works for me, works for you too, especially if folks think you're here to see *me*, not keep my daddy sweet."

"I don't know what you mean." Taylor's heart hammered.

Her lips twitched. "Taylor, all those times you've come to dinner, an' sat across from me… have you any idea how many times I've caught you lookin' at my tits? Not once. Now, either you are *superbly* good at not gettin' caught, or… my tits just don't do it for ya." There was no hiding her smirk. "Granted, they're not the best LaFollette has to offer—Trina Barron wins that prize, hands down, but then again, she's been winning that ever since middle school. But mine are not bad." Her gaze met his. "I guess it doesn't matter what they look like if you're not into tits—or girls…"

Holy hell in a handcart.

Taylor's throat seized up. His pulse was rapid, and his head spun.

Denise let out a sigh. "Damn me and my intuition." She put a hand to his shoulder. "Breathe, Taylor. You're safe. Honest."

He leaned on the sink, taking deep breaths. Her reaction wasn't what he'd expected. Denise rubbed his back in slow circles, the motion soothing, and eventually he got himself under control again.

Denise leaned in close. "Not everyone in this town is a bigot. Some of us were brought up to have an open mind. Which is something to think about for the future." When he gave her an inquiring glance, she shrugged. "So what if my daddy gives speeches for the Boy Scouts of America? Don't assume to know what's in a man's heart—or how he'll react. He might just surprise you." She cocked her head toward the door, dropped her arm, and reached for a drying plate as the door opened. Taylor twisted to look over his shoulder.

"I'm sure something was said about popcorn." The chief's eyes gleamed. "Especially if we have any of that caramel popcorn left."

Denise laughed. "I'll take a look. We won't be long."

"We? You staying, Taylor?" That look in his eyes...

Taylor smiled. "Sure. I'd love to."

The chief beamed. "Great." Then he disappeared from view.

"Thanks for that," Denise said softly.

"Still feels wrong, like I'm leading him on."

She shook her head. "You're not. You're just giving him more time to get to know you, that's all. And he won't be mad when he knows you haven't hurt me." She nudged his arm. "Now let's finish this, so we can go watch some chase movie." She rolled her eyes. "That they've both seen maybe a hundred times, and will probably fall asleep during. Personally, I give 'em half an hour."

"That's okay. More popcorn for us." Taylor had to admit, Denise's pragmatic approach went a long way to quell his fears.

Maybe telling the chief wouldn't be so bad.

Not that Taylor had any intention of telling him just yet.

Chapter Four

Friday, November 3

"Del? We got company."

Del jerked his head up from his task of polishing the trike and peered toward the glass door. A young man stood outside, nose pressed against the shop glass as he stared inside. Del looked him up and down. Not scrawny, with arms that had some definition to them, and a mop of curly hair. Then Del saw what stood behind the kid, and he grinned. "Well, look at that."

He got up from the workshop floor, strode across to the door and yanked it open. "That yours?" he asked, pointing to the motorcycle.

The kid beamed. "Sure is."

Del circled the bike, taking in the gleaming steel, faded, worn leather seat and the immaculate burgundy-and-cream paint job. "You've taken good care of her."

"She belonged to my granddaddy." The kid's voice quavered. "He left her to me, and I promised I'd keep her lookin' as good as new." He chuckled. "Well, maybe not *that* good, but I'm tryin'."

Del straightened and folded his arms. "What do you know about her?"

"She's a 1965 Triumph T120C. My granddaddy called her his Bonneville Scrambler."

"Did he ever race her?"

The kid's face lit up. "Sure! Before I was born, of course."

"Well, you sure as shit aren't here to sell her, so now we've gotten the important stuff out of the way—admiring the bike—how about you tell me your name and why you're here?" There were two days to go until the opening.

"The name's Chaz Monroe." The kid pulled himself up straight. "I see you're lookin' for help." He inclined his head toward the sign in the window. "Thought I'd maybe apply for the job."

Del got a good feeling about Chaz. "Well then, you'd best come inside and we'll have a chat." He gestured to the main door and waited until Chaz was inside before following him. Del pointed to the office doorway where Jon stood, watching the proceedings. "We'll go in there. Jon, could you find us a couple of Cokes?"

"Sure thing." Jon stood aside for them to enter, then left them alone.

Del indicated one of the two chairs facing his desk. "Take a seat. My name's Del Walters, by the way. How old are you, Chaz?"

"Seventeen."

"You live with your folks?"

"Yeah, but…" Chaz studied Del's desk. "I'm lookin' to move out, soon as I can."

Something in his voice and manner told Del to back away from that topic.

"Who taught you so much about bikes?"

Chaz jerked his head up, his smile back in evidence. "Me. I watched videos on YouTube. You can find most stuff on there. Plus, I saved up all the money I made from mowin' lawns an' makin' deliveries for the local convenience store. That way, I could buy the parts I needed. Not that I needed many. When my granddaddy passed, my grandma said I could have whatever I wanted from the outbuildin' where he kept the Triumph."

"Is that what you do? Gardening and deliveries?"

"No, sir. That's on top of my day job. My daddy owns a coffee shop in town. Some days I'm behind the counter, others I'm servin' the customers."

"Let me guess. It don't pay all that well."

Chaz huffed. "Not enough for me to afford a place of my

own."

Which explained why he wanted the job.

"How did you do at school?" Del wanted someone with some smarts about them. There would be more to this job than cleaning up the workshop and working on bikes. He was looking for a protégé.

"Finished top of my class," Chaz said with a half-smile. "Not that it mattered: I was always gonna work for my daddy."

Del sighed internally. In a different place, in different circumstances, Chaz would have been a cinch for college.

Jon appeared in the doorway, carrying two cans. "We don't have glasses."

"That's okay," Del told him. "We don't have a coffee machine yet, or cups, or a water cooler. That's on today's To Do list. They all need picking up." He gave Jon a meaningful stare.

Jon coughed. "Guess I'd better go get 'em then." He placed the cans on the desk and grabbed the keys to the truck. "Back soon." And with that, he left them alone.

Del indicated Jon with a nod of his head. "That's my brother, Jon. You'd be working with both of us."

"Seems like a good point to ask what the job would be." Chaz opened his can and took a drink.

Del had to agree. For the next five minutes, he ran through his view for the position, from initial duties to training to work alongside Jon. "I need to take on someone who's prepared to work hard and stick with it. The workload will increase, but then so will the pay."

Chaz regarded him with wide eyes. "Whoa. And there was me, thinkin' I was applyin' to sweep up an' be general gofer."

Del narrowed his gaze. "Too much for you?"

Chaz grinned. "Nope. Sounds perfect." He cocked his head to one side. "That is, if I've got the job."

Yeah, Del got a really good feeling about Chaz.

He stuck out his hand. "It's yours. But I'm gonna suggest we have a trial period of say, six months? If things are going well by then, we carry on. That way, if you change your mind and decide it's not for you…"

Chaz stroked his chin. "Let's see. Getting paid to work on bikes." His smile lit up his eyes as he shook Del's hand. "Sounds like heaven to me."

Del laughed as he pulled open a desk drawer and removed a generic application form. "Put your contact details on here, and I'll get a contract drawn up." He handed Chez the form and a pen, then sat back to enjoy his Coke.

"Can I ask you something?" Chaz seemed almost hesitant.

"Fire away."

"You had a sign in your window a while back. A colorful one, with the words Love is Love."

The skin on the back of Del's neck prickled. "That's right." His senses were suddenly on alert. "What about it?" *Well fuck*. He could almost hear Jon yelling 'I told you so.' What concerned him was the motivation for Chaz's remark.

"Oh, nothing. I just noticed it, is all." Chaz got on with his form filling.

This was *not* something Del could just let go. "Did it offend you?" Hell, he had to know such things. A lot was riding on this.

Chaz put down his pen. "No. Not at all. In fact, it kinda made me feel like we'd get along." He smiled. "Not that I didn't already know that when I first saw the name of the place. At least, I hoped I had it right. But then… you took down the sign."

Del nodded slowly. "I wasn't sure if putting it up was the wisest thing to do."

Chaz's eyes were bright. "Yeah, I think you had the right idea, takin' it down. There are plenty of assholes in this town who might… take exception."

Del decided to level with him. "Yeah. They're already crawling out of the woodwork." He pulled open another drawer and removed a plain folder. "We got these last week, couple of days apart." He handed the two sheets to Chaz. "Short, but not exactly sweet."

Chaz gazed at them, his eyes widening. "Aw, shit. Have you told the cops?"

"Nope." Del took the sheets back and stuck them into the folder. "They're not threatening us. Just making a point. 'No Queers here.' 'Abomination.' Not all that original, huh? At least there are no Bible verses." He shoved the folder back into the drawer.

"You sure about not goin' to the police?"

Del sighed. "If things escalate, then yeah. Only, I'm hoping it doesn't come to that."

Chaz studied Del for a moment. "Rainbow Racers…. That was *your* idea, wasn't it?"

Del snickered. "What makes you say that?"

Chaz snorted. "No offense to your brother, but you seem to be a lot more… comfortable in your skin than he does. And he doesn't seem a rainbows kinda guy."

Del shrugged. "That's his affliction to deal with." They both snickered at that. He peered closely at Chaz. "You're not out, are you?" Chaz's face tightened, then he gave the tiniest shake of his head. Del pressed a little harder. "And I'm thinkin' this is why you're looking to move out of your folks' place." He leaned forward, his hands clasped together on the desk. "Are you okay living there? I mean—"

"I'm fine," Chaz said quietly. "I'm just tired of not bein' able to be myself, that's all. Of hidin' all the time. Because there is no way I can tell them. Uh-uh. I *know* how that conversation is gonna go, and it'll end with me in the hospital."

Del's throat tightened. Fuck. Some people really didn't deserve kids.

He took a mouthful of Coke and cleared his throat. "Then this is your lucky day. You just found yourself a job, and a place where you can be yourself, among family." He locked eyes on Chaz. "You got that?"

Chaz swallowed hard, and his eyes glistened. "Got it."

Del rose to his feet, and Chaz copied him. "Then maybe this

is when I give you the five-cent tour, and show you where you'll be working. The workshop is out back. That's gonna be your first role—making sure the bikes get cleaned up and maintained once they come back in." He walked around the desk to where Chaz stood, and on impulse, gave him a brief hug. "Welcome to the family."

"Thank you," Chaz whispered, his face pressed against Del's broad chest.

Del released him. "I'm only gonna say this once, so listen up. If you have any problems at home, *anything* that makes it difficult for you to stay there, you tell me, all right? There are always solutions, even if it means you end up sleepin' on the workshop floor—not that it's gonna come to that."

Chaz wiped his eyes. "I'm glad you put that sign up. It was gone so quickly, I thought I'd dreamed the whole thing. But it made me come up here to investigate." He sighed happily. "And now look." His stomach rumbled, and Chaz pinked. "Sorry 'bout that."

"No apologies needed. I was about to get some lunch myself. You can join me, and we can talk some more." Del grinned. "You can give me a gay man's view of LaFollette."

"That's real easy. If you wanna be gay, go elsewhere, like Knoxville or farther afield. I know of no one else who's gay around here."

Del tapped the side of his nose. "Just because you don't know them, doesn't mean they're not out there."

What came to mind was the biker from the trail. Now *there* was someone Del would love to get to know better.

He led the way out of the office and over to the door. As he drew nearer, he spotted movement. "Looks like we could have some customers when we finally open our doors." A truck was parked up in the lot, a Honda, and three young guys were standing in front of it, staring at the shop.

Chaz tugged on Del's jacket sleeve. "Trust me. You don't want *them* as customers."

Del glanced at him. Chaz was watching the guys carefully, almost hiding himself behind Del's larger frame. Everything about him screamed tension.

"Who are they?" he asked in a low voice, taking a step back.

"You know I said there are plenty of assholes in this town? Well, there's three of 'em right there. The one in the red jacket is Pete Delaney. That's his truck. They were a few years ahead of me in high school. Just a bunch of mean, bigoted fuckheads."

When the guys clambered back into the truck and drove off, Chaz let out a long, shuddering breath. "Sorry, but they're bad news."

Del snickered. "Fuckheads was enough of a giveaway. Well, if they try anything, I'll just call the law on them."

Chaz snorted. "You may find the law is as bad as they are. And I'd say those boys could be your mystery letter writers, except that implies they can write."

Del's snort echoed Chaz's. He patted Chaz on the back. "Come on. Let's go eat and talk. Jon can join us when he gets back. I'll text him." He gestured to Chaz's bike. "You wanna come with me, or follow on your baby?"

That finally brought a smile. "I'll follow."

As Del pulled out of the parking lot, he thought about the faces of the three youths. Hard faces.

Don't you give me no trouble, boys. I'm not afraid of you.

Except now he had a business—and Jon—to think about. Then he remembered. There was Chaz too. His family had just gotten a little bigger.

Chapter Five

Monday, November 6

Taylor covered his mouth as he yawned, before signing the report. An earlier start to his day than usual, but a very satisfying one. A couple were in separate holding cells, and their stash of drugs was in the evidence room, the result of a dawn raid on their mobile home.

Stings like those weren't everyday occurrences, and they sure broke the monotony. Come to think of it, that was the third such raid Taylor had taken part in since he'd joined the department. So much of what the officers had to deal with these days was drug-related.

Thank God there were still folks out there who weren't prepared to put up with the increasing amount of drugs that found their way onto LaFollette's streets. An anonymous call had started the ball rolling, and police surveillance backed up the caller's claim. Once it had become obvious there was drug-dealing taking place, action was swift, hence two dirt-bags in jail. They were probably trying to lay the blame on each other from the get-go.

The aroma of coffee hit his nose, and Taylor glanced up to find Lieutenant Purdy placing a mug on Taylor's desk. "You looked like you needed this," he said with a smile.

"Thanks." Taylor took a sip. Delicious. "I think I need to be hooked up to a coffee IV."

"Hey, where's mine?" Brian Fogarty grinned. "I was up with the dawn chorus too, y'know." His desk backed onto Taylor's.

"Yeah, and you've already drunk two cups while Taylor here

was writing his report. So I think your caffeine level is just fine." The lieutenant leaned against the desk and addressed Taylor. "Is what Dale said true? Did those lowlifes really claim it was all for personal use?"

Taylor nodded. "Unbelievable. *Sure* it was—for the next couple of years." He glanced around the squad room. "Where's the chief?"

"Photo op." When Taylor gave him a quizzical look, he snickered. "We had some visitors this morning. The Barton sisters."

"Uh-oh. Now what?" The elderly Barton sisters, who had to be in their nineties, were stalwart churchgoers who appeared at the front desk now and again to inform the staff sergeant that they were praying for the police department. Taylor grinned. "Lemme guess. They wanna pray for the souls of those we've arrested."

"Not exactly. They've donated thirty Bibles, for all the staff and police officers. The chief is posing with them right now, then we'll post it on Facebook." Lieutenant Purdy's eyes sparkled. "And you know how much he *loves* Facebook."

Taylor snickered. "Just as much as someone out there will *love* to complain about us puttin' Bibles up there. Can't forget, y'know. Separation of church and state."

Some bright spark in Campbell County had come up with the idea of making the department social media-friendly. The chief hated that once a month, he went to a restaurant or coffee shop where members of the public would meet him, ask questions, or basically do whatever the hell they liked. 'Coffee with the Chief' had really taken off, however, and every month, for the week prior to the meeting, it was plastered all over Facebook. Along with every bit of promo the County could come up with, photos of arrests, details of arrests…

Here ya go, folks. Look. We're doin' our job. Taylor made sure to stay out of the photos. The internet was Forever, and the last thing he wanted was to finally step out of the closet during one of his Atlanta visits, and have some guy look at him and grin. *'Ain't I seen you on Facebook?'*

"So don't you forget to pick up your copy."

"Huh?" It took Taylor a second or two to realize Larry was still talking about the Bibles.

"Hey, maybe we should donate a copy to the new fags!" Mark called out from across the room, leaning back on his chair. "You know, an' underline the parts that say what they're doin' is an abomination."

Aw fuck. Was *one day* without hearing Mark's homophobic poison too much to ask? Taylor's stomach clenched, and he studiously avoided looking in Mark's direction. He couldn't miss the reactions of the others though.

Larry Purdy's face hardened. "I don't have a clue who you're referring to, but you will *not* use language like that in this department. Do you hear me, Officer?"

Mark stilled. "I hear ya. I mean, yes, sir."

"Good." Larry straightened. "I'll go see how the chief is doing. See if he needs rescuing yet." He gave Taylor a wink, before walking out of the room without so much as a backward glance toward Mark. Taylor snuck a peek at Mark to see how he was taking it.

"Well, where the hell does he get off, talkin' to me like that?" Mark stared after Larry with narrowed eyes.

"It's called rank. You know, that elusive country *you* are never gonna reach if you keep openin' your mouth before puttin' your brain into drive first." Brian rolled his eyes. "When are you gonna learn? You can't say shit like that nowadays."

"What—fag? What else am I supposed to call ''em? Queers? Fudge packers?" Mark let his wrist go limp. "Homosex-uals?"

Taylor fought the urge to puke.

Dale came into the squad room and scowled at Mark. "Boy, you don't have the brains you were born with. How 'bout you call 'em people? Now *there's* a novel idea. And for the record, I don't like 'em any more 'n you do, but unlike you, I keep my mouth shut."

"Will someone tell me what the fuck Mark is talkin' about?" Brian demanded.

"You know that new bike shop up on Central? The one they're openin' tomorrow? Christ, they got balloons and ribbons all over the place." Mark raised his eyes heavenward. "Ribbons."

"What about it?"

"I looked it up. The guys who own it have the same last name."

Brian looked blank. "Am I missin' something here?"

Mark threw his hands up in the air. "Oh, for fuck's sake. You seen the name of the place? Rainbow Racers? That makes it so obvious. We got ourselves a gay couple. Y'know—they put on a pair of wedding rings and think they can say they're married?"

Something deep in Taylor's belly roiled. Holy fuck. The guy he'd met on the trail—he was gay *and* married? The fear Taylor had pushed deep down during the last few days rose up, an icy cold fear that trickled down the back of his neck, down his spine and into his balls.

Whichever way Taylor looked at it, Del had the power to blow Taylor's carefully constructed life to smithereens. All he had to do was open his mouth. Because Taylor was sure of one thing, no matter how irrational it seemed.

Del Walters knew Taylor was gay.

Then a voice filtered through the layers of panic. "What do *you* think?"

Taylor blinked. "Sorry. Must've zoned out there. What do I think of what?"

Mark let out an exaggerated sigh. "Stick with the program, Taylor. I was just sayin' maybe we should pay 'em a visit." His eyes gleamed. "A sort of 'reverse welcome' if you get my drift. Just so they get the message."

"And what message would that be?" The chief's voice was deep and rumbling.

Mark paled, his lips pressed together. Taylor had to hand it to the chief. He had a knack for being in the right place at the right time.

"I just caught all that out in the hallway, and I have to say, I do *not* like what I heard." Chief Tillerson swept his gaze slowly around the squad room. "You will do *nothing* that could lead to this department being charged with harassment, do you hear me? No visits. No calls. I repeat—*nothing* that could bring this department into disrepute."

"Well, *someone* sure as shit is gonna do something, Chief," Dale said quietly. "You know it an' I know it. Hell, we all do."

"Fine. In that case, we will deal with whatever misdemeanors result. That's what we do, right? We deal with crime." One last glare, and the chief headed for his office.

Purdy gazed at the officers present. "You heard him. So don't make me have to repeat any of it."

Mark had recovered a little of his usual swagger. "It don't matter none. Once folks realize what's moved into town, we won't have to do a thing." He settled back once more in his chair, fingers laced behind his head, a smug expression in place. "You watch an' see. They'll be outta here so fast, your head'll spin. They'll go back to California, or some other liberal cesspool that breeds 'em like rabbits."

Taylor wanted to have enough balls to yell at Mark, "'*What's* moved into town'? You make 'em sound like they ain't even human." Except he knew he'd do no such thing. He stared at his fellow officers, hoping one of them would echo his disgust.

No one said a goddamn word. And everyone seemed to be doing a damn fine job of avoiding catching anyone's gaze.

Silence fell in the squad room, and Taylor was grateful for it. Little by little, his heartbeat returned to normal, but the incident left him with a sour taste in his mouth that coffee just wouldn't shift.

When Sharon from Dispatch entered a short time later, pushing a trolley laden with boxes, Dale looked up and smiled. "These our Bibles, Sharon?"

She dimpled. "Sure are. Help yourselves, boys." She left them by Dale's desk, and left the room. Dale opened the top box and removed one of the red-bound books, browsing through it.

Taylor couldn't resist. He got up, walked over to where Dale sat perched on the edge of his desk, reached into the box of Bibles and took one. He marched over to Mark's desk, placed it carefully in front of him, and tapped the cover. "Got just the right bit for you," he said confidently. "Mark's gospel, chapter twelve, verses twenty-eight to thirty-one."

Mark gave him a startled glance. "Oh. Sure." His brow furrowed, and he glanced at the others, seemingly bewildered. "Er… thanks, Taylor."

"Don't mention it." Taylor retook his seat and got on with writing his reports. Inside he was a mess. He'd always thought staying in the closet was an easy option. All he had to do was keep his mouth shut, right? Do nothing to attract attention, act like he was straight, keep his opinions to himself…. *Day-um*, but this was harder than he'd anticipated. He hadn't counted on the pressure to react when faced with such… hostility. The urge to treat Mark like the hating little shitbag he was, was so fucking *strong*.

"I had no idea."

Taylor jerked his head up, to find Dale observing him closely from across the desk. "Excuse me?"

"I didn't have *you* down for a churchgoer."

Taylor frowned, perplexed, until it hit him. "Oh. That. My grandma made a cross-stitch of those verses. She gave it to my momma when they got married. I grew up seeing that all my life."

Dale's eyes shone. "And thou shalt love the Lord thy God with all thy heart, and with all thy soul, and with all thy mind, and with all thy strength: this is the first commandment. And the second is like, namely this, Thou shalt love thy neighbour as thyself. There is no other commandment greater than these." He smiled. "Sounds like a good way to live your life." And with that, he strolled over to the coffee machine.

Taylor gazed sadly after him.

Not in LaFollette, apparently.

Chapter Six

Tuesday, November 7

"What do you mean, you're gonna be late?" Del yelled at his phone. "We got a shop to open, damn it." He kept his eyes on the traffic, thankful there weren't many vehicles on the road at that hour of the morning. Less than three hours to go before they finally opened their doors, and Jon was apparently up to his neck in some domestic emergency.

"And right now I got a kitchen full of feathers, 'cause Delilah dragged some poor bird in here that she'd stunned but not killed. It's obviously come to, and she's chased it all around the friggin' room. But can I find it? Hell no. It's probably cowering under a cabinet, too terrified to come out." Jon sounded like he was at the end of his tether.

"Okay, okay." Del made his voice soothing as he approached the turnoff from Central Avenue. "Just… find the damn bird, clean up the place, and then get your ass over to the shop as fast as you can. *After* you lock up Delilah." He disconnected the call. *Of all the days… That's the last time I bring that damn cat any kitty treats, that's for sure.* Thank God they were ready. There was nothing to do but put out the cold beverages, set up the coffee machine, get the signs ready, and—

What the ever-loving FUCK?

Del switched off the engine and stared in horror at the shop front. Across the expanse of glass, in blood-red paint of some kind, were the words FAGS GO HOME.

The first thought to cross his mind was *Today? They've had* weeks *to do this, and they chose today?* Then he groaned. Of *course* they did. Their first tries obviously had no effect, followed up by a couple more short but sweet letters containing nothing but Bible verses, so why not make it a stronger message?

The second thought was a surge of regret. Jon had mentioned CCTV cameras, and Del had balked at the idea, saying they weren't needed. In a big city, sure, but for a small place like LaFollette? *Just shows what I know.*

He got out of his truck, moving slowly like he was trying to wade through molasses. All that time and effort to make opening day perfect, and with a couple of strokes of a paint brush or a spray can, someone had…

Del let out a growl. *Not today, you hateful bastards.* He pulled his phone from his pocket and called Chaz. When the call connected, the kid sounded a little groggy.

"Hey. Am I… late or something?"

"Nope, but I need ya to do something for me. Go to the hardware store and buy whatever they got in the way of paint remover or graffiti cleaner. Keep the receipts. Then meet me at the shop."

"Graffiti—aw fuck. How bad is it?"

"You'll see when you get here. Right now I gotta call the cops." He disconnected, then took a couple of photos on his phone before he did anything else.

Whoever had perpetrated this sure did things on a grand scale. The letters had to be three feet high. *What did they do—stick the paintbrush on the end of a pole?* He scanned the ground in front of the window for anything untoward, but there was nothing to be seen, except for the occasional drip of red paint, like drops of blood.

Gimme five minutes with the bastards who did this. Then *there'll be blood.*

Except he knew it was bullshit. Del was a lover, not a fighter. That didn't mean he couldn't scare the living daylights out of someone if he had to, however.

Del unlocked the door and entered the shop, doing his best not to touch the glass. Not that it mattered—the shits who'd done this probably wore gloves. In less than a minute, he was talking to the police switchboard, demanding that an officer be sent out. When they told him an officer would be there shortly, he thanked them and ended the call.

Jon is gonna have a shit fit.

Del knew he'd done nothing to put the business in jeopardy—unless... *That sign. That goddamn Love is Love sign.* What were the odds on some lowlife seeing it before he took it down? Because if it wasn't that, it was the shop sign. Del could already hear Jon's voice.

I told you so.

He pushed aside such thoughts. Now was the time for damage limitation. Between him, Jon and Chaz, they could have the frontage cleaned before the first potential customers appeared on the scene. Once the police had investigated, of course. Not that Del had high hopes of them finding the perps. Not enough to go on.

He went into the office and set up the coffee machine, his heart heavy. *I had to do it, didn't I? I couldn't have chosen an ordinary, innocuous name for the business. I had to be different.* By the time he'd poured himself a cup, he heard the roar of a motorcycle engine from outside. Del left the office to find Chaz gaping at the new paint job.

"Fucking bastards." Chaz held up a plastic bag. "Here. They had this stuff that'll clean paint off anything. Says it's fast-acting too."

"It'll have to wait until the cops have done their stuff, and tell us we're okay to clean it off. They should be here by now." Del looked over Chaz's shoulder and sighed with relief. "Speak of the devil." The police car pulled up behind Del's truck, and two cops got out, walking slowly toward them.

"Mr. Walters?" The taller officer took off his cap and extended his hand. "Officer Abernathy."

Del shook his hand. "We haven't touched the windows, not

that I expect you to find much in the way of evidence." He glanced over at the second officer, who stayed behind Abernathy.

"This is Officer Cox. He'll take photos for evidence, then dust for prints, if there are any."

"Seeing as the last thing we did before leaving last night was to clean all the windows, any prints you find won't be—" Del blinked as Cox stepped into view.

Well holy fuck. Christmas just got here early.

"I'll get right on it," Cox said, with a brisk bow of his head, before walking toward the shop.

Del stared after him. Cox looked just as delicious in a uniform as he had in cycling shorts and a tight T-shirt—maybe more so. That ass was even more enticing in tight black pants, that was for damn sure.

"Del?" A cough.

Chaz was staring at him, clearly puzzled. Officer Abernathy waited, notebook in hand, his expression impassive.

Del stopped thinking with his dick. "Come on inside. I just made some coffee. You can have some while you take down the details." The thought of taking down Cox's particulars came at him out of nowhere, and Del struggled to get his libido under control. He led the way into the shop, Abernathy and Chaz following.

Del took them into the office, then indicated a chair. "How d'you take it, officer?"

"Just black, thanks." Abernathy took out a pen. "This is the first such incidence?"

"Nope. The first on this scale, sure. I got a couple of nasty messages last week. I ignored them. Then we got a few more." Del pulled open the drawer and handed Abernathy the folder. "I've handled these, as has Chaz here, and my brother."

"Your—" Abernathy blinked. "Where is he?"

"He got delayed. He'll be with us shortly."

"And the two of you run this business?" Abernathy scribbled down some notes.

Del nodded.

"So, you haven't received any phone calls? Just these notes?"

"No, no calls."

"And no suspicious characters hanging around the place?"

Del hesitated. It wasn't as if the three boys had done anything wrong. Then he reconsidered. *Fuck it.* "Three guys paid me a visit in a Honda last Friday. They didn't do anything except park up front and stare menacingly at the shop. I didn't pay much attention at the time."

"Do you have names for any of them?"

"I do." Chaz rattled off their names, while Abernathy wrote them down.

Del took advantage of Chaz's intervention to walk over to the office door and look out the shop window. Cox was peering intently at the glass, clearly looking for prints. Their eyes met, and Cox froze.

That one moment told Del plenty. He hadn't read Cox wrong at all, that afternoon up on the trail. But whatever the guy felt about Del was immaterial. Cox was well and truly in the closet. And right now he was panicking, like a rabbit caught in the headlights of an oncoming car.

Any ideas Del might have had about calming Cox went out the window at the sight of Jon's car. Del opened the door and went outside, saying nothing as he passed the officer.

"What the fuck?" Jon gaped at the frontage.

"Pretty much what I said, give or take." Del gestured to Cox. "Two officers are here, investigating. We'll wait until they've gone, then we'll clean all this shit off." He strode toward the door, pausing at the threshold. "Officer Cox, this is my brother, Jon Walters. He runs the shop with me."

Cox stared at him for a second, mouth open. Then he coughed. "Sure. Okay. Well, there are no prints. All I can do is take photos and report it."

"You got forensic labs, don't you?" Jon scowled. "Can't you take a sample of the paint for analysis? That might tell us something."

Cox gave him a patient look, and pointed to the ground, where a clear plastic bag lay, containing… a sliver of red paint. "Already in hand, sir."

Del bit back a smile. *A point to you, officer Cox.* The guy was obviously on the ball. Del indicated the office. "I got coffee on, if you'd like some. Your partner is having a cup. And I'm pretty certain I can put my hands on some pastries."

"Thanks. I'll say yes to the coffee. I don't have much of a sweet tooth." Cox appeared more relaxed, thank God.

I'll bet you're plenty sweet enough. Those pretty pink lips held so much promise that Del's heartbeat jumped around a little at the thought. *Down boy. In the closet, remember?*

Jon and Cox followed him into the small office, where Abernathy was examining the nasty letters. He looked up as they entered. "Did these come in the mail? If so, did you keep the envelopes?"

Del shook his head. "They were left in the gap by the door. Just folded and stuck in there. No envelopes." He poured Cox a coffee, and handed it to him. "Help yourself to creamer and sugar." Then he smiled. After making sure Abernathy's attention was focused on the letters, Del leaned closer and lowered his voice. "Oh, I forgot. You're sweet enough." He straightened as Abernathy put down the letters and gazed inquiringly at Cox.

"No prints, and I've taken a sample for the lab." Cox shrugged. "That's it, I'm afraid." He addressed Del and Jon. "I did notice you don't have CCTV cameras out there. Might be something you'd want to consider for the future."

"Now ain't that a good idea?" Jon glared at Del, his voice dripping with condescension. "Pity neither of *us* came up with that idea."

Del cleared his throat. "You'll have to excuse my brother, gentlemen. He's trying desperately not to say '*I told you so*'." That brought chuckles from Chaz and Cox. Jon flushed.

"Well, it looks like we're done here." Abernathy drained his cup, then placed it on the desk. "Thanks for the coffee, gentlemen.

We'll file a report, and see what the lab turns up. In the meantime, if you have any other incidents, please let us know." He paused, gazing thoughtfully at his notepad. "There *is* one thing you can do that might prevent such occurrences from happening again." He cleared his throat. "Maybe in all your literature and promotional material, you might mention the fact that you're brothers?"

"And why the hell should we do that?" Jon gazed at him with wide eyes.

"Because some folks around here are liable to see your sign, learn you both have the same name—and jump to the wrong conclusion. If you get my meanin'." Abernathy coughed.

Which explained Abernathy's startled reaction when Del mentioned Jon. Not that Del was surprised. It also explained why Cox had relaxed a little. *He thinks he got it wrong.* Del grinned to himself. *Oh sweetheart, I would* love *to prove to you that you nailed it. Maybe while I'm nailing you to my mattress.*

"Wait—what?" Jon blinked. He turned to Del, his eyes bulging. "They… they think we're married?" He burst into a peal of raucous laughter. "Hell no. I wouldn't marry you even if you *weren't* my brother." Chaz was laughing too, and Cox was smirking.

Del decided it was time to bring this conversation to an end before Jon revealed too much. Cox wasn't dumb. He had to know after their encounter that Del was *not* straight. That didn't mean Del wanted everyone else knowing too. For whatever reason, right now he had Cox at ease, which was just perfect.

"Gee, thanks for that." He rolled his eyes. "So much for brotherly love." Del held out his hand to Abernathy. "Thanks for coming so quickly. Please let me know if you turn up something."

"Of course." Abernathy shook it. "And remember to let us know if there are any developments."

"We'll bear your advice in mind, about the cameras and the, er… you know."

Abernathy smiled. "I think you'll find once word gets out, that'll be the end of it."

Del sure hoped so. He extended a hand to Cox, thanking him, before seeing both officers to their car. Once they'd pulled off the lot, he turned to find Jon and Chaz standing in front of the shop, Chaz clutching the container of cleaner and a couple of rags.

"Tell me I'm wrong," Jon began, "but does that older cop really think you're straight? I mean, seriously?" Even Chaz snickered.

"If he does, I'm not about to disillusion him."

"Say what?" Jon gaped at him.

"Think about it." Del put his hands on his hips. "Are you telling me cops are above being homophobic assholes? That they give unprejudiced support and aid to everyone, no matter what their race or creed or color or sexual persuasion?" He jerked his thumb back to where the cop car had stood. "If we get more trouble, I want 'em on our doorstep in minutes—not hours, because hell, it's only those fags callin', right?"

"You live here long enough, they'll soon know you ain't straight," Chaz murmured. "Word gets around."

"Fine. You're right, of course. But let's get our feet under the table and settle down a little before we disillusion them all. Okay? It's not like I'll be staying around anyhow, once the business is a success. Jon's the one who'll have to deal with them once I'm outta here."

"Whoa, wait a sec." Jon grinned. "What happened to Mr. *I'm not going back into the closet*? You didn't think this would happen, did you? You really thought you could plaster rainbows everywhere and no one would say a word. Geez, you've been living way too long in California."

Del speared him with a look. "I hardly think saying I'm not married to my brother constitutes moving back into the closet, do you?" And funny though the idea was, Del saw no reason to spell out his private life to a cop, or even a community he didn't know. "Besides, what did you expect me to say? 'No, I'm not married to my brother, but hey, I *am* gay, you know.'" And not wanting to hammer the point home so that he didn't spook Taylor, didn't constitute moving back into the closet either.

That was when Del realized what lay at the root of his decision. Taylor.

If I want him—only, there was no *if* about it—*I'm gonna have to be patient.* Because if Del had been interested before…

Officer Cox was an enticing challenge, all wrapped up in a pretty uniform blue bow.

And Del meant to unwrap every single layer.

"Give 'em time to get used to us." Del sighed. "Come on. We've got some shit to wipe off before people get here." They'd do it. There was no way Del was going to let this spoil their big opening.

Taylor would have to wait.

Chapter Seven

"So why do you think they called the place Rainbow Racers?" Dale asked as they pulled away from the bike shop, after reporting in to Dispatch.

Taylor stared out the windshield. "Beats me. Maybe they like rainbows. They might have something too. There are rainbows everywhere these days. It does kinda grab your attention, right? Maybe that was the plan." Not that he believed that for a second. Del was as gay as a three-dollar bill.

And for whatever reason, he's not advertising the fact.

Not that Taylor blamed him.

"Seems like a nice guy. They've taken on a local kid to work for 'em. He was telling me about the job while you were outside." Dale chuckled. "Do you wanna be the one to break it to Mark that they're not a couple, or shall I?"

"I'll leave that pleasure to you. I'll just make sure I'm nearby when you do."

"They don't look alike," Dale mused. "You can see why people would jump to conclusions." Then he snorted. "Hell, I look nothing like *my* brother."

"You had the right idea, though. Telling 'em to spread the word."

"And we can start the ball rollin'," Dale added. "Prevention is better than a cure, don't they say?"

Taylor wasn't really paying all that much attention. He was replaying Del's words over and over. As soon as he'd told them about Jon, the fear that had seized Taylor ever since Dispatch had called them, began to dissipate. He wasn't sure what he'd been afraid of. That he'd walk into the bike shop and Del would say something, make some comment about their meeting? When it became obvious that was *not* going to happen, the tension that had gripped him eased off, and he breathed normally. He found it laughable that Dale bought the whole 'not gay' thing, but then, Dale didn't have the benefit of Taylor's inside knowledge.

The man who'd flirted with him up on the trail was as gay as they come. And damn, it had been hot…

It doesn't matter. I'm safe. Del's not gonna out me.

Yeah, Taylor was breathing a whole lot easier.

"So how's it goin' with Denise?" Dale asked as they continued on their way back to the police department. "Or am I not allowed to ask such a personal question?" He chuckled. "You're a real quiet one. But they say it takes all sorts. Look at the department. We got Mark, bragging about how many girls he's bangin' on a regular basis, Ethan who says diddly about his private life, the lieutenant who says nothin' neither, and then there's you. We're all waiting for the chief to announce that you two are walkin' out."

Taylor laughed. "Sorry to disappoint you, but it's nothing like that. As least, not yet." He hated adding that last part, but self-preservation was a powerful force. "She's real nice, though. Can't think why someone hasn't snapped her up already."

Dale snickered. "If you weren't a cop, would *you* wanna date the police chief's daughter?"

"Only if I was doin' something I shouldn't," Taylor retorted.

"Yeah, well, the chief can be pretty intimidating. Plus, I hear she's smart. Maybe too smart for the lummoxes around here."

Taylor weighed up Dale. He was an old school cop, a by-the-book man, and one Taylor would trust in a crisis. "You're right. I'm not sure why she didn't go to college." Except he already knew why—her daddy.

Dale huffed. "I can answer that one. Heard the chief and Purdy discussing it years ago, when she graduated from high school. Hell, the chief was so proud of her. But—and here's the bit you don't share, you got that?"

"Got it."

"The chief was talking about some friends of theirs whose kids had gone off to college. The way he told it, when these kids came back after their studies, they were… different, somehow. If they came back at all. Seemed like the chief was afraid she'd change if she went off to college."

"But… different doesn't have to be a bad thing, right?"

Dale shrugged. "Maybe he thinks it's safer for her to settle down and start a family." He sighed. "He just doesn't wanna lose his little girl. Hell, no father wants that." His face tightened for a moment, then he relaxed as they pulled into the parking lot of the police department. "Okay. Back to the grindstone. You wanna get started on the paperwork for that paint sample? You never know— it might turn out to have been sold recently."

"That'd be something. I'll get it sent off to the lab." Taylor paused as he got out of the squad car. "Now, you *are* gonna wait till I'm back before you tell Mark, right?"

Dale hooted. "Would I deprive you of that pleasure?" He sauntered into the building. Taylor followed, heading for the evidence room. That brief spasm he'd noted across Dale's features was a reminder of how little he knew about the guy. They were often partnered together, and yet Taylor couldn't recall Dale ever talking about his family. He knew there was a daughter—her photo was on Dale's desk in a frame, along with one of his wife—but Dale kept silent on his family.

It's none of my damn business anyhow. It's not like I share stuff about my life, right?

Trusting Dale to back him up was one thing. Trusting him with Taylor's biggest secret was quite another.

By the time he got into the squad room, Dale had poured them both a cup of coffee and was watching Mark from across the room, a big shit-eating grin on his face. Unfortunately, Mark was in the middle of a phone conversation that took up all his attention.

"Taylor, you got a minute?" The chief peered at him from the doorway.

"Sure." Taylor grabbed his coffee, got out of his chair, and followed the chief to his office.

"Sit down." The chief walked around his wide desk and sat in his high-backed chair. "Just got a phone call from Del Walters of Rainbow Racers, thanking me for your prompt appearance and advice this morning. He liked how efficiently you and Dale dealt with the situation. Nice work."

"Thank you, sir." Taylor wasn't stupid. There was more to come.

The chief laced his fingers, twiddling his thumbs. "Look, I've got a personal favor to ask. Next week is my wedding anniversary, and it's a biggie. Twenty-five years."

"Congratulations, sir."

He chuckled. "I still remember it like it was yesterday." He reached across his desk, picked up a frame, and handed it to Taylor. "Just look at us."

Taylor gazed at the photo. The chief had changed very little in the intervening years—he'd been a stout man back then too—but the face seemed a whole lot younger. He had his arms around Mrs. Tillerson, and they were staring at each other, standing in what looked like a wild flower garden. Her lace gown was beautiful, cinched in at the waist, and she held a bouquet of cream, pink and white roses.

Taylor smiled. "Looks like it was a good day." He handed the photo to the chief, who carefully placed it back in its position.

"I'd only just joined the police back then. We were still living with the in-laws, saving up for a place of our own." He cleared his throat. "Anyhow, we're having a party a week from Saturday, and... well... we'd like you to come along."

"Me, sir?"

The chief arched his eyebrows. "Don't act so surprised. It was Denise's idea. She mentioned it last night, and I said I'd ask you. Well, this is me askin'."

Taylor didn't know what to say. He was unsure as to Denise's motives, for one thing. For another, it felt too much like getting his feet under the chief's table. Especially when there was no way on God's green earth anything was ever going to come of it.

Thankfully, the chief took his hesitation for the natural reluctance of a young guy to hang out with a bunch of older strangers. "Look, you don't have to say yes, just 'cause it's me askin'. To be honest, it'd be good to have someone there I could share a laugh with. They're a miserable bunch of sinners on the wife's side." Then he froze. "And you do *not* repeat that, you hear?"

Taylor bit his lip. Maybe he could throw the chief a lifeline. "I won't say a word, and… sure, I'll be there."

The chief beamed at him. "Aw, great. I'll let the wife know. And I promise, if it gets too dull, you can leave anytime. Just don't let on *why* you're leavin', okay?"

Taylor smiled. "I'll be discreet." He got up, still clutching his coffee cup. "Is that all you wanted me for?"

"Yeah. Keep up the good work, Taylor. And don't pay too much attention to the likes of Teagle in there. You got too much goin' on between your ears to be listening to his drivel." He narrowed his gaze. "And I didn't say that, neither!"

Taylor mimed zipping his lips, before leaving the office. No sooner had he gotten back to his desk, than a text popped up.

Warning. Daddy needs a favor. My fault. Just say yes.

Shaking his head, Taylor dialed Denise's number. "You're about five minutes too late."

"Damn, he works fast." She sighed. "Sorry. They started goin' on about the damn party last night, an' all I could think of was how deathly dull it was gonna be, an' how I'd prefer to stick pins in my eyes than put up with an evening of conversation with my relatives."

"Ew." Taylor winced.

Denise chuckled. "But it gets the point across, doesn't it? So?

Did you say yes?"

"You mean, did I agree to provide you with some alternative conversation? Of course I did." A pause followed his words, and Taylor had an ominous feeling. "What? What is it you're not tellin' me?"

"Just… well… expect a few questions, along with a whole lotta assumptions. Because you *know* Daddy will introduce you as my guest, and you *know* the connotations my family will apply to that statement."

Aw crap. He glanced around the squad room to make sure no one was in earshot, then lowered his voice. "I've just agreed to be your fake boyfriend for the night, haven't I?" Taylor hadn't seen it coming. He'd been too busy putting the chief out of his misery.

"Look, you are *not* coming to that party to make puppy-dog eyes at me, y'hear? Just act like you do when you come for dinner. That's all they're gettin'."

He loved the fierce note in her voice. "Gotcha. But… you are *so* gonna owe me, okay?"

"Oh, sure, whatever. You name it."

Taylor caught sight of the lieutenant firing an inquiring glance in his direction. "Okay, I gotta go. I'll see you at the party."

"Thanks, Taylor. I mean it."

They disconnected, just in time for Taylor to catch Mark's explosion.

"They're brothers? My God, that's *disgustin'*!"

He groaned inwardly. Some people couldn't drag their minds out of the sewer, apparently.

Chapter Eight

Thursday, November 9

Del handed over a wad of leaflets to Drew, the owner of the Common Ground coffee shop. "Thanks. I appreciate this."

"Hey, no problem. We small businesses gotta look out for each other. And if you want some business cards to place in your shop…"

Del was all for that. "Sure. Gimme a pile of 'em." Drew's words had given him an idea. "I don't suppose… What you said just now. I was thinking about organizing some kind of cooperative… a committee of community businesses… where we can come together and more importantly, work together." He gave Drew a speculative glance. "You think something like that would work here?"

"Don't see why not. Makes sense. You gonna mention it to other business owners?"

Del nodded. "I'll let you know if anything comes of it."

Drew deposited a pile of business cards on the counter. "There." He grinned. "If this takes off, we're all gonna need one of those plastic stands that holds cards."

Del liked that idea a lot. He placed the cards carefully in the inside pocket of his leather jacket. "And before I go, I think I'll have a large black coffee."

"Sure. Grab a seat and I'll bring one over. On the house." Drew's smile was warm. "Sort of a 'welcome to the community.'"

"Aw, thanks." Del turned to choose a table—and froze when he saw Taylor Cox enter the coffee shop. The cop stiffened momentarily, but recovered, touching the brim of his cap.

"Afternoon, Mr. Walters." He waved a hand. "Hey, Drew."

"Hey, Taylor. Your usual? I'll bring it on over."

"Thanks." Taylor chose a table in the far corner where he sat with his back to the wall.

There was no way Del was about to waste an opportunity like that.

He strolled over to Taylor's table. "Hey. I'm just about to have a coffee too. Mind if I join you?"

Taylor blinked. "It's a free country." Then he sighed. "Sorry. That came out all wrong. Course I don't mind."

Del took the empty chair facing him and sat. "I take it you're a regular here." He leaned back.

Taylor nodded. "The coffee's good. And if you have a sweet tooth, their carrot cake is to die for."

Del couldn't help grinning. "And there was I, thinking you didn't have a sweet tooth." When Taylor didn't relax in his chair, Del knew he had to do something. "I'm going around local businesses, asking if they'll display our leaflets for the shop. I figure it's a good way to spread the word." Lord, the boy was twitchy. Del abandoned his flirtation mode and flipped over to business owner. Anything to relax Taylor. "Did anything come of analyzing that paint?"

"The report's due in today or tomorrow. I was gonna call you." Taylor frowned. "You've had nothing else happen?"

"No. All quiet, thank God." That described the business too, but it was early days, and he knew it. "Those boys I reported seeing outside the shop... I got the impression you knew 'em."

Taylor's eyes gleamed. "Let's say I've had a few encounters. Nothing official, but enough that I wouldn't be surprised if they had a hand in it. We're keepin' a close eye on Pete and his little gang. They haven't crossed the line yet, but it's only a matter of time before they end up in a cell for some reason or other."

Del glanced around the coffee shop. "This seems like a nice place. I guess I'm still finding my way around."

At that moment, Drew brought across their coffees. "You two know each other?"

"Unfortunately, yes. I met officer Cox here when there was an incident at the shop. Not exactly pleasant circumstances to meet under." Del wasn't about to mention their first meeting. Taylor was skittish enough as it was.

"Yeah, I heard about that. Good luck catching the bastards," Drew said with a nod to Taylor as he walked away from them.

Taylor waited until Drew was back behind the counter. "Can I ask you something?"

"Well, that depends," Del said slowly, "on what you're asking."

"What brought you guys here? I mean, why choose LaFollette?"

Del dumped a packet of sugar into his coffee and stirred it. "Coming back to my roots, I guess. We were born in South Carolina, and then *one* of us wanted to go study as far west as he could manage." Del chuckled. "Jon still can't understand why anyone would want to do that, but then he's a Southern boy, balls to bones."

"You have your moments when the Southern slips through," Taylor countered. "California didn't breed it all out of ya." His eyes sparkled, and Del sensed the first easing of tension in Taylor's body language.

Del snorted. "That's what Jon says too. Anyway, when I finished college, I didn't want to go back home. Why would I? Christ, it had been bad enough growing up there. Momma complained plenty at first, but she was no fool. She knew how the land lay. And what she wanted most was for her boys to be happy. Jon stayed at home, so she had one of her babies with her at least."

"Your momma…" Taylor's brow furrowed slightly. "You keep using the past tense."

Del's chest tightened. "We lost her. Far too early, if you ask me, but cancer's a bitch, and lung cancer is a super-aggressive bitch."

"I'm sorry." Taylor spoke softly, and Del could hear the sincerity.

"We survive, right? Although losing her…" He couldn't finish. He might not have lived near her, but there were some ties that really did bind. Del stared into his coffee. "The short story is, I had a couple of companies and did pretty good out of them. Jon had tried his hand at running a few businesses over the years. Let's just say, he hadn't enjoyed a lot of success. So one day Momma called me up and asked, kinda out of the blue, if I'd ever thought of running a business with him." He gave a rueful smile. "I guess me laughing down the phone wasn't exactly the reaction she had in mind. But she must have sowed the seed in Jon's head, because not long after she passed, he started talking about that very thing." Del jerked his head up. "Now listen. Not that I *ever* think this would come up in conversation if, heaven help us, you're at the shop again, but…"

"Jon made it sound like it was all his idea, didn't he?" Taylor's eyes held compassion. "He didn't let on about your momma."

God damn it. Pretty *and* perceptive. Del was liking Taylor Cox more and more.

"Yeah," Del admitted simply. "And I've never let on that she mentioned it."

Taylor leaned back against the wall, his mug in his hands. "See, *now* LaFollette makes sense. Jon didn't want to stray too far from home."

"Got it in one. He did all the groundwork, all the research, and I let him. I had stuff of my own going on back in San Francisco, but I checked in from time to time to see how he was going. When he came up with this plan, I had to admit, I really liked it. I could see it taking off too. It was just…" Del swept his arm to encompass the coffee shop.

"Tennessee." Taylor bit his lip. "Yeah. Not the place I'd choose either."

Del took a drink of coffee before responding. "And yet

you're here too." He quirked his eyebrows. He didn't have to say any more than that. There seemed little point dancing around. They both knew the score here.

Taylor sighed. "My momma's here. That kinda sums it up, doesn't it?" He took a long drink of coffee. "And no, given the choice, I would not be here. For reasons I think we're both aware of, and not gonna mention."

And there it was, Del thought. As close as Taylor would get to confessing his orientation. Well, that was fine. Del could deal with that. Still, there was one more question he had to ask. "Your momma… does she have any idea…"

Taylor held up his hand. "She asks when I'm gonna settle down and make her a grandma. She asks if I've met any nice girls lately." He chuckled. "I tried to tell her the sort of girls I get to meet are *not* the kind to bring home to momma. Why, just last week, I arrested one lovely creature who was busy makin' crack with her lowlife boyfriend, and another who I busted for prostitution."

Del tried not to snicker. "I'm gonna take that as a no."

Taylor sighed heavily. "What makes it worse? I'm… well, I'm not *exactly* seeing the police chief's daughter, but I might as well be as far as my coworkers are concerned. And I'm pretty sure my momma is reading *all* kinds of things into that."

"And what is the chief's daughter's take on all this?" Del could understand Taylor being in the closet, but leading someone on?

Taylor huffed. "Let's just say things are workin' out to both our advantages. She's not dumb. If anything, her instincts are pretty much on the money."

"I'm glad you can be honest with her. I didn't think you'd be the sort of guy who'd mess someone around." Del couldn't account for the relief he felt at Taylor's words. Maybe there was something in him that was offended at the idea of a cop being duplicitous. Del knew corruption existed in the police force—he was just old-fashioned enough to want Taylor to be a good guy.

Taylor arched his eyebrows. "And you base that assumption on two short encounters? Three, if you count this one?"

Del studied him in silence for a moment. "How old are you?"

"Twenty-six."

He stroked his beard. "Well, I got twenty years on you, and that teaches you a lot about people. You mentioned this girl's instincts. I trust mine, every time, because I know I can, but that's just experience." He met Taylor's gaze. "And I trust 'em when it comes to you." No flirting, just a frank glance that Del hoped to God set Taylor's mind at ease.

A long breath shuddered out of Taylor. "Thank you for not mentioning our first meeting to my coworker."

"I wouldn't do that," Del said earnestly. "Okay? You got that? Your secret is safe with me." He smirked. "But *Lord*, you gave me a start. Seeing you there at the shop... like that..."

Taylor narrowed his gaze. "It was the uniform, wasn't it?"

Del coughed, then quickly drank some more.

Taylor raised his eyes heavenward. "What is it about a uniform that makes some grown men go weak at the knees?"

Del snickered. "Not me. I just think it's sexy. I'm not one of those who gets off on the whole idea of a cop...." He was going to stop *right there* because with what he was imagining right then? Maybe he *was* one of those guys after all.

It was Taylor's turn to study him, and Del had to wonder what was going through his mind. Then Taylor tilted his head to one side. "I'm guessing *you're* the one who... takes control." He swallowed, and just like that, they'd veered off the careful path they'd followed so far. Taylor's words came across as uncertain, but there was no disguising the hopeful look in his eyes.

Del kept his lips zipped, but inside his head was laughter. *Oh honey, if you only knew what I'm thinking right this second.*

The awkward silence was broken by a burst of static from Taylor's radio, and followed by a quick staccato conversation into his mic. Taylor gave a shrug. "Looks like my coffee break is over." He rose to his feet and extended a hand. "It was nice meetin' you again."

"Same here," Del said as he got up and shook Taylor's hand. "We might have to do this again some time. Maybe another coffee shop? There seem to be a few of them."

"Then it's a possibility." Taylor touched his cap, came out from behind the table, and went over to the counter to pay. Del sat in the seat Taylor had vacated, watching him leaning against the counter as he chatted with Drew.

What was rampaging through Del's mind were images that sent heat barreling through him, images that alternated between Del shoved face-down over the hood of a police car, while Taylor plowed into him, and those of a uniformed Taylor bent over Del's trike, his black pants round his ankles, while Del fucked him like they had all time in the world.

God, he'd be so fucking tight.

Del shoved such delicious images aside. *Never gonna happen, not in this town.* And now Del had yet another case of blue balls to contend with.

Enough. Time for a weekend trip to Atlanta.

Chapter Nine

Friday, November 10

"Got any plans for the weekend?" Dale Abernathy asked after wiping sauce from his lips. His lunchtime sandwich seemed to have more than usual. When Taylor gave him a questioning glance, Dale shrugged. "I saw the noticeboard. You're booked off from end of shift today." He grinned. "You can't *fart* in this town without somebody noticing."

"Good to know I'm providin' y'all with a topic of conversation." Taylor scrunched up the paper that had contained his lunch, and stuffed it into the plastic bag Dale kept in the patrol car for such purposes. He'd learned pretty fast that Dale could not abide an untidy car.

Dale snorted. "Come on. When Mark or Brian have a weekend off, we all know about it well in advance."

"That's 'cause they can't keep their fat mouths shut." Taylor drained half his coffee. "Some of us like to cultivate a little mystery." He waggled his eyebrows.

That got him a laugh. "Nothin' wrong with that. Course, you *know* they're all talkin' 'bout you an' Denise. Word is, you've got an invite to the chief's anniversary party." Dale's eyes gleamed. "Care to comment?"

"Nope." Taylor finished his coffee and stuffed the cup into the trash bag.

Dale chuckled. "I like that about you." When Taylor regarded him in surprise, Dale gave another shrug. "You keep your private life separate from your work. That's how it should be. Who says we have to spill our guts about every little thing that's going on in our lives?"

Taylor gave a hopefully nonchalant smile. "Maybe there's nothin' to tell," he suggested. Well, nothing he felt like sharing.

"Doesn't matter if there is or there isn't," Dale retorted. "It's *your* business." The bitter edge to his voice stilled Taylor instantly. This wasn't like Dale.

"Hey," he said quietly. "I'm not prying or anything, but… are you all right?"

Dale drank his coffee, grimacing. "Damn. Hate cold coffee."

Taylor took that as a warning. Whatever was going on, it was private.

"I saw the analysis came back on that paint from the bike shop incident," Dale said suddenly.

"Yeah. Turns out it's sold locally in about three different locations. A popular color too. Next step is to see if we can trace who's bought it recently. And maybe pay Pete Delaney a visit, find out why he and his little gang were there. I mean, the shop wasn't open at that point. A visit from us might put the fear of God into him, just in case he was *thinkin'* on doin' something." When Dale didn't respond, Taylor figured that was the end of the conversation. "Ready to make a move?"

"What do you think about these gays?"

The blunt question was so out of the blue that Taylor's breathing hitched. "Excuse me?" He glanced across at Dale, who was staring into his empty cup.

"I know what the preacher says about 'em. Had that fed to me my whole life. And you know what? You don't question it. You just… go along with it. But what if… what if something happens to *make* you question it? What if …suddenly, it touches *your* life?" The note of anguish in Dale's voice cut into him.

"Dale? What's wrong? What's happened?" Taylor ached to pat him on the shoulder, to let Dale know he wasn't alone right then, but he held back.

Dale reached across and dropped his cup into the trash. "You an' me... we get along, don't we? I mean, we can... talk about stuff?"

For one moment, Taylor went cold, convinced that somehow Dale knew his secret. Then he shook off the thought as illogical. He'd done nothing to give himself away. This had to be something else.

"What you said just now about your business being nobody's but yours," Taylor said gently. "That also gives you the right to share what *you* want to share. And you *know* I'm not one who lets his mouth run away with him. If... if talking to me helps, then you go right ahead an' talk, okay?"

Dale said nothing, and Taylor hoped to God he hadn't overstepped the mark. Then Dale took his wallet from his pocket, opened it, removed a photo, and held it out to Taylor.

He took it, recognizing it instantly as the same photo from Dale's desk. It was of his daughter, sitting on a pony, laughing, her eyes bright and her face flushed.

"That's my little girl, Zoe. Except she's not so little anymore. She was seven or eight in that photo—she's twenty now." He smiled. "Funny thing is, when I think of her? This is how I see her in my head."

Taylor said nothing, waiting for whatever was causing his coworker such pain.

"She's at college. Won herself a scholarship. We were so proud of her." Dale took back the photo and studied it. "About a year ago, she came home for the summer and told us she had some news."

Oh shit. Taylor had a feeling he knew where this was going.

Dale's voice shook. "She said... she'd met someone. Not that we couldn't tell. Lord, she was... *glowin'* with it. We figured this had to be someone pretty special. Then... she got out her phone, pulled up a photo and just handed it to her mom. It was of her and this girl, short black hair, glasses, and they were laughing their asses off. Then she showed us more photos of... Fran. Zoe didn't say anything, just scrolled through photo after photo after photo, like she was waitin' for us to get it, *waitin'* for us to see what was right there without her having to say the words, y'know?"

"What did you do?"

Dale took a breath. "Her mom cottoned on faster than I did. She just said, 'Oh, she seems… nice.' Then she asked if Zoe was gonna bring this Fran to meet us." He paused. "God, I was slow. I was like, 'why would we wanna meet her?' Zoe just… stared at me. Then she sighed and said, 'maybe because I love her.'"

Taylor's stomach clenched. "How did you react?" He recalled an earlier conversation, where Dale's mood hadn't made sense. *Oh Lord. He said something, and it wasn't good.*

"I couldn't help myself. It just sort of… popped out. I came out with all those lines from the Bible that I'd heard so many times, like I was on autopilot or something. And her face. I swear, I heard her heart break." The tremor in Dale's voice brought Taylor close to losing it. The pain there….

Taylor took a moment to get himself under control. "Has she been home since?" He already had a fair idea of the answer.

Dale shook his head. "Her momma's been to stay with her a few times." He cleared his throat. "It's only recently that I've started thinkin' that… maybe I got it wrong. I mean, I knew I'd messed up the second the words left my mouth, but somehow I just couldn't take 'em back. It's easy to say all that when it doesn't affect you. But when it does? I heard myself spouting all the things I'd heard growing up, only now they were hurtin' someone I loved. And I didn't know what to do. I mean, I couldn't just throw away everything I'd learned, right?"

"But something changed, didn't it?" Taylor sensed there had to have been something to cause a shift in Dale's thinking.

Dale nodded. "A couple of weeks ago, I saw something that made me think. It was a sign, all pretty colors, and it only had three words on it. It said Love is Love."

Taylor blinked. "Where did you see that?"

"That bike shop. Rainbow Racers. And it wasn't up for long, but I saw it." Dale snickered. "Those two are brothers, sure, but *one* of 'em is queer, I'd lay money on it."

"And yet you didn't say a word about that sign to me after we'd been there. Hell, that sign might be what caused the whole episode." Taylor stared at him incredulously.

"Probably was, but they didn't mention it. I could see why they might wanna keep that quiet. Like I said, that sign got me thinkin'. Supposin' the gays got it right all along? Supposing love *is* love, pure an' simple, an' *we're* the ones choking things up with hate an' prejudice?"

Taylor regarded him thoughtfully. "And if *that's* true, then maybe you can accept that your little girl is in love, and it doesn't matter who with." Another thought occurred to him. "There's something else too. You don't really think she got to college and they brainwashed her into thinking totally differently, do ya?"

Dale gave a slow shake of his head.

"You brought her up. You taught her right from wrong. You taught her about life, and that one day she'd find someone and fall in love, right?"

"Yeah."

Taylor pressed ahead. "And when this Fran came along, she knew, because of everything you taught her. She knew, and she accepted it. You did good."

"So you're sayin' that having a lesbian for a daughter doesn't make me a bad parent?" Dale chuckled. "Well, that was one angle I didn't expect." He gave Taylor a speculative glance. "I remember the day the chief told me I'd be partnering you. I'll be honest, I wasn't happy about it. You were young, and as far as I was concerned, that meant impulsive, loud, irrational and hotheaded." He smiled. "I'm glad to be proved wrong. And now we'd better get back to work, before the chief decides we're surplus to requirements."

Taylor couldn't leave it there. "And Zoe?"

Dale sighed. "Maybe it's time she came home for a visit. Not that it's gonna be easy, y'understand."

"A step at a time. Just remember, she's probably as scared as you." Taylor opened the car door and got out, taking the trash with him. When he got back in, Dale was just finishing a call. Taylor buckled up. "Where now?"

"We got an anonymous tipoff we have to follow up on."

That meant one thing—drugs.

Taylor couldn't wait for the weekend. He was going to chill, have more than a few beers, and relax in a place where he didn't have to be nervous.

A place where he could be himself. Not that *that* amounted to much. It meant simply that he could take in all the sights that weren't available to him in LaFollette.

And *that* was saying a lot.

Chapter Ten

Nearly midnight, Friday, November 10 - Atlanta

Del took a long drink of beer and surveyed the dance floor. It wasn't huge, but still, it was ten times better than anything that existed in LaFollette. And that rainbow flag outside had surely been a welcome sight. Inside Blake's on the Town, it was pretty much as he'd expected. The square bar had the added attraction of a couple of twinks dancing on it, gyrating to the music, their hips rolling fluidly as they leered at all the guys clustered below. The crowd on the floor was mostly men, but there were women too, and everyone seemed to be having a good time.

Del was *definitely* ready for a good time.

As soon as he'd checked into his hotel room, Del grabbed a quick shower, a clean set of clothes, then he was ready to roll. He had a list of places to investigate, but the siren call of loud music, cold beer, and shirtless men dancing proved too much to ignore. Blake's didn't disappoint. After a Caesar wrap and fries, plus a couple of beers, he was ready to take on the world.

Fuck, he'd missed this. Okay, so it was light years away from Magnitude, the huge dance party at the end of Folsom, but after weeks of no one but Jon for company, Del was more than content. He'd already danced his ass off, and was taking a breather, unable to miss the appreciative glances, not to mention the whistles and calls of 'Well, hel-*lo,* Daddy.' Enough heated glances to assure him he was *not* going to bed alone.

Thank fuck.

A bench ran along one wall, filled with guys watching the

floor show. Del perused the line-up, looking for his next dance partner. He ignored the barely legal, vacuous-looking pretty boys, who probably couldn't rub two sentences together; even though the objective of the night was to get laid, Del was picky. Then his heartbeat sped up as his gaze alighted on a familiar buzz cut in the farthest corner.

Well, well, well.

Del's night had just taken an interesting turn.

Taylor took sips from his beer and tried not to make eye contact with any of the men who walked slowly past him. They might not have said a word to him, but he felt their gazes on him nevertheless, like pinpricks on his skin. He was happy just to watch the parade. One day he'd get up enough nerve to meet one of those gazes, but for now, just *being* there was enough. Anything else was way beyond his comfort zone.

A shadow fell across him, but Taylor didn't look up. When the shadow didn't move, he began to get an uncomfortable feeling in his belly. *Now what?*

"Of all the gin joints in all the towns in all the world, she walks into mine."

Taylor jerked his head up at the familiar voice, and stared into Del Walter's eyes. "You have *got* to be fucking kidding me!"

Del smirked. "Good to see you too, Taylor." He laughed. "God, I always wanted to quote that line."

Taylor was barely listening, too distracted by the sight before him. Del was fucking *hot*, wearing a pair of black leather pants that clung to his muscular thighs, and a white T-shirt that hugged him above the waist. Hell, everything about the man screamed 'bear'.

Then Taylor reclaimed control of his mouth. "Are you following me?"

Del guffawed. "Nope. Apparently it's a case of great minds thinking alike." He glanced around the bar. "This is actually my first visit here. You?"

Taylor gave a shrug. "I come here once in a while." The guy next to him chose that moment to vacate his spot, and before Taylor could get a word out, Del was in there. He leaned back against the wall, his gaze trained on Taylor.

"So..." Del speared him with a look. "Can we talk about that thing we can't talk about back home?"

In spite of his nerves, Taylor had to smile. "You knew I was gay when we first met, didn't ya?"

Del snickered. "Well... yeah." He arched his eyebrows. "I mean, come *on*. Tell me you didn't bend over to put down your helmet, knowing what a view I'd get of your perfect ass."

Nailed.

Then Del's words fully registered. "I have a perfect ass?"

Del rolled his eyes. "Like you don't know." Taylor didn't know where to look. Thankfully, Del changed the subject. "So, what do you do when you're in Atlanta?"

"Not much. I go to gay bars. Sometimes I eat out in the gay district." That was enough.

"Have you checked out the bathhouse? That's on my To Do list."

Christ. Taylor erupted into a raucous cough, and Del patted him on the back. When his eyes stopped watering, Taylor anxiously awaited Del's next words, aware of the thoughtfulness in his gaze, like he was mentally assessing just how far he could push.

"Do you dance?"

Okay, that was *not* what he'd expected.

Taylor cleared his throat. "I just watch, to be honest. I'm not that good a dancer."

Del's eyes widened. "Who says you have to be good at it?" He got to his feet and held out a hand. "Come on. We're here, right? Then let's do something different. Liberating. Stress-relieving." He grinned. "Sexy."

That hand didn't move, and Taylor could only stare at it.

"Taylor?"

He raised his chin, to be confronted by those same blue eyes that had looked through him that day up on the trail. Only now, they were warm.

"Dance with me."

He could say no. He could leave. Except in the end, he did neither of those things, but stood, his heart quaking, his stomach tense, and let Del lead him through the throng of guys to where a space opened up for them, as if by magic.

"By the way," Del said, leaning forward so Taylor could hear him above the music, "I'm a great dancer." And before Taylor could respond, Del began to move, his arms flailing like some demented Kermit, his body jerking as if on strings, Del seemingly oblivious to the spectacle he presented.

Taylor couldn't help it. He burst out laughing, tears pricking his eyes, his sides aching. Del came to a halt, grinning, and in that moment Taylor knew for certain that he'd done it on purpose.

He chuckled. "I think I can follow that." He moved from one foot to another, in time to the music, and Del mimicked him, with no goofing off this time.

"You don't think I'll win any dance contests then," Del asked, his eyes twinkling.

"Put it this way. I wouldn't expect any scouts from America's Got Talent to come knocking on your door, if I were you. Not that you don't have a style all of your own. And it's definitely… unique." It came as a surprise when Taylor realized he was having fun. He forgot about his nerves and concentrated on the rhythm and the pulse of the music, moving to its beat, and feeling…

Safe. I feel safe. That was down to Del.

They danced facing each other, each one's movements a reflection of the other's. When the music wasn't too loud, they talked, mostly about where to eat in Atlanta. It wasn't until they'd been dancing for at least an hour that Taylor realized they were gravitating closer to each other. Not so close that he couldn't insert a cigarette paper between them, but close enough that he could feel

Del's body heat, his nostrils filled with Del's scent, a mixture of cotton, musk and some underlying fragrance that seemed to connect with Taylor's dick. Del said nothing, but swayed to the music, his gaze focused on Taylor, like he was the only guy in the room.

It was heady as fuck.

"See?" Del murmured. "It's not so bad, is it? Moving around the floor together…"

Taylor licked his suddenly dry lips. "Maybe it's not that big a deal for you, but…"

Del's gaze grew more intense. "How do you feel?"

Taylor pushed down hard on the butterflies dancing in his belly, and thought about it. "Good," he admitted truthfully. "I'm kinda glad you convinced me to get up." He gave a shy smile. "For all the times I've been coming to Atlanta? This is my first dance."

Del came to a halt. "You wouldn't have done this if I hadn't been here, would you?"

"Nope. I'd have stayed for a few drinks, made 'em last all night, an' watched everyone havin' a good time."

Del frowned. "So what do you do when someone hits on you?"

Taylor grinned. "What makes you think someone would want to hit on me?"

That got him a blink. "Come over here a sec." Del led him off the dance floor and back to the corner where he'd been earlier. Del leaned against the wall, regarding him thoughtfully. "Can I be honest?"

"Sure." Taylor's heartbeat sped up.

"I wanted to hit on you the first time we met. But… when I saw you tonight? Everything about your body language screamed 'stay away.' It was coming off you in waves. I only came over because I know you."

"I'm glad you did," Taylor said honestly. The yawn overtook him before he could rein it in.

Del chuckled. "Seems to me like you're all done for the

night. Let's get you back to your hotel."

Oh fuck. Just like that, the butterflies in his stomach morphed into a herd of stampeding buffalo.

"A good night's sleep is just what you need," Del continued. "Then we can meet up for brunch tomorrow at that place you were telling me about. Cowtippers?"

It took a moment for his words to register, and then a feeling of relief swamped him. "Sounds good. And yeah, I'm ready to go."

They headed for the door, and the cool night air hit him in the face as soon as they were outside. Del walked with him the couple of blocks to the hotel, and paused at the main door.

"Give me your phone, and I'll add my number. That way, if you change your mind about brunch, you can let me know. No hard feelings, by the way, if you do. Okay?"

Taylor didn't hesitate. He handed over his phone, and Del went to Contacts. Taylor half expected a request for his number, but it didn't come. Instead, Del handed the phone back, then put his arm around Taylor's shoulder and gave him a one-armed hug. "Now get some sleep. I'll see you tomorrow."

Taylor couldn't hold back his smile. "Thank you," he said sincerely.

Del merely waved his hand and walked away. Taylor stood and watched him, his nervousness evaporated. Del might have pushed him out of his comfort zone in the bar, but Taylor still felt like he was in a safe place.

And that was definitely down to Del.

He entered the hotel and headed for the elevator, wiped out but happy, and looking forward to brunch the following day.

Del got into bed and switched off the light, faintly amused at his situation. Okay, so the evening hadn't exactly gone to plan, but he could deal with that. He didn't even mind the fact that he wasn't sharing his bed for the night.

He had other things to think about. Well, one thing. Taylor.

Del folded his arms under his head and stared up at the ceiling, where lights from passing cars danced across the surface. Taylor's reaction to the question about the bathhouse told him one thing—there was a ninety-nine percent probability that when it came to guys, Taylor was a virgin. Everything about him yelled inexperience. He had good instincts—that teasing reveal of his ass up on the trail was proof of that—but that was about it. Del wondered how many visits Taylor had paid Atlanta so far.

Does he come here to acclimatize himself? To get comfortable around gay men?

All Del knew was he wanted to see more of Taylor. To get to know him more. And then he realized they had the perfect opportunity to do just that.

He comes here. I come here. Why not arrange to come together? It would add a delightful edge to his weekends in Atlanta. What hadn't escaped him was that Taylor was attracted to him. That had been obvious too by the end of the night.

That was just fine by Del. It gave him a goal, and he was in no hurry to achieve it.

I want him. I want to be the first to kiss those soft-looking lips. I want to see those beautiful pale brown eyes widen when I touch him, caress him. I want to be the one who makes him moan, who shatters him with his first orgasm.

Del closed his eyes, an image of Taylor *right there* as he spat into his palm before reaching beneath the sheet to palm his rigid cock. He moved his hand rapidly up and down his shaft, lost in a vision of Taylor astride him, head thrown back, belly taut, Del's hands on Taylor's hips as he drove up into that tight, hot hole...

Del shot hard, caught unawares by the swiftness and force of his release, warmth spattering his belly as his climax shook him. He threw off the sheet and lay there in the semi-darkness, his grip still tight around his dick.

Holy fuck.

He cleaned up and settled down to sleep, his body's needs

sated. As he sank deep into the welcoming blackness, his last thought was that he wished Taylor was beside him, a warm body to wrap around, to hold throughout the night.

Now that *would be bliss.*

Chapter Eleven

Monday, November 13

Taylor propped his bike up against the garage door, then went around the house to the back porch. He opened the door and yelled, "Hey, lady, got anythin' worth stealin'?"

As always, his momma giggled. "Only my shotgun, an' it's aimed right atcha."

It was their standing joke, except Taylor knew she kept a loaded gun within easy reach. He found her in the living room, watching TV, a glass of sweet tea on the table next to her. She smiled as he walked over, proffering her cheek for a kiss.

"Just finished your shift? There's more tea in the refrigerator."

"Thought I'd call in on the way home. And I'll pass on the tea. It's been a long day, an' there's a shower calling my name."

Momma chuckled. "But you thought you'd check up on the old lady first." She gestured to herself. "Still here, still breathin'." She paused before taking a sip of tea. "I missed you this weekend."

Taylor flopped down onto the couch and picked up the TV guide, leafing through it. "I had some things to do. I did tell ya. And I went to Knoxville on Saturday night." Okay, it was a lie, but one she wouldn't query.

"Ah, with some of your coworkers? Well, no wonder. You had better things to do than visit an old lady." She grinned. "Just as long as you behaved yourself."

"I was in bed before midnight," he said, crossing his heart. There had been that heart-stopping moment when he'd truly believed he wasn't going to bed alone, but he was far happier the way things worked out. Saturday had been a lot of fun. He and Del had eaten a huge brunch, then walked it off while they looked at Atlanta. Another night of dancing had followed, only this time Taylor found his groove and danced his ass off. When it came time for each of them to head back home Sunday, Taylor had been reluctant to leave. For the first time since he'd been going there, he'd had fun.

Before they parted company, however, he rectified things. He gave Del his phone number.

Momma put down her glass. "That's fine. You can make up for it by havin' supper with me this Saturday instead."

Aw crap. "Thanks, Momma, but… I kinda got invited to the chief's anniversary party."

Momma regarded him in silence for a moment, then picked up the remote and switched off the TV. "Something you wanna tell me, son?"

He put down the TV guide and met her steady gaze. "No, ma'am. Not that I'm aware of."

Momma narrowed her eyes. "I am *not* stupid. You've been havin' supper there for a while now. You tryin' to tell me the chief keeps askin' you to supper because he thinks you can't feed yourself? 'Cause you sure ain't no orphan child who needs feeding, last time I looked. Or are you buckin' for a promotion? I didn't think you were the type to suck up. So I figure it's to do with the girl, but you ain't said diddly squat about her neither." She cocked her head to one side. "What's goin' on, Taylor?"

His heart quaked. His momma had always had the ability to see right through him, but he thought he'd have longer before her overriding curiosity got the better of her. "Momma, there's nothing to tell," he said gently. "Denise is a nice girl an' all, but… I guess what I'm tryin' to say is… don't read more into this, all right?"

"She's a nice girl, but she's not the one, is that it?" Momma gave a wry smile. "Lord, you're as picky now as you were in high school."

"What does that mean?" Taylor feigned ignorance.

"It means no girl was ever good enough to bring home to momma." Her eyes sparkled. "You'd date someone a couple of times, but I'd never get to meet 'em. Something would always happen and you'd break it off. Not that any of 'em lasted more 'n' a couple of dates."

Two or three dates was as far as Taylor would get before the question of sex reared its head. Making out didn't present a problem—with his eyes closed, it could have been anyone—and once or twice his hands had gone where they'd never gone before, but that was it. Anything else was out of his league and more than he felt capable of doing. It had also sealed in Taylor's mind that he was definitely *not* bisexual.

He opened his mouth to tell her there was nothing wrong with being choosy, but she got in there first. "You moved back here because of me, didn't ya?"

Taylor frowned. "Momma?"

She sighed. "Like I said, I'm not stupid, so don't you go lookin' at me like I've gotten a second head or something."

"No, I'm lookin' at you because *you* were the one back then who was askin' why I wasn't workin' in LaFollette. Or did you forget that part?" He'd been happy living in Nashville. There'd been a gay cop on the force, and everyone seemed to get along with him just fine, enough that Taylor had contemplated coming out. There'd been more potential for Taylor to hook up with a guy too—word getting back to his momma's ears would have been unlikely. But he knew the real reason he'd moved back had been her health. Not that she was at death's door or anywhere in its vicinity, but she struggled with her breathing.

"But if I wasn't here? Would you have stayed in Nashville?"

Shit. "Where's all this leadin', Momma?"

She took another drink of tea. "I guess I just have this feelin' that… you're not happy here. And if that's the case, well… if you think you'd be happier elsewhere, then you should go there. Don't tie yourself to LaFollette because of me, not if there's a chance you could have a better life someplace else."

Impulsively, Taylor got up from the couch, went over to her chair, leaned forward and kissed her forehead. "You are one sweet lady, you know that?"

She huffed. "Ain't nothin' sweet about me. I jus' know that… it's not that I think you're hidin' something exactly, it's just…. Maybe you're not tellin' me the whole truth." She sighed. "I hoped you'd find a girl. Love cures a lot of ills."

It was a cure Taylor didn't dare seek. And maybe that was the problem. Living a lie was proving more difficult than he'd anticipated. He thought back to how he'd felt that past weekend, how liberating it had been to let himself go and not be afraid of being seen.

I loved it. I could… breathe.

"Love does do that, but only when you've found someone who fits," he said quietly. He kissed her cheek. "I'll call in later this week for supper, how's that?"

She nodded, her eyes bright.

Taylor regarded her closely. "You might wanna think about gettin' out more too, y'know."

"Pfft." She waved her hand.

Taylor was not going to be put off. "I'm serious, Momma. You're not even sixty yet. You got years left. I'm not sayin' go dancing every night, but… there have to be places where you can meet people your own age. And I don't mean your church."

She chuckled. "Taylor Cox, are you suggestin' your momma should date?"

"Why the hell not? Why should you be alone? And let's face it, you're beautiful." She kept her blond hair shorter than she used to, and her skin was smooth and pale.

Pink stained her cheeks. "Get outta here. Go on home and eat your supper. I'll see you later in the week, but only if you have the time."

"I'll make time," he whispered as he kissed her smooth forehead. Taylor straightened. "G'night, Momma." He left her and headed out to the garage. As he drove through the streets, he went over the conversation.

She knows. Deep down she knows, but she's afraid of sayin' something in case it somehow makes it all come true.

It was times like these when Taylor thought about living as an openly gay man that he dreamed it could really happen. The thought usually lasted for about ten to fifteen seconds before reality kicked in.

You see how things are. What makes you think attitudes will change?

There was only one answer to that. Hope.

Lord, I'm really fucking this up, aren't I?

It had started really well, a meeting with his friend Jake at Common Ground to catch up over a coffee on what had been going on since Taylor had seen him last. Taylor had wanted to hear all about Jake's latest trip to Atlanta, particularly the gay strip club he'd visited with his friends. What had changed everything had been Jake's revelation.

The news that he had a boyfriend had been enough of a shock, but learning it was Liam had frozen Taylor to his chair. Jake was dating his dead brother's ex? *Shit*, that was *all* kinds of wrong. And it had only gotten worse the more he watched Jake, saw how deep Jake's feelings ran for Liam. Because there was no denying what he saw.

Jake was head over heels in love, and fuck, Taylor wanted to know what that felt like.

He should have congratulated Jake.

He should have wished him and Liam all the best for the future, because, hell, they were gonna need it, especially if they intended spending any time in LaFollette. Taylor could only imagine the comments and glances they were going to get, walking down the street. As if being gay wasn't bad enough—Jake had to date an African American? It was like he had a death wish or something.

Taylor should have forgotten his own feelings and been happy for Jake and Liam.

In the end, he did none of those things, and probably lost his friend in the process. Taylor's own words still rang in his head.

"For one thing, this seems awful fast."

"Caleb has only been dead six months, Jake. Six months. An' now Liam's datin' you? I guess that's my real concern. Who does he see when he looks at ya? You—or Caleb? 'Cause he's got to be missin' Caleb like crazy. I mean, how long were they together? Six years?"

"What concerns me is that you're *the one who's gonna get hurt in all this."*

That last one…. Taylor hadn't been thinking about Jake. He'd been thinking of himself. Of everything he was missing out on. And then he'd really gone and stuck the knife in.

"So… I'm sure Liam has told ya he cares for ya. Hell, he may have told ya he loves ya, an' I don't doubt for a minute that he feels all those things—now. But…what if he's just on the rebound?"

"You have to ask yourself, why is Liam attracted to you? Is it because of you—or because of Caleb?"

Those last words burned in his throat, a remnant of the verbal poison he'd spilled into Jake's ear. Because Taylor *knew* that for Liam to be with Jake, they had to have something pretty amazing.

And here they were, Jake staring at him, so still and so pale that Taylor began to worry. "Are we okay?"

Jake's incredulous gaze said it all, and Taylor thought they were finished right there, but then Jake took a deep breath. "You jus' told me my boyfriend is basic'lly gonna dump me 'cause it's too soon after his ex—my brother—died, an' *then* you ask if we're *okay*? Whadda ya *think*, Taylor?"

Christ, he'd *really* fucked this up, and all because he was jealous. Taylor envied Jake his happiness, his first love, the fact that he'd found someone who loved him back. He opened his mouth to spill his guts, to say he was sorry, but Jake got in there first.

"Tell you what. Ask me again when I've calmed down, an' pref'rably after I've talked to Liam, jus' to make sure you really *are* talkin' a load of hogwash."

"Trust me, if I'm wrong? It'll make my day." Taylor meant those words with all his heart. He still couldn't find the words to tell Jake the truth. Jealousy was such a strong but immature emotion. Instead, he told a half-truth. "Let me know how it goes? 'Cause you know I'll only worry 'bout ya if you don't."

Yeah, he'd worry, all right—that what he'd said had split them up. Because in spite of his jealousy, Taylor really didn't want that to happen.

"Sure." Jake patted Taylor's shoulder. "An' thanks. You could've kept your mouth shut, but ya didn't, an' I know that's 'cause you're a good friend."

Some friend, Taylor thought glumly as he left the coffee shop.

He'd never been so ashamed of himself his entire life.

K.C. WELLS

Chapter Twelve

Wednesday November 15

Del gave the trike one last wipe over with a soft rag, while keeping an eye out for customers. Chaz had an appointment, but he'd be in later. Jon had gone into town, and so far that morning, there had been two customers, returning bikes after a two-day rental. Two *happy* customers, thank God. Del gave them the spiel about leaving a review on Trip Advisor, seeing as the business was relatively new, and they'd seemed more than happy to do that.

The sound of an engine had him looking up, just in time to see a police car park in front of the shop. Del straightened and walked over to the workshop door, rag still in his hand. When only Taylor got out, he smiled.

"Hey. I was gonna text you later." He chucked the rag aside onto a pile of them.

Taylor gave a half-smile. "There you go. I've saved you the trouble. Got some news on your unwanted paint job."

Del gestured toward the shop. "Then step into my office. You got time for a coffee?"

"Not really."

There was something about him that didn't seem right, an air of fatigue or maybe even depression. Del opened the door for him and followed him into the shop. "You know the way."

Taylor headed for the office, and once they were inside, he sank into one of the customer chairs, before digging his notepad out of his pocket. "The analysis came back. The paint is a common brand, sold locally in two or three different stores. Two spray cans were sold recently, but they used cash in both cases. Clerk couldn't remember who'd bought them."

"Didn't the stores have security video?"

Taylor sighed. "One did, but it was awaitin' repairs. The other said it's just for show. The camera's a dummy."

It wasn't like Del could say anything about that, not with his track record on the CCTV. "So we're no closer to finding out who did it."

Taylor shook his head. "With no prints either…"

Yeah, Del had always known the chances of finding the scumbag were close to zero. "Well, we had to try, right?"

"Maybe you need to think about CCTV cameras, like we discussed." Taylor held up a hand. "I know you don't think it'll happen again, but just in case it does…"

"Yeah, yeah, I got the message." Hell, Jon had been saying the very same thing. Frequently. "I'll look into it," he said with a sigh of resignation. It made sense, after all.

"So why were you gonna text me?"

Del leaned against the desk. "First off, I was curious if you had any plans for the weekend." Del had been thinking about this since their meeting in Atlanta. He hadn't brought up his ideas because it seemed like Taylor had been having a big enough task just relaxing. But the weekend had gone well, and that had given Del the impetus to put together a plan.

Whether Taylor would go for it remained to be seen.

"I'm going to a party."

Del chuckled. "Yeah. You're real excited about it. I can tell."

Taylor regarded him with scrunched up brows for a second, then he snickered. "It shows, huh? It's the chief of police's anniversary. Not my first choice for a Saturday night, but hey…"

"I guess it's a duty kinda thing?" A light bulb went off in Del's head. "Unless this has something to do with the chief's daughter?"

Taylor's brows knitted together. "It's… complicated." He bowed his head as though his neck could no longer support its weight.

Del gave Taylor a keen glance. This wasn't the same guy who'd laughed and joked all through Saturday and Sunday. *This* Taylor had the weight of the world on his shoulders. "You wanna talk about it?" he asked softly. "Whatever it is that's on your mind?"

Taylor raised his head to meet Del's gaze. "Not really. I... I messed up, and tellin' you just how *badly* I messed up is not gonna make it any better."

"No, but getting someone else's perspective on it might not be a bad thing. Maybe it's not as fucked up as you think it is." Del laid his hand gently on Taylor's shoulder. "I'm not prying. I'm just trying to help." He kept his voice low and even, sort of... soothing.

Lord, the pain in Taylor's pale brown eyes...

Just then his radio screeched into life, and Taylor sighed before answering. When he was done, he got to his feet. "I gotta go."

Del stood too. "Sure. You got bad guys to catch. Doesn't mean you can't stop for a coffee at some point this afternoon, does it? Because that was the second reason for texting you. Common Ground again?" He smiled. "I'll treat you to a slice of carrot cake." He kept his gaze focused on Taylor. *Come on, honey. Say yes.*

Finally, Taylor's tension melted. "You know what? That sounds great. Not sure when, so I'd have to text you later when I got a better idea of the time."

"Not a problem. Jon can run things here." Impulsively, Del gave Taylor a brief hug. "It'll be okay," he whispered. To his surprise, Taylor leaned into the embrace, and Del was aware of his scent, a reminder of the weekend. He released Taylor, just as Jon walked into the office.

"Good mornin', officer." Jon's voice held an edge of surprise.

Taylor stepped out of Del's reach, and touched his cap. "Gentlemen." He walked out of the office, shoving his notepad back into his jacket. Del watched him get into the police car, his heart heavy.

Not certain if I can do a damn thing in the time it takes to have a coffee and some cake, but I'm sure as hell gonna try.

Jon cleared his throat, and when Del turned to look at him, Jon regarded him with arched brows.

"So what was that?"

Del feigned innocence. "Huh?"

Jon smirked. "Don't give me that bullshit. I'm not blind. You got something goin' on with that cop, don'tcha? Unless you're huggin' *everyone* these days." He folded his arms across his chest. "How the fuck do you do that, hmm? You just happened to find yourself a gay cop?"

Del took a breath. "First off, there is nothing going on. I swear."

Jon narrowed his gaze. "Maybe, but you'd sure *like* there to be something, right?" He gave Del a smug glance. "Go on, tell me I'm wrong."

Del couldn't do that, not when he wanted it to be true.

"Okay," he said quietly. "Yes, I like him. Yes, he's gay, but he's not out. In fact, he's so far in the closet, he's in Narnia. So you're not gonna say a word."

Jon's expression was solemn. "I wouldn't do that."

Like Del didn't know that already. "And I hugged him because... he's got something on his mind, and I wanna help. And that's the truth."

Jon said nothing for a moment, then nodded slowly. "Just... be careful, all right? I don't wanna see you get hurt."

"How's that gonna happen?"

Jon widened his eyes. "You fall for a cop who can't come out, an' you are in for a *lot* of pain, bro. Because I can *not* see that ending well. Can you?"

Del gave him a hug. "Love you too, bro. All we're doing right now is sharing coffee and dancing our feet off." He glanced over Jon's shoulder. "And right now, *we* got customers, and a business to run." He patted Jon on the back and went out to greet them.

Time enough to think about Taylor later.

Del parked his motorcycle in the parking lot behind Smith Ace Hardware, and stowed the helmet. The lot was a huge space with Ollis Creek running along one side of it, and he could walk through the hardware store to get to the coffee shop. There were maybe twenty or more cars dotted around, and no one in sight.

Well, he couldn't see anyone, but he could sure hear something going on. From the far end of the lot came raucous laughter, and the sound of breaking glass. Del craned his neck to see what was happening, and saw three guys standing around a car. Two of the three guys were smashing tire irons into the car windows. The windshield was already shattered.

"Hey!" he yelled, and broke into a run. "You stop that right now!" He didn't break pace as he sprinted toward the car, trying to take in details of the guys. They took one look at him and started running toward the creek, still clutching the tire irons. By the time Del reached the car, they were out of sight.

"Fuck." He bent over, winded, and sucked in air. The car was a mess, with boot prints covering the hood, and dents where they'd obviously jumped on it. Tiny pieces of glass covered the car and the ground surrounding it, and there were deep scratches in the paint on the doors.

What really pissed him off was that he hadn't gotten a clear look at the bastards. They were younger, that much he could tell, and a helluva lot fitter than Del, but that wasn't saying much: he was carrying more weight than the three skinny guys.

"Oh my God."

Del straightened and found himself faced with a tall, slim figure. The guy was maybe in his early twenties, his skin a russet brown. He dropped his plastic bag onto the ground and rushed forward, his dark brown eyes wide with horror.

"No need to ask if this is your car," Del murmured.

The young man jerked his head in Del's direction. "Who're you?"

"The name's Del Walters. I run a bike shop up on Central. There were three guys who did this, but I only got a quick look at 'em. They ran off when I yelled."

"Thanks for that."

Del waved a hand. "Anyone would've have done the same."

The guy met his gaze, and Del's scalp prickled. "Ya think? Then you have more faith in human nature than I do. Specially around here." He glanced back to the car. "Bastards. Fucking low-life bastards."

Del cocked his head to one side. "You sound like you got an idea who did this."

The guy snorted. "Pick anyone from my high school. Not that they ever went *this* far back then. They wouldn't have dared." His tone was bitter.

"Okay, then let's be practical. You need to report this to the police—I'm sorry, but it feels weird talking with you and not knowing your name."

The guy smiled. "You're right. I'm sorry. I should've introduced myself, but good manners go out the window when scumbags trash your car." He held out his hand. "Kendis Sesay."

Del shook it. "Pleased to meet you. Okay, *now* you call the police." On first impression, Kendis was an intelligent guy.

Kendis let out another derisive snort. "Sure. Not that they'll do anything. I mean, have you *seen* some of the old guys who drive around here in patrol cars? I step off the sidewalk in front of them, an' you can tell they're *dying* to do a stop 'n' search."

There were some things about the South that hadn't changed since Del was a kid, which was a pity, because they were the kind of attitudes that needed to be relegated to the past, as far as he was concerned. Then it hit him.

"Not all of 'em." He got out his phone and scrolled through, pressing Call when he found Taylor's number. "Hey. You there already?"

Taylor laughed. "Christ, I just walked through the door. You want me to order for ya?"

"Actually? Can you come to the parking lot behind Smith's on North 1st Street? I need you in an official capacity."

Taylor's brisk reaction was exactly how Del had imagined it would be. "Be there in a minute." He disconnected.

Del pocketed his phone. "Okay. I have a friend who's a cop. We were about to meet up for coffee, but he'll take down details and make sure this gets reported. Meantime, you need to get the car towed someplace."

Kendis rubbed the scruff on his chin. "There's B&B Auto Repair. I've used them before." He gave a half-smile. "You'd probably like 'em. The shop sign is held by a bear."

Del almost choked. Okay, that told him something about Kendis. He coughed to clear his throat. "You tell it like it is, don't you?"

Kendis chuckled. "It's the only way to be." He glanced around Del. "This looks like it's your friend."

Del turned to greet Taylor, whose eyes widened when he saw Kendis. "Hey, I know you. Kendis Sesay, right? You and your brother played for the Cougars." Taylor addressed Del. "Kendis was a few years after me, but he went to the same high school. He played basketball for the school team." He extended a hand. "How you doin'?"

Kendis shook it, then gestured toward his car. "I've been better."

Taylor gazed at the car, wincing. "Ouch." He got out his phone and took pictures of all the damage. "You got any idea when this happened?"

"Just now," Del interjected. "I saw three guys, two of them with tire irons. They ran off toward the creek when I started running and yelled at 'em to stop."

Taylor's lips twitched. "Lord, I bet that sight alone scared the shit outta them."

Del narrowed his gaze. "Meaning what?"

Taylor grinned. "You forget, I've seen you dance."

Kendis looked from Taylor to Del, then burst out laughing. "You two really are friends, aren't you?"

Del flashed Taylor a glance, but he appeared calm. "We met in much the same way I'm meetin' you. I got called in to investigate an incident at his bike shop. Then we discovered we like the same coffee shop." Taylor got out his notepad. "I'll need you both to come in and make statements. Del, could you identify them if you saw them again?"

"I doubt it. They were too far away, and running in the wrong direction. I can tell you they were young, and what they were wearing. That's about it."

"It's better than nothing." Taylor made a note, then regarded Kendis. "You got any idea why they chose your car? I mean, I'm not askin' if you've gotten anyone pissed enough to wanna wreck it, but…"

"Maybe they didn't like the way I played ball," Kendis suggested, that bitter note still evident. "And no, I've not made any enemies, far as I know." He shrugged. "Maybe someone just doesn't like the way I look. Wouldn't be the first time." He got out his phone. "You know what? I'm gonna call B&B and have 'em tow this away. 'Cause right now I can't bear to look at it."

Taylor patted him on the arm, before handing him a card. "This is my number, if you ever wanna call. Just sayin'." He attempted a smile. "Even if you just wanna talk over a coffee sometime."

Kendis's eyes glistened for a moment. "Thanks." He slipped the card into his phone holder.

Del tugged on Taylor's arm. "Ready for that coffee now?"

"Sure." Taylor gave Kendis a last glance. "You okay?"

Kendis nodded. "I'll be fine. After all, it was only my car that got busted up, right?"

On impulse, Del got out his wallet and removed a business card. "And this is so you can reach me. I like coffee too."

Kendis took it. "Well, looks like LaFollette isn't comprised *totally* of assholes." He gave them a weak smile. "Thanks, guys. I may take you both up on that offer at some point."

"Looking forward to it." Del gave Taylor's arm another tug. "Come on."

They walked off toward Smith's hardware, leaving Kendis gazing at his car, his phone to his ear.

Del still had a puzzle to solve—what had brought Taylor so low that morning. And he didn't plan on leaving the coffee shop until he had the answer.

Chapter Thirteen

They took the same table in the corner, and Del smirked. "You like sitting where you can see what's coming, don't you?"

Taylor chuckled. "I guess it goes with the job." He stared out the window toward the town beyond. "I was just thinking about Kendis. This can't be the easiest place to live. I mean, look around. It's almost a sea of white faces out there. He and his brother must've stood out like a sore thumb in high school."

Del had been thinking the same thing. "I wonder what circumstances brought them here. Why LaFollette of all places?"

"I can answer that." Taylor clammed up as Drew came over with their coffees and cake. He thanked him and waited until he was back behind the counter. "This happened after I'd graduated, but it's a small town. You get to know everything. Kendis and his brother were transferred to the high school to play ball. That was it, pure and simple. The coach wanted a couple of hot players, and he went out of state to get 'em."

"Seriously?"

Taylor nodded. "Kendis, his brother, and his mom moved here so the boys could play ball. The school found their mom a job, but unfortunately, Kendis's part of the deal wasn't so sweet."

"Did they face a lot of racism?"

Taylor shook his head. "Word got around. The school needed 'em to win the championship, so everyone was to play nice. So to speak. So no, they didn't get racist threats or attacks. They just got… silence. Avoidance. It was like they weren't there, apparently. I guess now he's graduated, people feel freer to do what they like."

That gave Del a sour taste in his mouth. "You think he'd ever be physically attacked?"

Taylor shook his head again. "That's not how things work here. It's more a case of 'ignore it an' it'll go away.' Don't get me wrong. I don't doubt the vandalism to Kendis's car was racially motivated, but I don't think they'll sink to violence."

Del hoped not. Kendis seemed like a real nice guy. He relayed Kendis's comments about older cops and their attitudes. "Do you think he's right? About the way they act around him? Because thinking about it, that would make sense."

Taylor frowned. "What do you mean?"

"People are the same wherever you go. It's not only intellect and wisdom that hopefully grow with age—lots of prejudices grow too, especially if those concerned aren't doing so well, financially or socially. You can be virtually indifferent to certain groups when you're younger, but if life doesn't treat you so well, and you get older and more bitter, with more hate in your heart..." Del shrugged. "I can see some older people being the most hostile. And talk about a double whammy," he added quietly. When Taylor's brows knitted, Del sighed. "I think he's gay too." He repeated Kendis's comment about the bear sign. To his surprise, Taylor's face tightened.

"Oh Lord. I didn't need that today." He wrapped his hands around his mug and drank.

"Suppose you tell me what got you so messed up this morning?" Del suggested softly. "And I'm not gonna judge you. You should know me better than that by now."

"I do. It's just...." Taylor leaned against the wall, his mug still in his hands. "I met up with a friend recently. He had some... news for me, and I didn't take it very well."

"Tell me." Del kept his tone gentle.

Taylor took a deep breath, then let it all out. Del listened to Taylor's words, but he watched Taylor's facial expressions too, noting the way his breathing sped up, the hard swallows he took, the way he wouldn't meet Del's gaze. When Taylor was done, Del said nothing for a moment, trying to make sense of it all in his head.

"Do you believe everything you told Jake?" he asked at last.

Taylor's reply was barely audible. "No."

"Then why did you say it?"

Taylor raised his chin, and Del gazed into troubled brown eyes. "I... I was jealous."

"Because he has a relationship?" When Taylor nodded, Del leaned forward, his hands clasped together on the table. "And who says you can't have that?"

Another hard swallow. "I can't." Taylor's voice was low.

"But why not?"

"I can't be gay. Not here."

Del got that. He truly did. What he didn't get was how Taylor couldn't see the solution. "Then don't. You got Atlanta for all that."

Taylor frowned. "I've been going to Atlanta a while now. But it—"

"And how do you feel when you're there?"

Taylor shuddered out a breath. "Like I can be... free."

Del nodded. "You feel comfortable in your own skin. Free to be yourself. But I've seen you there. You're like a cat on a hot plate. How many visits did you pay before you got up and danced like you wanted to? Hmm? It was only 'cause I asked you that you did it. So... don't stop. Explore."

Taylor's breathing hitched. "Excuse me?"

Del took a drink of coffee. "I had this idea last weekend, and I've been meaning to talk to you about it. No one says you have to come out, all right? That's your decision. But that doesn't mean you can't live the life of a gay man in Atlanta. And you know exactly what I mean."

"Do I?" Taylor sipped his coffee.

Del snorted. "Remember what I said a while back. I got twenty years on you, and there isn't much I haven't seen. I trust my instincts, and right now those instincts are tellin' me you're not just jealous of Jake 'cause he's in a relationship."

"Why else would I be jealous? Certainly not of the fact that his boyfriend is gonna bring him a world of hurt if Jake ever takes him home."

Del shook his head. "What eats you up is everything that comes with a relationship—stuff you think you're missing out on. Like intimacy. Lust. Sex." He met Taylor's gaze and locked him there. "Tell me I'm wrong. Because I recall the way you looked at me that first time up on the trail. Like you wanted to lick the leathers right off of my body."

Taylor paled. "Fuck. You... you *saw* that?"

Del smiled. "Hell yeah. Of course, I was busy havin' similar thoughts about you. Like bending you over my bike." He saw little point in hiding now. If this was going to work, they needed to be honest.

Taylor flicked a nervous gaze around the coffee shop, and Del pounced.

"And that reaction right there is why you need to come with me to Atlanta, on a regular basis. You can't live the way you want to here, and I totally get that. So I'm suggesting that once a month—hell, every five or six weeks if you like—you and I go to Atlanta for the weekend. The goal is simple. I take you around. To places you might not go on your own. I get you to push at your envelope, and experience what it's like to be a gay man. And I'll have your back. I'll keep you safe." Del leaned forward. "Most importantly—what happens in Atlanta stays in Atlanta."

Something hot and hungry uncoiled in Taylor's belly, sending tendrils of warmth spreading through his body. Because Del had nailed it.

Taylor looked at his situation and despaired. He wanted all those things, with no chance of getting them in LaFollette. And yeah, he was jealous of Jake because Jake was clearly getting what he needed.

He also knew that Del was right. A healthy dose of fear had kept him from doing anything in Atlanta beyond drinking in a bar or watching a drag show. That wasn't living either. That was watching from the sidelines. And there *were* places Taylor longed to go, places that tugged at him, called to him…

He wasn't stupid. Sure, he believed Del would take him to all those places—and more—but he also knew what would be in Del's mind while they were there. Talking about bending Taylor over his bike didn't leave any room for doubt, right? Del wanted him, and that was just fine, because while he was being honest like this, Taylor could admit that fuck, he wanted Del too. No illusions there.

But the idea of spending time in Atlanta with Del as a kind of safety net appealed to him. *I could let go. Really let go. And Del would be there for me.*

That line about stuff staying in Atlanta might have been corny, but Taylor clung to it. No one back home would know. He could let loose and spend forty-eight hours in ways he could only *dream* about in LaFollette.

"Taylor."

He blinked. "Huh?"

Del grinned. "Not sure what planet you were on right then, but judging by your expression, it was a lotta fun." He pushed the plate of carrot cake toward him. "Eat, before Drew thinks there's something wrong with it."

Taylor took a forkful of cake and ate it absently, his mind still on Del's proposal.

"You like the idea, don'tcha?" Del said simply.

He didn't trust himself to speak, just nodded.

"Yeah, me too. And if you wanna save on hotel bills, we can share a double room." Del held up his hands. "You in your bed, me in mine." His eyes sparkled, however, and Taylor wasn't fooled for a second.

Yeah right. Not that the idea didn't send more warmth

pulsing through him.

"We… we can talk about that," he said as nonchalantly as he could manage. He finished the cake and drained the rest of his coffee.

"Now I'm sorry you got that party to go to this Saturday." Del was almost pouting, and Taylor realized it was for his benefit.

He laughed. "Yeah, well, Atlanta will have to wait. And don't forget next week is Thanksgiving. So that's gonna be out too."

"You gonna spend it with your momma?"

"Yeah. I try to do as much as I can when it comes to helping her with dinner. She's nearly sixty, but her breathing ain't so good, an' it wears her out. How about you? Gonna get together with Jon and cook?"

Del's eruption of hearty laughter sounded good, even if a few heads turned in their direction. From behind the counter, Drew regarded them with interest. Taylor signaled to Del to lower the volume a little, and Del dropped his voice into a whisper. "Oh my God. Only if we wanna end up in the hospital with food poisoning. Sure, we'll spend it together, but everything edible will be of the 'shove in the oven or microwave' variety."

Taylor chuckled, then glanced at his phone. "Damn. Time I was outta here. I need to get back and file a report on Kendis's car."

"I'll come with you." Del stood.

"Why?" Taylor was seized by a moment of irrational fear, before he got a hold of himself. *What the hell am I afraid of?*

Except he knew the answer to that. *What if someone sees more than I want them to see?*

Del put a hand to his arm. "Relax, Taylor. I'm coming in to give a statement about those guys I saw. I can describe their height, build, hair color, and what they were wearing. So what if I didn't see their faces—at least you'll have something to go on." His expression grew serious. "And I can be as distant and polite as I need to be."

Relief surged through him. "Thanks. Not that I thought you'd walk in there—"

"With my arm around your shoulders?" Del snickered. "Yeah, I can see *that* being well received. Let's get going, before I have Jon complaining that I'm never there." His eyes twinkled. "My turn to pay, 'cause you paid last time." He went over to the counter.

Taylor checked in on his radio, while Del paid. When Del gave him the thumbs up, they left the coffee shop. What came to mind was how different this encounter felt compared to the last one. Taylor had been uneasy then, unsure of Del.

This time had felt like the meeting of two friends, and Taylor liked that just fine.

What got him warm all over was the thought that they could be more than that.

Chapter Fourteen

Saturday, November 18

"Dear Lord, here we go again," Taylor whispered as he caught another glance in their direction. He handed Denise her glass of wine, then deliberately turned his back to the observer. "Is she still looking this way?" He'd recognized that spark of interest in her eyes as she gazed around the room.

Denise snickered. "'She' is my cousin Abigail, and yeah, she's still lookin', so be afraid. Be very afraid. Biggest gossip in all of Campbell County."

Taylor groaned. "According to you, *all* your relatives are gossips."

Denise coughed. "Yeah, well... I *may* have exaggerated a little... just a little...." He glared at her, and she smirked. "What? I was havin' fun!" Then she straightened. "Abigail's coming this way."

He snorted. "Yeah, like I'm gonna believe a word you say from now on." The panicked look in Denise's eyes, however, spoke volumes, and he turned around to find himself face to face with cousin Abigail. Taylor pasted on a smile. "Good evening. Y'all havin' a good time?"

Abigail's eyes were bright. "I had to come over and meet Denise's young man. I hear you're a police officer." She looked Taylor up and down, and he worked hard to maintain a neutral smile.

"You got that part right, Abi, but Taylor is *not* my young man," Denise insisted. "He's a friend, is all. Now, why don't you go in the kitchen? Momma is putting out some more—"

That was as far as she got before Abigail made a beeline for the kitchen.

"How did you get her to do that so fast?" Taylor demanded. "I was expectin' a full-on interrogation."

Denise winked. "If there's one thing Abi loves more than gossip, it's food. One hint is all it took." Then she beamed over his shoulder. "Hey, Daddy. You enjoyin' your party?" Her lips twitched.

Chief Tillerson gave her a mock glare. "And there I was, thinkin' I raised an intelligent daughter." He chuckled, then turned to Taylor. "I'm not a social animal, Taylor."

He couldn't resist. "I'd never have guessed, sir, not after seein' you at your monthly Coffee with the Chief meetings." He bit back a smile.

Denise let out a very unladylike snort. "My, but he does know you, Daddy."

His eyes glittered. "Mm-hm. Meanwhile, I've been gettin' remarks and questions all night about you two. What a cute couple you make. Asking how long you've been goin' steady. Wondering if we might expect an announcement." He gave her an evil smile. "Now, I *could* continue with what I've been doin' all evenin', and tell 'em there's nothing *to* tell, *or* I could send them in your direction."

"You wouldn't." Denise stared at him in horror.

The chief leaned in and kissed her cheek. "No, I wouldn't, but it's awful temptin'." He glanced around the room, which was packed with people, all chattering loudly, glasses in their hands, the faint strains of Frank Sinatra barely audible above the noise. "Don't know why I bothered with the music. All this chatter just ruins any chance of listenin' to Frank." He leaned closer to Denise. "If your momma asks, you haven't seen me." He kissed her cheek again, before heading toward the back porch.

Denise laughed. "He's gonna take a spell in the yard where he can smoke in peace. You *really* wanna get in his good books?"

"That can't hurt none."

Denise left him for a moment, then returned with two cold cans of beer. "Go take him his favorite brewski, and have one with him. I'll do the dutiful daughter thing and mingle."

Taylor took them, and carefully made his way through the guests, heading for the back door whilst avoiding any direct gazes. He found the chief in the gazebo at the far end of the yard, sitting on a bench, his legs stretched out in front of him.

"Thought you could do with one of these." Taylor held out a can.

The chief's eyes gleamed in the solar lighting. "As my daughter says now and again, you rock." He took it and shifted along the bench to make space. "Join me. I hate drinkin' alone."

Taylor sat, opened his own can and took a refreshing gulp.

The chief sighed. "Ain't nothing like a cold beer, even on a night like this. It always hits the spot." He rested his head against a wooden post. "Do you like parties?"

"They're okay, I guess. I don't have a lot of experience going to them nowadays."

The chief chuckled. "Hell, that's no bad thing in a police officer. Better to be like that, than out every night, tomcattin' around."

Taylor knew he was referring to Mark Teagle, but said nothing.

They chatted about inconsequential topics, like Taylor's plans for Thanksgiving and the holiday weekend, before moving on to more personal matters like his momma. But through it all, Taylor knew what was coming, felt it like an undercurrent, deep and relentless, tugging him gently but firmly in one specific direction.

"So... how are things goin' with you an' Denise?"

And there it was, the jagged tip of the iceberg, its mass hidden in the depths.

Taylor didn't want to lie, because giving the man false hope was just plain *wrong*, but at the same time, he didn't want to upset the status quo. Denise was content with the situation, as it kept her parents off her back, but Taylor knew he couldn't keep this up forever.

"I like your daughter, sir," he said truthfully.

The chief snorted. "Lord, I hear a 'but' in there somewhere."

Crap. He was no dummy.

"It's obvious she likes you too. I guess what I wanna know is, if this is goin' somewhere. I figured you'd have a better idea of that by now."

"Frank? What in the world are you doin' out here when we've got guests?" Mrs. Tillerson's hiss crept out across the garden, and the chief groaned quietly.

"So much for a quiet beer," he murmured. "Come on. We'd better get back inside."

Taylor could have kissed Mrs. Tillerson right then.

Once inside, one of the male guests came up to the chief, grinning. "A little bird tells me you got a new box of cigars this week. Any chance of tryin' one?"

The chief laughed. "I guess it *is* that time." He raised his voice. "Any of you gentlemen wanna join me for a smoke? And of course, ladies. We don't discriminate around here." That brought a ripple of laughter.

"Oh, get in there, so we can all talk about ya," Mrs. Tillerson said with a wave of her hand. All the women around her chuckled.

Denise came over and whispered into Taylor's ear. "I forgot to tell you about this part. All the men disappear into Daddy's man cave to talk big important man stuff. Lucky you—you get to go too."

"I heard that." The chief gave her a mock glare, before gesturing to Taylor to follow him.

The 'man cave' turned out to be a large room lined with pine, with hunting trophies on the wall, which amounted to a couple of deer heads and a fox. Big, squashy couches lined three of the walls, and there was a fireplace set into a stone-covered chimney breast, beside which was a big old armchair that had to be the chief's seat of choice. Glasses were filled, only this time with whiskey, and cigars handed around to the seven or eight guys who'd followed the chief in there.

Taylor declined to smoke, but took a finger of whiskey and stood next to the fireplace, watching. The men were a mixture of relatives by marriage, and friends, and Taylor was certain he recognized some of them from businesses around LaFollette. What amused him was their attitude. Gone were the pleasantries and chat from the party: it was as though that had been an act for when in mixed company.

The Great American Male in his natural habitat, Taylor thought with an internal grin. It was like watching a documentary on animal rituals.

"So, Frank, you gotten a look at the couple of fags who moved into town a few weeks ago, sweet as you please?" The man seated opposite the chief lit up, and puffed out a whole load of smoke into the room with a satisfied air.

Taylor stiffened, but did his best to act like someone hadn't just poured freezing water over his balls.

The chief frowned. "Cal, you *sure* you're Elaine's brother? 'Cause I always thought your family had brains. You appear to have lost yours somewhere." Snickers and guffaws followed his words.

Cal persisted. "Oh, come on. We've all seen the sign. 'Rainbow Racers,'" he said, hooking his fingers in the air. "Ain't that nice?"

The chief rubbed his chin, before meeting Taylor's gaze. "Didn't you say they're brothers?" Taylor nodded, and the chief glanced at Cal. "Taylor here had cause to visit the shop before they opened. So it looks like you're talkin' out your ass—again." Yet more laughter ensued, and Cal narrowed his gaze.

Taylor had met enough bigoted assholes to know the signs. Cal wasn't about to back down.

"I don't care what they *say*. You just gotta look at the big guy. Drives around in leathers on that big bike of his, gets himself a nice little boy to work there…. Fucking pervert, if you ask me. I tell ya, it's like watching those TV shows about all those degenerates in California. All you see is guys like him."

"You watch a lot of those, do ya, Cal?" someone commented, and a fresh eruption of snorts and snickers followed.

"And what idiot rides a motorbike and *doesn't* wear leathers? Nothin' wrong with protecting your ass." More chuckles. "Hell, *I* wear leathers when I go ridin'. Does that make me one, too, Cal?"

"Hey, wait a sec." One of the guests straightened. "Are we talking about Del Walters? Christ, I've met him. The guy seems all right, if you ask me. He's tryin' to organize all the local businesses into some sort of committee, to offer support to each other, you know, like networkin'." Murmurs of agreement echoed around him.

"An' *maybe* that's just an act, to get y'all on his good side. Look, what does it say in Corinthians, about Satan masqueradin' as an angel of light?" Cal's face was twisted.

Another guy snorted. "So he's gone from being a queer to the Devil himself?" He rolled his eyes. "Cal, you are so full o' shit. An' I get to say that, 'cause I'm your cousin."

Taylor listened in growing horror to the verbal diarrhea Cal was spouting, aching to say something, *anything*, to defend Del. As others spoke positively, and he saw that Cal was definitely in the minority, he grasped his courage at last.

"Can I ask you a question?" Taylor's mouth was suddenly dry, and he took a sip of whiskey.

Cal blinked. "I s'ppose."

"This guy, Del Walters… will his business impact on yours in some way?"

Cal's brow furrowed. "Well… no."

"Then what does it matter what the guy chooses to do in the privacy of his own bedroom? What bearin' does it have on *your* life?" Taylor was past caring what the dickhead thought, although his heart pounded.

"Of *course* it matters!" Cal declared loudly. "What he's doin' is just wrong."

"Hey, now, Taylor has a point," someone else said. "He's not harming anyone."

"Yeah, an' the way you described him, well... that ain't right. He's taken a kid to train in his business. You made it sound like he's... pimpin' him out or something."

Taylor welcomed the surge of relief that flooded through him.

Cal's cousin chuckled. "Shit, the way you go on an' on about him... something you wanna tell us, Cal?" That got the biggest laugh of the night.

The chief cleared his throat, and just like that, silence fell. He aimed his steely gaze at Cal. "Don't we have enough hate in this world without you addin' to it? Because as far as I can tell, this guy is just goin' about his business, gettin' local enterprises to band together.... That tells me all I need to know about the man." He took a puff of his cigar. "And to tell the truth? I was always partial to rainbows myself." He grinned.

The men around him chuckled, with the exception of Cal, but Taylor wasn't bothered. What heartened him was the support they'd offered Del, and the lack of prejudice and hate. Most of all, he liked the chief's words.

Maybe Denise had it right all along. He recalled her words of a few short weeks ago.

So what if my daddy gives speeches for the Boy Scouts of America? Don't assume to know what's in a man's heart—or how he'll react. He might just surprise you.

Taylor was really open to being surprised right then.

Chapter Fifteen

Thanksgiving, November 23

Del took another peep at the turkey through the oven's glass door. "Isn't it done yet?"

From the living room, Jon snorted. "Will you leave it to cook? The last time I shoved a thermometer up its butt, the damn thing was nowhere near as hot as it should be. Now, I don't care if it looks like you could eat it right this second. Until that thermometer says, 'Hey, y'all! It's safe to eat now!' we don't touch it." Del caught more mumbles, something along the lines of how they should've stuck with their original idea.

Del laughed. "If we'd stuck with the first plan, we'd be eating hot dogs, slaw and chips right now. This is better, isn't it?"

Jon appeared in the kitchen doorway, Delilah in his arms. The cat stared at the oven, licking her chops. "I guess. There has to be a first time for everything."

Del smirked at the cat's obvious interest. "Well, *someone* wants the turkey as is." Across the room, his phone vibrated on top of the countertop. He picked it up and smiled. "It's Chaz." Del connected the call. "Hey. Happy Thanksgiving." When a muffled sob caught his ear, Del went cold. "Chaz? You okay?"

"Del…. Where are you right now?" Chaz sounded terrible, almost as if he was mumbling.

"At Jon's. Why? You need something?"

"Can… can I come over?"

Del held his phone against his chest. "We're about to have company."

Jon frowned. "Is he all right? And sure, if he needs to see us, tell him to get his ass over here."

Del resumed the call. "Okay, I'll send you the link for Jon's address. You on the bike?"

"Yeah."

"I've got a better idea. I'll come pick you up." Del really didn't like the way Chaz sounded.

"No, it's…. I can get there, all right?"

"Then go easy. No accidents, okay?" He sent the link.

"Got it. I'll be there soon." Chaz disconnected.

Del pocketed his phone, deep in thought. *What the hell?*

"Del?"

He looked up to meet Jon's concerned gaze. "Something's wrong. Sounded to me like… he'd been crying."

"Aw shit." Jon's jaw set. "You *know* what I'm thinkin', don'tcha?"

"That this is something to do with his parents? That was my first thought too." He gazed around the kitchen. "Well, if he's gonna stay for Thanksgiving, there'll be plenty of food. Eventually."

Jon rolled his eyes. "Lord, you have no patience. The fact that you've never found a guy who'll stay the distance now makes a lotta sense." Then he froze. "Hey, Del… I… I didn't mean it to come out like that."

Del said nothing for a moment. *Maybe he's got a point. Maybe I've been complainin' all this time about not finding someone, and it's been my own fault.* He thought he'd found someone, but Lane had turned out to be a lying, cheating bastard. *Was it me? Was there something in me that pushed him away?* Then he shoved that thought aside. No, that mess was all down to Lane. *Other* messes, he was less sure about.

Finally Del became aware of the awkward silence. Jon was regarding him anxiously, still holding onto Delilah who was straining in his arms to get to the oven.

"It's okay," he reassured Jon. "You just made me think,

that's all."

"Then it's *not* okay." Jon's earnest expression made his chest tighten. "You're a good man, an' don't let anyone tell you different. Any guy who gets you in his life is gonna be a lucky SOB, you got that?"

Del gave him a warm smile. "I'd hug ya, but you've got your arms full of cat."

Jon snorted and deposited Delilah on the tiled floor. "*You* rate more than the damn cat any day." He gave Del a firm hug. "Besides, who am I to talk? I ain't got nobody in my life neither."

"Yeah, but you like it that way. An' Delilah is probably the only female you could put up with."

Jon snickered. "You got me there." He broke away and turned his head toward the back door. "Sounds like our company has arrived." He opened the door and stepped outside.

Delilah chose that moment to wind in and out of Del's ankles, purring loudly. He wasn't fooled none—he was standing next to the oven. "That will *not* get you some turkey any faster," he told her, before shaking his head. "Look at me. Talkin' to the cat."

"Jesus Christ!"

The alarm in Jon's voice cut through him. Del bolted toward the door and out onto the driveway. His stomach clenched when he saw Chaz, Jon's arm around him as he helped him walk to the door. Chaz's face was a mess, a sea of cuts and bruises, and he was holding one arm up against his chest.

Del was at Chaz's other side in a heartbeat. "How in the hell did you drive with a bad arm?"

"Not my arm, it's my wrist, an' it fucking *hurt*! Thought I was gonna pass out at one point."

Chaz looked like that might happen at any second. "Let's get you inside," Del said, his voice soothing, "and then we can decide how best to treat you. We might be talking the Emergency Room." Jon nodded in agreement.

Chaz shook his head. "They'd ask too many questions." He winced, and Del could see why: his lip was busted.

"Then we'll make do with my first aid kit." Jon helped him into the house. "The kitchen's full of food, so let's go to the bathroom. I can clean you up better in there." Then he paused. "You know what? Del's better at this than I am. I'll go pour us some tea. We can talk when you're patched up and you've taken some Tylenol."

Chaz attempted a smile. "That last part sounds good."

Del took him into the bathroom, let him sit on the toilet seat, then rummaged in the cabinet under the sink for Jon's green first aid zip bag. "Here we are," he said triumphantly, pulling it out from under rags, sponges and God knew what else. He paused at the sight of Chaz's poor face in the harsh light, and took his phone from his pocket. Del activated the camera, then paused. "Trust me. I've seen enough people in your position to know that while you might not wanna use them *now*, photos can be useful later on."

Chaz let out a sigh of resignation. "Go ahead. It's not like I could stop you anyhow."

Del took a couple of pictures from different angles, including ones of Chaz's arm. "Is there anything else I need to see?" he asked quietly.

Chaz hesitated, then pulled up his shirt with his good arm. There were bruises over his chest and belly.

Del went cold inside. "Are you sure we shouldn't be taking you to the Emergency Room? What if you've got internal bleeding?"

"I'll make you a deal. If I feel worse, you can take me. But right now, I'm just sore. And I don't wanna answer their questions."

Del took a couple more photos, then he put the phone away, and as carefully as he could, cleaned and dressed Chaz's cuts and bruises.

"Jon's right," Chaz mumbled. "You're good at this."

"That's because I did some training back in San Francisco. I was running a business where no one was trained in first aid. So I did it." He opened the mirrored cabinet door, took out the bottle of

Tylenol, popped the cap, and shook two into Chaz's good hand. Then he poured a glass of water and waited for Chaz to put them in his mouth before handing it to him. When he was done, Del rinsed the glass and took one last look at Chaz's face, before lowering his gaze to his arm.

"Now, how bad are we talking? Broken? Fractured?"

Chaz shook his head carefully. "I twisted my wrist when I— you know what? You don't need to know that."

"Gotcha." Del searched through the box until he found a support bandage, which he carefully unrolled over Chaz's hand and wrist. "That's the patching up all done. Now I got a few questions to ask." He peered at Chaz's face. "You took quite a pounding. You got a headache?" Chaz shook his head. Del held up a single finger. "Okay, follow this with just your eyes." He watched Chaz's eye movement carefully. "You feeling confused or dizzy? Seeing stars, like in the cartoons?"

Chaz smirked at that one. "No, sir."

"No ringing in your ears? Feeling nauseous?"

"Just sick that this happened in the first place." Chaz's face was a picture of misery.

Del patted his shoulder. "Okay, well, I don't think you've got a concussion, but we'll keep an eye on you anyhow. Let's go get that tea Jon promised." He helped Chaz stand, then hovered while he walked slowly into the living room.

Jon stood by the couch. "You make yourself comfortable. You don't have to move again this evening, except to answer the call o' nature. And when you're tired, I've got a guest bed with your name on it."

"Seriously?" Chaz's eyes filled with tears, and he wiped them away quickly. "Sorry. Not usually this—"

"You have nothing to apologize for," Del told him firmly. "Now sit down, put your feet up, and let two old guys fuss over you."

Chaz snickered. "Old guys my ass." He eased himself down gingerly onto the couch, then visibly relaxed.

Del sat beside him. "Now tell me who I need to go beat the crap out of."

Chaz's eyes widened. "Uh-uh. You're not getting your ass thrown in jail because of me. You gotta promise me, Del."

Del studied his face, the anxiety there. "Okay," he relented. "I promise."

Chaz let out a sigh of relief. "Thanks." He sniffed the air. "Something smells good."

"Well, you close your eyes and take a nap," Del advised. "By the time you wake up, it'll be ready to eat. Just let the Tylenol do its stuff." He picked up the remote and put the TV on in the background, not too loud, but enough to provide some distraction.

"'Kay."

"And by then you might even be hungry," Jon added. Then he nudged Del.

"What?" Del lowered his gaze.

Chaz was already asleep.

"D'you think it's safe to let him fall asleep like that?"

Del gazed at Chaz's peaceful expression. "I think he's just worn out by it all. Let him sleep." He signaled to Jon to go into the kitchen, then got up off the couch as carefully as possible, so as not to disturb Chaz. When they were in there, he silently closed the door after them. "Lord, he's a mess."

Jon started pacing. "He's a sweet kid. How could they do this to him? An' what the hell set 'em off? Chaz always seems like the careful sort, y'know? He wouldn't leave stuff lyin' around for his folks to find."

Del had to agree. "Whatever happened must've been major." The aroma of roasting turkey filled the room, but his appetite appeared to have fled. In fact, what he really needed right then was some fresh air.

"I'm going for a ride," he announced. "Not for long. I just need to get some air in my lungs. Unless you need me here?"

"To do what? Watch the turkey roast? Get outta here." Jon swatted Del's backside. "There's nothing to do here. I'll keep an eye on Chaz, but right now, sleep is probably the best thing for him."

Del agreed. He grabbed his leather jacket from the hook beside the back door, made sure he had the keys for his bike, then left.

He knew exactly where he was headed.

Del sat astride the bike and stared out at the town. The view from the Tank Springs trail had become his favorite. He supposed it would look quite different when covered with a blanket of snow; it had changed since his last time up there, now that all the fall colors were gone, the leaves long since shed.

It all looks so peaceful down there. Except now he knew better. The surface of LaFollette might appear as calm as a summer lake, but beneath the stillness were strong emotions that could stir up the waters in a heartbeat.

Del chuckled to himself. *Since when was I so… poetic? Philosophical?*

"This is getting to be a habit."

He jerked toward the voice, aware of the burst of happiness inside him. "What happened to Thanksgiving with your momma?"

Taylor arched his eyebrows. "Good to see you too. There's an hour before we eat, and I needed a break. So I came here."

"Great minds." Del got off the padded seat and walked over to where Taylor stood, holding onto his bicycle. He smirked. "You're wearin' a lot more than the last time we met here."

Taylor snorted. "That's 'cause I wanna keep my nuts where they are. It's a damn sight colder than it was then." He folded his arms across his chest. "So… what are you an' Jon having for Thanksgiving? Let me guess. Turkey sandwiches."

Del waited until his snickers had passed. "I'll have you know, we're dining on roast turkey and *all* the trimmings. Well, as many of the trimmings as we could find that were already prepared. The bird, however, we are roasting from scratch."

Taylor beamed. "I am impressed. Meanwhile, I survived peelin' and choppin' vegetables. You got any that want doin'? I'm your man."

Del couldn't help smiling at that. "I'll bear that in mind." Then he recalled Chaz, and the urge to smile left him. "We got ourselves an unexpected guest." When Taylor frowned, Del recounted how Chaz had arrived.

"Dear Lord. Is he all right?" The genuine note of concern in Taylor's voice touched Del.

"I'll know better after he's had some sleep and something to eat. And before you ask, he hasn't said one word about what happened, although we can guess."

Taylor stared out at the landscape beyond. "Funny how we both ended up here."

"I'm glad." A thought occurred to him. "You know what? One Sunday, we oughta take a pair of trikes and go find a new trail. Make a day of it. Although not any day soon. Snow might be on the way."

Taylor grinned. "In LaFollette? You're more likely to rust through all the rain than get snowed in. December's the worst month for rain too. Still, a Spring picnic? Sounds good. And there are plenty of trails." He shivered. "Only, let's do it when we're not freezin' our butts off?"

Del snickered. "That depends how cold it gets around here during Spring."

"It'll be warm enough. Besides, I got somewhere else I'd rather be until then." Taylor's eyes gleamed, and Del relished the slow release of heat that uncoiled inside him.

"Speaking of which…how long you wanna wait until we hit the streets of Atlanta again?"

Taylor bit his lip. "What are you doing next weekend?"

Del burst into laughter. "Lord, you remind me of me. You got it. Want me to book the hotel?"

"If you don't mind."

Del didn't mind that one little bit. "Leave that to me." He cocked his head to one side. "Wanna ride with me on the trike? Makes more sense than both of us taking two vehicles."

Something flashed across Taylor's face, so fast that Del almost missed it. But it didn't take a genius to know what was on his mind.

"Here's an idea," he said quietly. "You pack a bag, put on your leathers and a helmet, and bike up to the shop. We can leave from there. Who's gonna know it's you in a crash helmet with the visor down?"

Taylor pursed his lips. "You're right. And I've been wantin' to ride that baby ever since I saw you—it."

Del said nothing at the slip, but God, it was tempting. "I'll be ready to go at five. If you can get there a little earlier, even better." He sighed. "I suppose I'd better get back. You too."

Taylor's eyes twinkled. "Oh, I don't know. I got something to look forward to now. I think this next week is gonna fly by."

Del wasn't gonna argue with that. "Then go home to your momma and make sure she enjoys her Thanksgiving. You have no idea how many more of them she'll be around for." His first thought that morning as he and Jon had started preparations was that he wished his momma could have seen that. *She'd have probably wet herself laughing.*

Taylor put on his helmet, got astride his bicycle, and raised his hand in a wave. "See ya." He pushed off, and Del admired the view as he pedaled away, that firm ass looking as delectable as ever. Then a thought occurred to him.

Next weekend there would probably be nothing to hide that delectable ass from Del's sight.

Holy fuck.

Dinner was over, the dishwasher was groaning at its seams, and Jon had poured them a drink. Chaz had made a valiant attempt to eat all his dinner, but it was obvious his heart wasn't in it. Del waited until they were all seated in the living room, before bringing up the elephant standing smack dab in the middle of it.

"So what now?" he asked Chaz. "I'm not asking you to tell us what happened. Jon and I are not stupid. We've already got a fair idea of who did this and why. At least he didn't send you to the hospital."

Chaz's eyes glistened. "Let's just say he found somethin' I thought had been well hid. Apparently not. An' it wasn't exactly somethin' that could be explained away either."

"Did they kick you out?" Jon sounded aghast.

Chaz nodded. "Didn't even give me time to pack a bag or nothing. Said if I wanted anything, I'd have to go back for it another time. If I dared."

Del started going over his contacts in his head. He had to know *someone* who'd help Chaz out.

"Okay then," Jon announced suddenly. "You're gonna move in with me."

Both Chaz and Del gaped at him.

Jon frowned. "What? It's the obvious solution. I got the room, there's just me an' Delilah, an'—"

"Well, for that matter he could stay with me," Del retorted.

Chaz bit his lip. "Do I get a say in this?" Then he winced. "Ouch." Before they could speak, he held up his good hand. "Jon, thank you for the offer. You're a great guy an' I already love your cat." Delilah was presently curled up in his lap like a giant furry, purring cushion.

Jon blinked. "That it?"

"That's it. Del…" Chaz sighed. "You're a great guy too, but you know what? I just have this feeling that staying with Jon is the way to go. Things around you tend to get… complicated. Besides, you might not be on your own for much longer, an' I don't wanna get in the way."

"You know something I don't know?" Del quipped, although his heart pounded. Because he'd been thinking the very same thing.

He knew it was selfish, but…

Chaz just stared back at him. "I'm not stupid either. That's all I'm gonna say. Now, as long as Jon has a new toothbrush for me, we're good to go. My stuff can wait a while. There's always Goodwill."

"Failing that, there's Del's credit card," Del said seriously. "No employee of ours is gonna lack for anything."

Chaz wiped his eyes. "You're good people." He yawned, covering his mouth with his palm.

Del got to his feet and held out a hand. "Bed, young man. You've had a crazy day. And you get a long holiday weekend of doing nothing but eat leftovers." He helped Chaz to his feet. "Jon'll show you to your room. Get some sleep." Impulsively, he kissed Chaz's forehead.

Chaz swallowed. "Best thing I ever did, applyin' for that job." He followed Jon from the room.

Del waited until the door closed before sinking back into the couch. *What kind of low-life beats the shit out of a seventeen-year-old kid and then throws him onto the street? And what kind of mother lets him?*

People sucked. And not in a good way.

Chapter Sixteen

Sunday, November 26

By three in the afternoon, Taylor had done his laundry, cleaned the house, and checked for the fifth time that there was absolutely *nothing* worth watching on TV. Outside was a blustery day, but with no rain, and ordinarily he'd have been happy to stay indoors, but something was gnawing at him, and he couldn't figure out what. He'd spent Thursday with his momma, worked Friday and Saturday, leaving his Sunday free.

To do what? Clean? Organize my sock drawer?

There were times when being single truly sucked, but he couldn't lay the blame for that particular status on anyone's doorstep but his own. Making friends had never come easy to him, even when he was a teenager. He'd spent a couple of years of high school totally smitten with a guy a few years older than him, and hiding those emotions took a toll on him. How could he be himself when he was hiding what he truly was?

At least with Del, he didn't need to hide. Denise didn't know him well enough for him to feel comfortable talking about his sexuality, and besides, the only times they met were in her home, and no way was Taylor going to discuss anything so personal there. *Walls have ears, right?*

Taylor switched off the TV, grabbed his thick jacket and headed for the back porch. Maybe some bracing, fresh air was what he needed. As he opened the door, and the first rush of cool wind caressed his face, he reconsidered and grabbed his beanie too.

The streets were virtually empty as he cycled through the

town. Not that he was going anywhere near civilization. He headed for Lonas Young Memorial Park, a quiet green space popular with campers in the summer. Except in late November, there'd be no campers, just the chance to enjoy the scenery.

Taylor cycled past the Cedar Hill Baptist Church, not bothering to check out their noticeboard. Nothing had changed about *that* since he was a kid. His momma went now and again, but with nothing of the fervor of earlier years. Then he took Demory Road, and was thankfully surrounded by green. The road crossed over Norris Lake, passing the Big Creek ramp, where motor boats launched. The road clung to the edge of the lake, and in its center was an island of bare trees, a ribbon of sand running around its perimeter.

He took a right turn onto Lake View Lane, grateful for the expanse of evergreens in the otherwise gray and brown winter forest, the trees towering over him as he cycled toward the creek where he'd played as a kid. Now and again he glimpsed houses, set back aways from the lane, hidden by the trees, and as he got closer to the creek, there were fewer trees and more houses, though never an overwhelming number. The lane ended abruptly, he got off, and from then on, walked the bike, through the trees to the sandy spit of land he knew awaited him.

Taylor laid the bike down and walked to the edge of the water. The surface was calm, disturbed now and again by the wind that sent ripples trickling across the creek, accompanied by the gentle swaying of the trees. The only sounds were the birds, and for a moment he felt as though he was the only person for miles around. He scanned the rough sandy ground for stones to launch across the creek, but couldn't see anything flat enough. Instead, he stood at the water's edge and gazed out over the serene landscape, at peace.

This was what I needed.

Except he knew that was a lie. The calmness had brought him brief respite from whatever was nibbling away at him, but it wouldn't last. And as if to confirm that diagnosis, he caught the sound of footsteps coming toward him.

I can't even manage more than five minutes of quiet.

Without turning around, Taylor picked up his bike. There were other spots he could reach, though none as peaceful as this one.

"Don't go on my account."

Taylor jerked his head around at the familiar voice.

Del grinned at him. "I mean, you only just got here." He wore his leather jacket over jeans, a soft-looking gray scarf around his neck, and a leather cap on his head.

Taylor couldn't deny he was pleased to see him, but the chances of this meeting being coincidental were too great. "Okay. This time, you *must've* followed me."

Del arched his eyebrows. "Sure. I spend my Sundays just waiting around for you to show up so I can stalk you." He smirked, then pointed toward the trees behind him. "I live there." That grin was back. "So who, exactly, is following who?"

Taylor stared at him for a second, then saw the funny side. He laughed. "Sorry, but this is gettin' to be a habit."

"Come on up to the house. Not that it isn't pretty out here, but I'm freezin' my nuts off."

Taylor murmured in agreement, before walking his bike over to where Del stood. "This is a great place to live. I used to come here when I was a kid." They strolled toward the trees.

"I like it," Del said simply. "The house was exactly what I was looking for." He pointed ahead. "That's it there."

Taylor had to admit, the place was striking. Not to mention cute.

Above the front door was a small dormer window, and above that was an observation deck that ran around a many-sided top floor. Taylor couldn't tell if it had seven or eight sides. A white veranda ran around the first floor, with steps leading up onto it from the front door.

He leaned his bike against the railing, while Del opened the door. "Welcome to my little hideaway. You're its only visitor, apart from Jon, and that doesn't count 'cause he was helping me move in."

"So you don't live together?"

Del guffawed. "Lord no. I work with him. Besides, I know enough about him from living together when we were kids to know that ain't ever happening again." He pushed open the door and stood aside for Taylor to enter.

The glass double doors were covered on the inside with a layer of sheer white gauze, and they opened onto a wide, open space with hardwood flooring and lots of light. There wasn't much in the way of furniture. To the left sat a dark brown couch, in front of which was a plain beige rug and a coffee table. To the right was a small dining table with four chairs, and beyond that Taylor could see through an archway to a pale green door. Wooden posts stood at regular intervals in the center of the space, going up into the roof. The kitchen was on the right, sectioned off with a low partition. Ahead of them was a spiral staircase, rising up through a second level that was surrounded by dark wood railings.

"This is awesome," Taylor murmured. At the foot of the staircase sat a single armchair that had obviously seen a lot of use. A lamp stood beside it, and a footstool squatted in front of it, its angle perfect for watching the TV on its unit. No bookshelves, no knickknacks, no pictures.

Taylor bit back a smile. "I'm guessing you like the minimalist look, huh?"

Del hung up his jacket and scarf, and chuckled. "Come with me." He led Taylor up the spiral staircase, where it opened out onto a second level. Two futon chairs sat there, a table between them. Light spilled into the space from three dormer windows, and the railings followed the same shape as the observation deck above them. As they reached the top of the stairs, Taylor realized there were in fact eight sides. A futon sat below the windows that went the whole way around the deck, with a french door set into them to allow access to the outside deck.

Taylor was captivated. It was a simple, uncluttered space, and not one he would have associated with the gruff bear standing beside him. "I love your house," he said quietly.

Del gazed at his surroundings. "Me too. I always tell myself not to get attached to property, because you never know when you're gonna have to sell up and move on. But this place? Yeah, it's felt... right, from the moment I saw it." He beckoned. "Let me show you one of my favorite parts." Del led Taylor carefully down the staircase, and when they reached the bottom, he headed through the archway. The green door opened to reveal a bedroom, with floor-to-ceiling windows along one side, in the middle of which was a sliding patio door that led to the veranda. A large bed sat in the center, with rugs on three sides.

Taylor hesitated at the threshold. Del's bedroom was an unknown quantity.

Del turned to look at him. "It's okay, you can come in. It's not like I have man-traps all over the floor, or sexual devices hanging from the ceiling." His eyes glittered.

Taylor pouted. "Not sure if that disappoints me."

Del pointed to the door at the end of the room. "And that is where I go after a long day."

Taylor wandered over, and peered around the door. It was a bathroom, with corner windows, below which sat a bath that filled the available space. Jets were set into the porcelain, and Taylor grinned. "Now I see why you like this room so much." There was also a shower, but it was a normal-sized cubicle. *Not exactly big enough for two.*

He withdrew from the room, and took another look at the bedroom. Unlike the rest of the house, photos covered the wall space, and he walked over to peer at them.

Del joined him. "Most of these were taken in San Francisco." He snickered. "I keep them in here because heaven forbid I scare any visitors."

Taylor wondered what on earth he meant by that—until he took a closer look. "Oh... my." He was seeing photo after photo of men in all shapes and sizes, usually not wearing all that much, and what they *were* wearing left little to the imagination. Then there were the naked guys, not to mention a naked woman—until he looked closer and realized she had a *very* large dick. *How could I miss that?* In one photo she was standing in a window, while a mass of guys watched her getting sucked off.

"That's my friend, Danni," Del said with a chuckle. "You can't really miss her at Folsom, not with that cock and those tits." He cleared his throat. "Recognize anyone?"

Taylor scanned the photos, searching. Then he found it. Del wore a leather jockstrap that barely contained his dick. He was standing with a group of similarly attired men, and he was smoking a fat cigar. His broad chest was covered with hair, and his firm belly glistened in the sunlight. He looked… happy.

"Do you miss all this?" Taylor asked him.

For a moment Del didn't reply. Finally he sighed. "Sometimes. I miss being able to walk down Castro Street, and if I met up with a friend, I'd kiss him. Couldn't do that here. Couldn't even hold his hand." He snickered. "During the last elections, there were a couple of guys campaigning in the Castro. They wore gold sequinned socks—and *not* on their feet. That was the only item of clothing. They just stood on the street corner and chatted to people, not a care in the world."

"Now I know why you go to Atlanta, apart from the obvious."

Del nodded. "It's the closest thing to being back in Cali."

"Did you… did you have someone back there?"

Del's face tightened. "I thought I did. Turned out I was wrong." He coughed. "Hey, I'm being a dreadful host. Would you like some tea, coffee, whatever?" His eyes lit up. "Or there's hot chocolate."

Taylor grinned. "*Now* you're talkin'." He followed Del out of the bedroom and into the kitchen area, leaning on the partition while Del prepared the beverages.

Del glanced across at him. "What are your plans for today?"

Taylor huffed. "I got out of the house because I had no plans.

And there are only so many times you can clean a kitchen before you start taking off the work surface."

Del laughed. "Been there. Well, I was just gonna say… I have no plans either, beyond watching movies and eating pizza. So I wondered if you'd like to join me."

For one irrational moment, Taylor's heartbeat raced. He couldn't. He just… couldn't. His pulse quickened, and his throat tightened.

It took him a second or two to realize Del was saying his name.

"Taylor." Del's voice was soft. "No one knows you're here. It's just pizza and a movie. You can relax here. You can be you."

That last statement pierced him. *I don't have to hide here.*

And there it was at last, what had been gnawing away at him. The need to hide all the time, to present this… persona of Taylor the straight cop, the straight son.

A persona he was finding increasingly difficult to live with.

"Thank you," he said, his voice as soft as Del's. "I'd really like that."

Del beamed. "Besides, you know you're safe here. You got to see my bedroom and nothing happened." He winked.

Taylor snorted. "I'm not sure if I should be relieved or insulted." But Del's words went a long way to putting him at ease.

I need some time with a friend. And Del was proving to be a good friend.

Taylor turned out the light and pulled the comforter up over him. He'd stayed at Del's as late as he could, unwilling to leave the couch where he and Del had sprawled all evening, watching movies and eating popcorn, not to mention drinking a couple of beers. Del wouldn't let him drink more than two, claiming he didn't want Taylor to be arrested on his way home for driving under the influence while in charge of a bicycle.

Yeah. Friends look out for you.

It was obvious Del didn't want him to go either. It was only when Taylor pointed to Del's clock that they'd both reluctantly agreed it was time for Taylor to leave. Del helped him into his jacket, and Taylor could still feel those hands on his shoulders. It made him feel…safe.

"I could take you home. It's not that far."

Taylor had smiled. "No, that's okay. You stay in where it's warm. Besides, before you know, I'll be textin' to say I've made it home in one piece." He chuckled. "Without falling off my bike. Can't have you thinkin' I can't hold my liquor."

Del's last words before Taylor departed still rang in his head, sending a pleasurable shiver through him. He'd moved in closer, until their bodies were almost touching. His voice had been deep and husky.

"Next time I get you in a bedroom, we'll be in Atlanta. I might not be such a gentleman then."

Lying in his bed, Taylor closed his eyes and let those words play over and over again. He knew that the following weekend brought with it the very real prospect of losing his virginity—in every sense of the word—and that thought made him shiver anew. But it was more than that. He'd be with Del.

Taylor couldn't help himself. He wrapped his fingers around his dick and tugged gently on it, his mind full of Del. The size of him. The way he wanted Del to hold him, to take care of him. Taylor imagined being enveloped in Del's arms, that firm body cradling him, Del's lips against his neck, his large hands moving slowly over Taylor's body, leisurely caressing him. Taylor spread his legs and reached down to squeeze and play with his balls, before venturing further south. When his finger came into contact with the hot, tight pucker, he gripped his shaft and increased his pace, tilting his hips to bring that hole closer.

When Del's lips met his, Taylor came, his load warm against his belly, one hand still cradling his sac.

Please, let the real thing be just as good, if not better.

Chapter Seventeen

Friday, December 1.

Taylor regarded their surroundings with approval. "Nice room."

Del snickered. "It has the essentials. Two beds, a walk-in shower—which is way better than a shower over the bathtub—TV and room service." He grinned. "Because I don't know about you, but *I* always get the munchies after dancing all night."

Taylor wasn't thinking about dancing, but he figured if things went the way he wanted them to, he could see them working up an appetite. Then Del's words registered fully. *Dancin'? Does he really wanna go* dancin'? Sure, Taylor had really enjoyed himself the last weekend in Atlanta, but things had changed since then.

Hadn't they? Or had he imagined that conversation in the coffee shop? He certainly hadn't imagined that bike ride. Nearly four hours on the trike, holding onto the seat when what he *really* longed for was to wrap his arms around the hunk of a bear in front of him.

"I guess there's something we need to discuss before our weekend kicks off."

That got through to him. "Yeah?"

"Yeah. It occurred to me on the way here that sharin' a room is a great idea, but... it could make things a little... awkward."

To Taylor's mind, there were only benefits to the situation. "Like what?"

Del shrugged. "Well, here's me sayin' I'd help you to push at that envelope. Suppose you do... and suppose you hook up with someone…" He gestured to their room. "It's not exactly ideal, is it? So I was thinking, if that was the case, I'd make myself scarce an' give you a little privacy."

Suddenly the shine vanished off Taylor's weekend. "I guess that makes sense," he said slowly.

"Not that *anything's* gonna happen until we get out there," Del said, his eyes gleaming. "We've freshened up, so what are we waitin' for?" He grabbed his jacket from the bed. "Ready?"

"Ready." Taylor pasted on a smile. As they left the hotel room and walked along the hallway to the elevator, he attempted to push down hard on his frustration and disappointment.

I didn't want my first time to be with some stranger.
I wanted it to be with you.

It didn't take Del long to work out something was wrong, and it didn't take a genius to work out it was all Del's fault.

Why the fuck did I say that?

Stupid question. He didn't want Taylor to feel obligated. So what if he wanted to nail Taylor to the nearest flat surface and fuck his brains out? That wasn't what he'd promised, was it, when he'd arranged this weekend? And just because *he* might want something, didn't mean Taylor was on the same page.

Del knew he should have said something when Taylor launched into the shots like they were going out of style. Especially when he hadn't eaten a thing. Del resisted the urge to tell him to slow down, because hell, Taylor was an adult, right? Besides, Del wouldn't let Taylor drink himself into oblivion.

Then there was the dancing. Taylor threw himself into it, but it wasn't like last time. Then, they'd danced together. Okay, not holding-each-other together, but close enough that Del could feel Taylor's body heat, could look into his eyes, and that had been just fine. This time, it was like Del wasn't even there.

What shocked Del was how much that *hurt*.

He watched as several guys made eye contact with Taylor, and each time Del's chest tightened, because damn it, this was *not* what he wanted. But for all their flirting with him, surprisingly, Taylor didn't return their interest. He gave plenty of smiles, but none that promised a damn thing, which only confused Del even more.

What the hell is goin' on?

It didn't help that all night long, Del hadn't exactly been starved of attention either. Guys approached him, all armed with hands that apparently had minds of their own, trailing fingers over Del's biceps, stroking his beard. It was as if he was wearing an invisible sign that read Touch Me. And every time, Del politely but firmly removed their wandering hands, before returning his attention to Taylor.

Lord, the irony. He could have filled his bed a dozen times over, but the one man he wanted in it was totally oblivious.

Del put up with it for as long as he could, but by the time midnight arrived and Taylor showed no signs of slowing down, Del had to do something. When Taylor headed once more to the bar, Del strode over to him and put a hand on his arm.

"I get it," he said loudly, striving to be heard above the music. "I fucked up. Now, can you give your liver a break? We can talk about this tomorrow."

Taylor said nothing for a moment, and Del hoped to God he wasn't going to insist on staying. Finally, he gave a single nod, and Del heaved an inward sigh of relief.

The walk back to the hotel was in silence, and Del began to dread the rest of the weekend. *Lord, I hope I can fix this.* By the time they reached their room, and Del flicked on the lights, he'd made up his mind. Never mind about waiting until the next morning—he had to say something. But as soon as Taylor emerged from the bathroom, he let loose with all cannons.

"Jus' what the fuck are you playin' at?"

Del gave a start. "Look, I know I said we'd talk about—"

Taylor's eyes widened. "You confused the hell out of me.

One moment you wanna fuck me over your trike, the next... 'If you wanna hook up with someone.'" The mimicry was obvious.

Del gaped. "I did *not* sound like that."

"That's not the fucking point!" Taylor yelled.

"Then what is?" Del was at a loss.

Taylor launched himself across the room and grabbed hold of Del's face. He stared into his eyes, then gave a low growl. "Fuck it, it's now or never." Then he kissed Del full on the mouth.

For one moment Del froze, the breath knocked out of him by the swiftness of Taylor's action, but then sanity returned, because *Jesus*, he wanted that too. He slid his arms around Taylor's lean frame and grabbed his ass, molding Taylor against his body while he returned the kiss with all the heat and passion he could give. Taylor's long, low moan was music to his ears, and Del squeezed his firm, jeans-encased butt.

"Fuck, yeah," Del whispered against Taylor's lips, aware that Taylor was pushing him backward toward the bed. He had no problem with that, and when his thighs hit the mattress, he fell back, taking Taylor with him, spreading his legs to give Taylor room to lie between them.

Taylor's tongue demanded entrance, and Del opened for him, happy to let him take the initiative. The hunger in him was all too evident, and Del couldn't hold back his response. He pushed up with his hips to meet Taylor's hardness, their lips still connected as they explored each other, Taylor feeding him moans of desire as he rocked against Del's erection.

Taylor wasn't quiet, he couldn't keep still, and God, it was heady as fuck. He buried his face in Del's neck, seized him in a tight hold, and picked up speed, dry humping him, his breathing harsh and erratic. Del couldn't keep still either, matching Taylor's movements, desperate to give him what he needed.

When Taylor froze above him, expelling a long breath, his body suddenly limp in Del's arms, Del knew they'd passed the point of no return. His nostrils flared as he detected the tell-tale scent, and he waited to see which direction Taylor took. His own body ached with the need to come, but Taylor's needs came first.

Del didn't have long to wait.

"Oh my God." Taylor sat up, his face tight, and launched himself off the bed and toward the bathroom. He slammed the door shut and Del heard the catch as he locked it.

Aw crap.

There was no way Taylor was leaving that bathroom tonight.

He gazed down at his jeans, aghast. *I fucking came in them, like a little kid. What'll Del think of me?*

A soft knock on the door startled him. "Hey, come on out."

At least he was still there. Not that Taylor was going to comply. Nope. Uh-uh. He was gonna sleep in the bathroom.

Another knock. "It's okay, honest."

Taylor snorted. "Not okay in *my* book."

Del chuckled. "You've been on shots all evening, you're horny as fuck... we've all been there."

Taylor stilled. "Even you?"

Del snickered. "Lord, you should've seen me on my second date. Man, I was three sheets to the wind, with a boner that would not quit, and I tried to hump the guy's leg, like I was a little dog and he was the mail-man."

Okay, that made him smile. Cautiously, Taylor opened the door. Del stood there, his face kind. Taylor bit his lip. "I hate to break it to ya, but there is no way on this planet that anyone could confuse *you* with a little dog."

Del chuckled. "Yeah, but you get the picture, right?" He gestured toward the bed. "Come sit with me, and I'll order us something to eat, which is what I *should've* done at that bar, instead of letting you get drunk. Then we'll watch a little TV, and by then we'll probably be ready to sleep. Tomorrow is anothah day, Scarlett." His eyes twinkled.

Taylor gestured to his clothes, grimacing. "Any chance I can get out of these before room service arrives?"

Del's eyes twinkled. "You really don't wanna know how it feels when things get a little… dried on." He winced theatrically.

Taylor rolled his eyes. "There ya go, remindin' me. Trust me, I don't need remindin'." He unfastened his jeans, but paused in the act of removing them, his gaze on Del. The thought of undressing in front of him had given Taylor a ripple of excitement before that evening, but now?

Del chuckled. "You do what you have to, while I get on the phone to room service. A couple of club sandwiches and some Cokes should be plenty at this hour. Then I'll see what's on TV." He turned his back on Taylor, sat on the edge of the bed, and reached for the phone.

Taylor squirmed out of his jeans, still grimacing.

This was not how I wanted the weekend to start.

Once he was in a pair of sweats and a T-shirt, sprawled on the bed beside Del, eating a club sandwich and arguing quietly over who was eating the most chips, both of them trying not to laugh out loud at an old, (not intentionally) comical horror movie, he felt much better.

Not that the shame of his earlier… performance had left him. Fuck. It was like he'd been in heat. Then he remembered the way Del had kissed him. There had been no disguising the obvious need in him.

He wanted me too. Then a wry thought crossed his mind. *And if I hadn't dry humped him like it was an Olympic event, he'd have had me.*

Maybe this weekend wasn't going to be a complete bust after all.

Del was snickering at the horror movie, but to Taylor's mind, there was a space between them that needed closing. Experimentally, Taylor shifted closer and laid his head on Del's broad chest, his hand resting on that firm belly.

Del stilled, and Taylor craned his neck to look up at his face. Del gazed at him, his eyes not giving anything away, and Taylor wondered if he'd gone too far. Then he reasoned *fuck that.* After shooting in his briefs, this was nothing.

Then Del smiled and put his hand on Taylor's back, rubbing him in slow, soothing circles while he went back to watching his movie.

So soothing, in fact, that Taylor drifted off to sleep.

Chapter Eighteen

Taylor opened his eyes, aware that the room was brighter. Apart from that, nothing had changed: apparently he and Del had fallen asleep sprawled out on one of the beds. His head still rested on Del's chest, and Taylor had to admit, it made for a great pillow.

Then Del stirred, and Taylor shifted across the bed to the other side. Del opened his eyes and blinked. "Where'd you go? That felt good." He peered down at their bodies. "I guess we were both tired last night if we didn't even bother getting into our own beds." He gave a drowsy smile. "Either that, or the movie bored us to sleep."

Taylor was suddenly wide awake. "Oh God." He glimpsed his jeans in a huddled pile on the floor by the bathroom door. "I hoped that part was a dream."

Del rolled onto his side to face him. "And before you say another word, don't you go kicking yourself over what happened. Like I said, I fucked up. If I'd... explained myself properly, you wouldn't have downed all those shots on an empty stomach." He paused, his eyes more alert. "Although... holy fuck, that was *hot*."

Part of Taylor wanted to hear more, but he still needed answers. "What would you have said differently?"

Del sighed. "I didn't want you to get the wrong idea, like, I'd brought you here just to have my wicked way with you."

Taylor smirked. "But... you did, didn't ya? Or did I misinterpret the part when you wanted to bend me over your trike?"

Del rolled his eyes. "For Christ's sake, of course I wanted to fuck you. I mean, you're fucking *gorgeous*! But that kinda assumed you wanted the same thing. And so I made that stupid remark about giving you space…"

"It wasn't stupid," Taylor said simply. "You were bein' a gentleman an' givin' me an out. I get that now." He grinned. "Not that I *wanted* one, but hey, the thought was there." His heart was still pounding in reaction to Del's words. *He wants me.* Not that Del's kiss the previous night had left him in any doubt about *that*.

Del heaved an exaggerated sigh of relief. "I'm glad we got that cleared up. Because now…" He locked gazes with Taylor. "I get to have my wicked way with you." He got up off the bed, grabbed the hem of his T-shirt, and slowly pulled it up his body, over his head and off, revealing a wide chest covered in salt-and-pepper hair, broad, muscled shoulders, and a firm belly with yet more hair covering the center of it in a soft-looking down. A dark trail led the way down beneath the waistband of his jeans, and Taylor couldn't look away as Del popped the button there, before sliding the zipper down, just a little, to reveal the dark fuzz of his pubes.

Oh fuck. He's gone commando.

"Taylor?"

With a start, Taylor jerked his head upward. Del was grinning at him. "I said, I'm gonna grab a shower. You get the bathroom after me." And with that, he lowered the zipper all the way and pushed his jeans down past his hips and knees, bending over to remove them completely. Del straightened, and his dick bobbed up, pointing at Taylor like an accusatory finger—a really *big* finger—almost as if it was saying, 'See the state of me? Your fault.'

Del walked past Taylor into the bathroom, his cock pointing the way, and Taylor got the rear view. Del had a broad back and an ample ass, his cheeks jiggling as he entered the bathroom. The door closed, and soon after there came the sound of water hitting the tiled floor.

Taylor flopped back onto the bed. *Oh my God.* Reality was way better than his imagination.

His teeth brushed, Del was going for the fastest shower in recorded history.

Not that he was missing bits. Every inch of him came into contact with the apple-smelling bodywash, only some bits got a more thorough seeing-to than others.

It was only as he was toweling off that Del realized they really had missed out on an important conversation. Not the condoms—they were in Del's bag, along with the lube—but the delicate topic of who was gonna fuck the cum out of whom. Taylor couldn't possibly have misinterpreted Del's declaration, and Del couldn't recall hearing vehement cries of 'No no no, stay away from my virgin ass.'

But if the previous night had taught him anything, it was that you didn't make assumptions.

He wrapped the towel around his waist, gave his hair one last comb-through with his fingers, then opened the door to let steam puff out into the room. Taylor darted past him so fast, Del almost missed it, left with an impression of golden skin, a flat belly and nicely toned arms and chest. Then the door closed.

Del chuckled. Just as well he could talk through a door.

He got the condoms and lube from his bag, placed them on the second bed, then went back to the bathroom door. "I don't know about you," he said, leaning close and raising his voice slightly to be heard above the torrent of water, "but I came prepared."

A second or two later, he caught Taylor's reply. "Oh. Good. Me too."

"And I know we haven't discussed who is doing what to whom, but..." Del leaned against the door frame, his eyes closed, his mind conjuring up an image of Taylor in his uniform, his cap on, his boots gleaming, dangling a pair of handcuffs from his index finger, and telling Del to 'Assume the position.' Del's dick strained against the towel, and he reached down to grip it.

"You're thinkin' about me in my uniform again, aren'tcha?" Taylor's wry chuckle followed.

Del blinked and hastily withdrew his hand. *How the fuck...?*

The water switched off. "S'okay, can't say I haven't been thinkin' the same thing."

Del liked the way this was going.

The door opened and Taylor stood there, his buzz cut virtually dry, but beads of water left on his chest and belly, the smell of apple bodywash and mint toothpaste still clinging to him. The white towel encircled his hips, riding low on them, low enough that Del could see dark-blond fuzz above the point where the towel swelled out, thin enough that the head of his cock was plainly visible.

"But I've been thinking too." Taylor swallowed, before reaching out to stroke a finger along Del's erection. "And I know where I want this. For this first time, anyhow." He smiled. "We'll save the uniform for another occasion."

Del grinned. "I like a man who knows what he wants."

Taylor's eyes gleamed. "I have a list."

Del knew what he wanted too. With one brisk hand movement, he undid Taylor's towel, allowing it to fall to the floor, freeing his long, slim dick that promised to reach *all* the right spots. Del removed his own towel, held out his hand, and led Taylor to the pristine bed. He sat on the edge of the mattress, his legs wide, and pulled Taylor to stand between them, after placing his towel on the bed.

Del looked up at him, his lean body trembling slightly. "You're beautiful," he said simply. Before Taylor could react, Del leaned forward to press gentle kisses onto his belly, his hands sliding over warm, damp skin to stroke Taylor's back. Taylor placed his hands on Del's shoulders and shuddered out a sigh of pleasure.

Del reached up, cupped Taylor's nape, and pulled him down into a kiss. Taylor responded with an eagerness that had Del wanting more, and he shifted further onto the bed, beckoning for

Taylor to follow. They lay together, arms wrapped around each other, touching and caressing as they kissed. The hitches in Taylor's breathing, the brief shivers of desire, the way he tentatively sucked on Del's tongue…

Del loved every fucking second of it. He stroked Taylor's arms and chest, exploring his mouth with his tongue, and breathed him in, his warmth, his sensuality, and his light caresses. He loved the way Taylor shifted until he was partly lying on Del, undulating his body against Del's, soft, happy noises escaping from his lips.

Del raised his arm, presenting Taylor with his pit. "Here. Kiss me here."

Taylor didn't hesitate. He pressed his face against the furry pit and kissed, lightly at first, but then more deeply, before moving a little lower to Del's nipple. Del held his breath, awaiting the first touch of Taylor's tongue there, that first tug on his sensitive nub. He arched his back as Taylor flicked it, before sucking on it, his teeth grazing it.

"Fuck, you're a fast learner."

Taylor raised his head and grinned, before shifting across to play with the other nipple, sending darts of exquisite pleasure piercing through him. Del shuddered violently, loving the feel of Taylor's hands on his neck and chest, continually stroking him, while his hot mouth worshipped Del's nipples.

Taylor lifted his chin. "Time for a new lesson," he said quietly, then kissed his way down Del's body, steering away from his shaft, until he was planting kisses on Del's thighs. Del's cock jerked up to meet him, and Del laughed.

"Something likes that idea. Lick a line up the underside of my dick, nice and slow."

Taylor complied, and Del closed his eyes at the feel of that warm, wet tongue on his cock. When Taylor reached the head, he gave it a flick, and Del's cock rose up to meet him as he took it in his mouth. Taylor slid his lips down the shaft, about halfway, before rising again, picking up a little speed as he sucked and licked, playing with it, until Del lay beneath him, unable to suppress the shudders that coursed through him. Taylor was on his hands and knees, his own dick stiff, his head bobbing as he sent waves of pleasure surging through Del.

"My balls," Del gasped out. "Feelin' kinda... neglected."

Taylor chuckled around his cock, and the vibrations were delicious. He carefully took one testicle into his mouth, running his tongue over it and sucking on it, until Del was shaking with need.

"My turn," he ground out, scrambling up off his back and pushing Taylor onto his. Del leaned in and kissed him, their tongues once more in play, while he slid a large warm hand down Taylor's body to where his dick was standing at attention. Del didn't break the kiss as he pulled gently on Taylor's cock, noting the low moan that rippled through Taylor.

He knelt over Taylor's shaft, pulling it toward him, before allowing it to spring back and slap against his belly. He did it again. And again. And again, and each time the meaty thud made his mouth water. Then he lavished the same care and attention that Taylor had shown, holding his dick around the base while he took it deep, Taylor pushing up into his mouth.

"Oh fuck," Taylor said weakly. "That feels... amazin'. Fuck, don't stop."

Del chose that moment to hum a little tune with his mouth full, and Taylor's moans grew in volume and frequency. When Taylor's tremors were almost constant, Del flipped him onto his belly. "Hands and knees, ass in the air," he demanded.

The speed with which Taylor did as instructed was evidence enough of his need.

Del knelt on the bed at Taylor's head, brushed his cock against Taylor's lips, and Taylor opened for him without hesitation, taking about half his length into his mouth. Del kept still and let him do the work, but it wasn't long before he was sliding deeper and deeper, hips pumping, his mind already on what he was going to do to Taylor's ass.

The same ass that was sticking up in the air, round and inviting, its crease slightly parted, as if teasing him...

Del pulled free of Taylor's mouth, pushed his head to the mattress, then leaned over his back to spread those cheeks wide. Muffled against the bed, Taylor's breath caught, and Del grinned.

"You want my tongue in your ass?"

Taylor's loud moan was answer enough.

Del didn't wait, but licked over his hole, a long, leisurely lick that only gave him a taste for more. Roughly, he tilted Taylor's ass higher, before reaching down to grab Taylor's rock-hard cock, pulling on it as he rubbed his beard between Taylor's cheeks. Then he pushed his tongue against the tight ring, getting it wet enough to slowly press one finger inside. More tongue, only this time he went a little deeper, alternating between his finger and the soft scrape of his beard over the tender flesh.

Taylor turned his head to one side. "Oh, God, Del. You got me shakin' here."

Del sank a finger deep into that hot hole, and Taylor groaned. "When I got you *beggin'* me to fuck ya, *then* you'll know what shaking is. Wait until I slide my cock inside this tight hole."

"Do it," Taylor urged.

Del ignored him, shifted position until he was kneeling at Taylor's ass, then went back to rimming him, sucking and licking, adding another finger, until Taylor was pushing back, riding those fingers while Del fucked him with them.

"Del, please." Taylor arched his back, his body jerking as he tried to get Del's fingers deeper inside him. His low cry of frustration when Del pulled free of his body told Del it was time.

Del spread the towel out and sat on it. He reached for a condom and the bottle of lube, and gloved up. He lay back against the pillows, his legs stretched out in front of him.

"You're gonna ride me."

Taylor tried to get his breathing under control, but the prospect of Del sliding that thick cock into him just sent more shivers through him. Del placed a hand on his hip, his touch warm and reassuring.

"Put your feet on either side of me, and squat," Del told him.

Taylor eyed him with incredulity. "You do *not* wanna be saying that word right this second."

Del snickered. "I know, it's gonna feel… weird. But that's what the towel is for. Not that we're gonna need it, but better to have it there, right?" Then he tugged Taylor down into a long, lingering kiss. "Can't wait to feel you on my cock," he whispered against Taylor's lips.

That was all it took to raise Taylor's internal temperature to scorching.

He squatted above Del's dick, feeling its head graze his hole, and shivered.

Del's hand was on his thigh. "Your pace, baby. As slow as you like. You're gonna reach back and guide me in, then once the head's inside you, I don't move until you say so." Taylor drew in a deep breath, and Del stroked his cock, the motion gentle and leisurely. "My fingers felt good, right? Well, that's only a fraction of how good my cock is gonna feel. I promise." He grinned. "Why do you think I can't wait to have you fuck me?"

That was all Taylor needed. He reached back, grasped the slippery shaft, and held it steady while he eased himself onto it, gasping at that first stretch of his hole to accommodate it. Del lay immobile, save for his hand still pulling on Taylor's dick, his gaze locked on Taylor.

"Fuck, you're tight."

"An' you ain't exactly small," Taylor flung back at him. "God, it's like fuckin' myself with a beer can."

"At least it's *warm* beer," Del said with a grin. "Although…"

Taylor was barely listening, conscious only of the thick cock stretching him wide. "I am *not* sticking anything cold up there!" He groaned as he sank a little lower. "It's gotta be all the way in by now." Taylor balanced on one arm as he explored with his fingers. "Oh my fucking God." He could feel the skin stretched tight around Del's dick, feel where the shaft disappeared inside him.

"We're past the halfway point, trust me."

"Sure don't feel like it." Then he remembered to breathe evenly, and suddenly his ass connected with Del's warm skin.

"And the crowd goes wild," Del whispered, his hand on Taylor's hip. "Balls deep, baby." His touch was light, soothing.

Taylor leaned forward and planted his palms flat on Del's chest. "So full."

"I know. Give it a sec. Get used to it."

Taylor took several deep breaths before he tried moving. He ignored the discomfort, knowing that Del wouldn't lie, and sure enough, it wasn't long before each movement was sending trickles of pleasure through his body, trickles that swelled into a stream of bliss. Del kept his word, lying still while Taylor moved, his hands tight on Taylor's waist as he helped him to bounce up and down on his dick.

"Ready to let me drive a little?" Del asked. When Taylor nodded, he drew him down into a deep kiss, his hands on Taylor's back, sensual and arousing. Del spread his legs and bent them, planted his feet onto the mattress, then proceeded to thrust up into Taylor's ass, grabbing Taylor's ass cheeks and pulling them apart so his cock slid deeper inside him.

"Holy fuck." The breath was punched out of him with each drive of Del's dick into his hole, and Taylor knew he couldn't last much longer. When Del's thrusts sped up and his breathing grew erratic, Taylor knew he wasn't the only one. He buried his face in Del's neck, hands holding on to the edge of the mattress, while Del wrapped his arms around his back, and fucked him with short, quick strokes. Taylor's dick lay trapped between their bodies, sliding through their mingled perspiration, the friction bringing him hurtling to the edge.

"Lord, you just got real tight around my cock," Del gasped out.

Taylor cried out as warmth erupted between them, and he held on to Del, his limbs trembling. Del kissed him, his hips still moving, and then his mouth opened in a wordless cry as his dick throbbed inside Taylor. Del didn't let go of him, his arms still tight around him, but he lay still, occasional jolts shaking them both.

Bliss gave way to a warm, sated feeling that permeated every part of him. Taylor kissed Del, their kisses taking the place of words, which felt unnecessary. Del grazed his knuckles over Taylor's short hair, his cock still buried deep in Taylor's body. Eventually he eased out of him, disposed of the condom, then returned to the bed.

"Bathroom, now. Trust me."

Taylor wasn't going to argue.

When he came back into the room, Del was lying on the bed, his arm flung wide. Taylor lay beside him and snuggled up to him, perfectly content.

When they'd lain like that for a while, Del sighed. "We can't stay like this, you know."

"Mm-hmm."

"We have to get up."

"Mm-hmm."

Del's stomach growled, and they both chuckled. "See, it's not just me that thinks so," Del said with a smile.

All Taylor knew was that this felt wonderful and he didn't want it to end. He was warm, at peace, and lying in Del's arms, he felt like he was the most precious thing in creation. He glanced at Del who lay with his eyes closed, his chest rising and falling.

Do you know how good you make me feel?

Then Del opened his eyes and kissed Taylor's cheek. "We have time, Taylor. Lots of time."

Right then Taylor wasn't planning on doing anything that required leaving their room before it was time to go back home.

He didn't want to risk losing this.

Chapter Nineteen

Saturday, December 2

"What's taking so long?" Christ, how long did it take to try on a pair of jeans?

From behind the curtain, Taylor chuckled. "Impatient much? They're a little tight."

That sent several images rattling through Del's mind. "Need any help in there?"

Taylor's guffaw drew looks from the guys who were shopping. "I don't think so. One, I am perfectly capable of dressin' myself, an' two, if you were back here, we'd prob'ly end up getting arrested."

Okay, that last point was a valid one, but still…

Any more thoughts Del might have had on the subject fled his mind as Taylor drew back the curtain and stood there. "Well?"

Holy Mary Mother of God.

Del's mouth dried up, and swallowing became a real chore. "I… I could've sworn you had underwear on when we left the hotel." Because it was obvious from Taylor's crotch that he wore nothing beneath the jeans. His dick pointed up toward his right hip, the fabric molded around it like a second skin.

Del was trying his hardest not to drool, because *day*-um…

Taylor snickered, and pointed to a pair of black briefs on the floor. "I was gonna ask, can you choose me a couple of jocks to try on? I need some new underwear. You can pick the color."

Del grinned. "Really?" His gaze flickered down. "You're a medium, right?"

Taylor arched his eyebrows. "Either you peeked, or—"

"Let's just say I'm been around enough guys' asses." Another flicker downward. "And you're definitely not a small." Before Taylor could reply, Del headed into the store to the underwear section, still grinning. It didn't take him long to find exactly what he was looking for, and he went back to Taylor, clutching his prizes.

Taylor was regarding his reflection. "I know I wanted skinny jeans, but damn, these really fit." He lowered his gaze to his ass, molding his hands around it. "So how does—"

"Do not *ask* me how your ass looks," Del ground out. He thrust the underwear into Taylor's hand. "Here."

Taylor stared at the items. "Rainbow stripes and little racing cars?" He smirked, then peered closer at the next one. "Wow. I might as well not be wearing anything." The fine black mesh pouch would leave little to the imagination.

Del was fine with that.

"Do I get to see you try these on too?"

Taylor's gaze met his, and he smiled. "How about I do a show later, just for you? In the meantime, I think I'll wear these back to the hotel." He turned his back on Del and presented him with a view of that tight little ass. "I think I need to wear 'em in a little."

It was on the tip of Del's tongue to tell him to wear them while he could, because once they were back in the hotel, Taylor's ass was gonna be bare within seconds. Instead, he gave Taylor a grin. "You do that."

Had to allow the boy *some* illusions, right?

The plan had been to do a little late afternoon shopping, then grab some food. It wasn't long after the jeans-buying expedition that Del realized Taylor had another plan entirely. Instead of walking at his side, as they'd done on their previous visit, Taylor walked ahead, and Del got to watch that fine ass in action. Then there were the occasional stops where Taylor would pause to bend over and examine something on the sidewalk, a flower growing through the cracks, an interesting *rock*, for God's sake…

Taylor wasn't fooling Del. He wanted to get fucked, and he was going the right way about it. What pleased Del no end was Taylor's confidence. By the sixth time Taylor had put his gorgeous ass in the middle of Del's line of sight, Del had had enough.

"Hotel, now," he gritted out.

Taylor regarded him with a would-be innocent look. "What about food?"

"Food can wait. Besides, you'll be ravenous by the time we're finished."

That slow grin was sexy as hell. "Finished what?"

Del speared him with a look. "Ever heard the phrase, 'Don't poke the bear'? Because you're about to find out why that can be a dangerous practice."

"Lord, I'm terrified." Taylor smirked.

That was it. Challenge accepted.

They got to the hotel room, and Del locked the door. He waited until Taylor had deposited his shopping bag on the desk, and removed his jacket, before he pounced. He pushed Taylor up against the door, his face pressed against the smooth wooden surface.

"Don't. Move."

Taylor's breathing grew more rapid, hitching when Del reached around and unfastened his new jeans. He tugged hard on them, trying to get them past Taylor's hips, but the damn things were sprayed on.

"You got ten seconds to get out of them," he ground out. "Then I want that ass bare, and ready to get fucked." Del shrugged off his jacket and dove across the room for supplies, before making sure the heating was turned up.

The speed with which Taylor rid himself of his clothing was highly amusing.

"Hands to the door," Del barked out.

"Am I bein' punished for something?" Taylor asked, twisting to peer at Del over his shoulder. Del took a moment to admire the smooth, broad back that tapered to a slim waist, before swelling into the object of sheer temptation that had lit a fire in him.

"You have to ask? After you flaunted this ass in my face all afternoon, bending over here, stretching there? And don't even bother telling me you weren't doing it on purpose, because I will laugh my fucking ass off."

"You're still wearin' clothes," Taylor observed.

"That's 'cause the only thing *I* need to get bare is my cock." Del popped the button on his jeans, lowered the zip, then freed his shaft. "Now show me that ass," he demanded, slowly pumping his already rigid dick.

Taylor arched his back and tilted his hips, and Del didn't waste a second. He got on his knees behind Taylor, pulled those firm cheeks apart, and dove right in there with his tongue.

"Jesus, warn a guy!" Taylor shuddered. Del chuckled against his hole, and shivers visibly rippled through him. He rubbed his beard through Taylor's crease, getting his face right in there, before resuming his teasing tongue-fuck.

"Del." It was almost a whimper.

Del got up, spun Taylor around, and seized his mouth in a fervent kiss, reaching behind him to wedge his fingers in Taylor's crack, tapping his middle finger against Taylor's hole. Taylor moaned against Del's lips, and Del grabbed his hand, dragging it to his own stony cock. "Play with my dick. Make sure it's good an' hard."

Taylor slid his hand up and down the shaft, all the while pushing back, clearly wanting Del's finger in his ass. Del snickered. "Not so fast." He spun him around again, pushing him face first against the door, before slicking up his bare cock and sliding it between Taylor's cheeks. Del rocked gently, making sure his shaft brushed over Taylor's hole, while he reached around to wipe still slick fingers over Taylor's exclamation point of a dick.

"Fuck, you're hard."

Taylor groaned. "What did you expect, when you've had your tongue an' fingers in my ass?" He rocked back against Del, who wrapped his arm around Taylor's front, resting it lightly against his throat. "C'mon, Del. Fuck me already."

Del laughed. "Boy, you're not listening, are ya? You ain't the one in charge here." He removed his arm, took a step back, and undressed, in no hurry. When Taylor let out a noise of sheer exasperation, Del snickered. "Keep it up. Won't make me fuck you any faster."

"Del."

Del snorted. "And saying my name like that won't do it for ya neither."

Taylor stood still at that point. "How do you want me?"

Pride swelled in Del's chest. "That's better." He sat in the wide chair and swiveled it around, before pushing it to some distance from the desk. "Head on the desk, ass high, legs spread. Show me that hole."

Taylor complied, presenting Del with the perfect view of his pucker. Del pulled his cheeks apart, and slowly rubbed his nose down through Taylor's crack, before reversing the motion and dragging his beard over Taylor's contracting hole. He pushed one finger all the way into him, up to the knuckle, then sawed it in and out, until Taylor was trying to ride it.

Del caught sight of himself in the mirror that ran along the wall above the desk, and grinned. *Now* there's *an idea.*

He leaned forward, grabbed Taylor's chin, and lifted it. "Look at yourself. Look how beautiful you are when you're getting fucked."

Taylor's eyes were huge, and he groaned, pushing back harder onto Del's finger. Del added another and watched Taylor's reflection, noting how he closed his eyes and expelled a long breath as Del filled him. It was mesmerizing, sliding his fingers deep into Taylor and seeing the result in the mirror. Taylor's gaze locked onto his, and he nodded. "More," he begged.

In spite of telling Taylor he was not to be hurried, Del couldn't wait any longer. He gloved up, wiped a slick hand over his cock, and filled Taylor to the hilt in one long thrust.

"Oh, fuck." Taylor bowed his head briefly, then jerked it up to stare into Del's eyes. "Yes. Again."

Del pulled almost all the way out of him, then drove his dick all the way home in one slick motion. Then repeated it, and repeated it, until he was withdrawing completely, before spearing that dark hole again and again with precision, accompanied by Taylor's grunts and guttural noises of pleasure.

"You like that?"

"Fuck, yeah. More." Taylor's face was a mask of bliss as Del thrust in him up to the hilt.

A delicious thought occurred. Del pulled free, then grabbed Taylor and tugged him toward the door. He pushed him until his back was flat against it, then grabbed Taylor's ass. "Arms around my neck, and hold on tight."

Taylor did as instructed, and Del hoisted him up into his arms.

"Now hook your legs around my waist."

Taylor's eyes grew wider. "Aw, fuck, I've always wanted someone to do this." He wrapped his legs tight around Del, and Del took one hand off his ass to guide his cock into position.

"Sit on it, all the way down." Carefully he let Taylor's weight do the rest, until his dick was buried in Taylor's hot ass. Then his hands were full as he began to bounce Taylor up and down on his cock. Del stepped back from the door, Taylor clinging to him as he impaled himself on Del's dick again and again.

"Oh... my... fucking.... God," Taylor gasped out.

"Name's Del," he gritted out, tilting his hips and thrusting up into Taylor's body.

Taylor let out a joyous sound. "Not... anymore. Now? ... It's ... God." He shuddered. "Fuck, you're deep."

Del snickered. "It's called... gravity. Not me... doing all the work, believe me." Talking was a real effort.

Taylor wrapped his arms tighter around Del's neck, holding on. "Like fuck it is. Look at... these arms... your muscles... strainin'..."

Del held onto his ass with one hand and pressed the other flat to the door, Taylor suspended between them, his legs wrapped around Del's hips, anchoring himself to him. "Like this?"

Taylor's eyes rolled back. "Aw, fuck, that's so hot." He sank a little too fast and a full groan tumbled from his lips. "Lord.... so full."

Del got into a rhythm, letting Taylor drop and then pushing up to meet him. "Still think... I'm God?"

Taylor threw back his head. "The Alfuckingmighty."

Del laughed. His muscles ached, and his thighs shook from the effort required. He carried Taylor to the bed, holding onto his precious cargo. He lowered him gently onto the mattress, his ass just hanging over the edge. "Now I gotcha." He penetrated him with a measured slow glide in and out, his focus on Taylor's face. "Feel good?"

Taylor nodded, his hand reaching for his dick. "So good." His eyes widened once more as Del filled him completely. "God... so full. That was amazing. The way you felt, like... you were *everywhere*... surroundin' me... fillin' me...."

"Fucking *love* the way you take my cock," Del said quietly, leaning over him, his hand cupping Taylor's nape as he lifted his head toward Del for a kiss. Taylor grabbed hold of the back of Del's neck and clung to him yet again, the kiss hot and urgent. He drew up his legs on either side of Del, and Del let his arms take his weight as he rocked into Taylor's body, slow and easy. Taylor grabbed hold of Del's forearms, nodding, not breaking eye contact, the two of them locked into each other.

Then Del laced his fingers under Taylor's head, supporting it as he picked up speed, only his hips moving as he fucked him faster. "Gonna make you come now," he gasped out. "Go on, touch yourself. Wanna see you shoot."

Taylor wrapped his fingers around his shaft and tugged hard. "Kiss me?"

Like Del needed to be asked. He bent over and locked their lips together in a fierce kiss, not breaking rhythm as he drove

Taylor closer and closer to the edge. When Taylor cried out, come pulsing from his dick onto his belly, Del kissed him again, only more softly this time, before lowering his head to the mattress.

Del grabbed Taylor's thighs and lifted one leg up to rest Taylor's ankle against his shoulder. Then without a word, he drove into him hard and fast, not stopping until he knew he was there. Del shuddered, his fingers digging into Taylor's thigh as he filled the condom, loving the blissful state of being that always followed a really good climax.

He eased out of Taylor, bent over, and licked up the come from his belly. Taylor watched him, open-mouthed, then reached out to cup Del's head again and drew him into a long, sensual kiss as they shared the taste of Taylor.

Del broke the kiss. "Shouldn't really have done that, but I figured with your job, you get tested for everything pretty regular."

Taylor chuckled. "You got that right."

Del caressed his cheek. "Then maybe next time you get tested… you show me your results, I'll show you mine." He waited for the implication to sink in.

Taylor stilled. "Oh my."

Del kissed him sweetly. "You didn't think this was it, did you?" When Taylor's breath caught, Del gave him an inquiring glance. "What is it?"

Taylor bit his lip. "That list of mine… I sorta hoped we'd get through it all, just in case—"

"In case this weekend turned out to be all there was?" Del suggested, his intuition kicking in. Taylor's sheepish look was answer enough. "Honey, this isn't it, not by a long shot. There will be more times, I promise. Just the two of us."

Taylor swallowed. "I think… that sounds awesome."

Del couldn't agree more.

Chapter Twenty

Monday, December 3

Taylor walked into the squad room, conscious of Del's parting shot the previous night.

"Where's your horse?"

"Huh?" Taylor stood just inside the bike shop door, his bike in the workshop. Time to go home.

Del grinned. "You're walkin' like a cowboy. I just wondered where the horse was."

Taylor speared him with a look. "I don't know about any horse, but I've been ridin' you for most of the weekend."

"You'd better hope you're in a squad car tomorrow, and not on a bike." Del's eyes sparkled. "And if you wanna give your ass a rest next time, I'll take one for the team. Purely in the interests of saving your tush, of course."

"Oh, of course." Taylor rolled his eyes. "Why'd you have to go an' say something like that, just when I'm leavin'? Now you got me all fired up again."

Del glanced through the glass front, but it was dark out there, with no one around. He pulled Taylor toward the office, tugged him inside, closed the door behind them without switching on the light, then stepped toward him in the darkness. "Then I guess you're gonna have to learn patience," he said softly, before taking Taylor's lips in a tender, lingering kiss. Taylor cupped Del's head and gave as good as he got.

When they parted, Taylor sighed. "I see a lot of cold showers in my future."

"And making sure you got a good supply of lube 'n' cum towels," Del added. He leaned in for another kiss, and fuck, Taylor just melted in his arms.

It had been a real effort to tear himself away.

"Hey, how was the weekend?" Brian called out as Taylor helped himself to coffee.

From across the room, Mark snorted. "He ain't gonna tell you shit about it. He never kisses 'n' tells, don't you know that by now?"

"Ain't nothin' wrong with keepin' your personal life private." Dale looked up from his desk, his eyes gleaming. "You might wanna think about that, next time you strut in here with tales of your... exploits." His gaze caught Taylor's, and he gave him a warm glance. "Don't you tell him nothin'."

Mark smirked. "If y'all are gonna live such borin' lives, I see it as my goal to bring a little... spice to liven 'em up." He preened.

Terry Donnelly guffawed. "Hearin' 'bout you an' a pair of twins will *not* spice up my life." He winked at the others. "Though it might cause me to upchuck my lunch." Laughter erupted, and Mark glared at them.

"Okay, enough foolin' around. Y'all have work to do, don't ya?" Lieutenant Purdy aimed a firm stare around the room, before going over to Dale's desk. "We've had a call you an' Taylor might wanna check out. Seems Rainbow Racers took your advice an' installed CCTV. Well, last night they had some... visitors."

Dale reached for his cap. "Let's hope it's our little pals. I'd love to put those bastards away. All they ever seem to do is get drunk and cause a disturbance. Come on, Taylor."

He put on his cap, grabbed his jacket, and followed Dale to the parking lot. It was news to him about the cameras, but then he reasoned that Del's business hadn't exactly been high on their schedule of topics to discuss.

The thought of seeing Del had his stomach in knots. Chiefly on his mind was whether he could act professionally, when all he could think of was a naked Del, balls deep inside him, a sheen of sweat on his chest as he—

Down boy. This ain't helpin'.

As they pulled out of the lot, Dale gave him a brief glance. "So… I know it's been a while since we talked about this, but…" He cleared his throat. "I called Zoe."

Taylor beamed. "Really? That's great!" Then he tempered his reaction when he realized Dale wasn't jumping up and down. "Isn't it?"

Dale shrugged. "We're talkin'. That has to be an improvement, right?" He peered through the windshield at the leaden sky. Rain had been falling since dawn. "Looks like we might have more than a couple inches by nightfall."

Taylor knew evasion when he heard it. "How was she? When you spoke to her?"

Dale was silent for a moment. "A little stiff at first, I guess."

"Did you tell her what we talked about? About how you've been seeing things a little differently?" Then Taylor gave himself a swift mental kick. "You know what? You don't have to tell me anything. Like you always say, it's your private business."

Dale sighed. "Talkin' to you last time really helped. Anyhow… I must've said something right, because she's talkin' about coming home for the holidays." His voice was calm and even.

"I'm happy for you," Taylor said truthfully. He couldn't help being more than a little envious, however. "She's lucky. You might not be happy with the situation, but you're willin' to put aside everything you've been taught, because you love her, and family is what is important."

Dale regarded him with wide eyes. "You have a way of puttin' things, like you can really see how things are. Yeah." He pulled off Central Avenue and onto the parking lot that served all the stores there. He groaned as they neared Rainbow Racers. "Aw, would you look at that?"

Across the glass frontage were letters in blue paint, and Taylor's stomach clenched. FUCK OFF QUEERS. "Maybe they ran outta red."

Dale switched off the engine. "Well, if they've got CCTV footage, we've got 'em. Let's go see." They got out of the car and hurried toward the door, the snow coming down heavier. Inside, Del was standing at the counter, conversing with Jon. He appeared miserable, which was understandable in the circumstances.

"Hey. Admiring our new work of art?" He grimaced. "They must've done this sometime during the night, because Jon was here yesterday, catching up, and it wasn't there then." His gaze flickered briefly in Taylor's direction, before he addressed Dale. "Jon's got it all cued up on the monitor, ready for you. And there's coffee if you want it."

"Want me to start on getting a sample?" Taylor asked Dale.

"Sure. I'll get a printout of their faces if we're lucky enough to have something we can use." Dale followed Jon into the office, Del behind him. Taylor opened the door and shivered as the wind chose that moment to pick up. He wasted no time taking a photo of the letters, before scraping off a sample of the blue paint. Unlike the last time, the words were closer to the ground, and there was a profusion of paint splatters everywhere.

Taylor peered closely at the paint, then took a photo of it. There were differences there too. He pocketed the camera and evidence bag, then hurried inside.

Del came out of the office, holding a mug of coffee. "Here. Warm your hands on this."

Taylor took it gratefully. "We got any clear headshots?"

"We sure do. Your coworker is one happy bunny."

Taylor snickered. "Can't think of a single person who's less bunny-like."

"I just wanted to make you laugh."

Taylor blinked at the unexpected revelation. "I didn't think I'd be seeing you so soon," he said in a low voice.

"I'm not complaining. Except, of course, that we have more paint to clean off. At least this time we can nail the bastards." His eyes focused on Taylor's. "Missed you last night." The words were barely a whisper.

"What about 'What happens in Atlanta stays in Atlanta?'" Taylor swallowed.

"I wasn't quite ready to leave it all there. Some things I wanted to hold on to a while longer." Del shifted a little closer. "What about you?"

"What about me?" Taylor's throat tightened.

"Did you miss me?"

Just then the door opened, and Dale strode out, beaming, a sheaf of paper clutched in his hand.

"Yes," Taylor whispered quickly, before walking toward Dale. "Looking good?"

Dale nodded. "Pete, Mike and Dan, oh my." He grinned. "They weren't stupid enough to look directly at the camera. Then again, maybe I'm crediting them with too much intelligence. Because to my mind? I don't think they even realized the cameras were there."

"That's 'cause they looked like they were off their faces." A young man came out of the office, holding a coffee mug. "I doubt they knew the cameras were even there. An' they sure ain't got the brains to look for 'em."

Taylor winced at the sight of the bruises on the young man's face. "*Day*-um. Are you okay?"

He attempted a smile. "You should see the other guy." Then he shrugged. "Looks worse than it is."

Del gestured to him with a flick of his head. "I don't think you two were introduced last time. Taylor Cox, this is Chaz Monroe, our trainee."

Taylor gave Chaz a brief nod. "You're probably right. They seem to do a lot of drinkin'." He looked to Dale. "We gonna bring 'em in?"

"You said it. We'll head back and write this up, then we'll get the paint sample to forensics. It'd be good to tie the paint to them, not that we need to with evidence like this." He studied Del for a moment, and Taylor wondered what was the reason for such scrutiny.

"Something else you might wanna think about." Del gestured to the sheaf of papers in Dale's hand. "Okay, so it was night, and those are black and white photos, but…. they might easily be the three guys who busted up Kendis Sesay's car last month. Not that I could swear to it, you understand."

"We got a description of their clothes," Taylor said quickly. "There must be *some* physical evidence to tie 'em to the scene."

Dale was beaming. "Oh, I'm really likin' this." He extended a hand to Del. "Thanks for the coffee. We'll be in touch."

"Thanks for the quick response," Del said as they headed for the door. "Good to know our local police force works so hard to support small businesses." He walked at Taylor's side.

Taylor wasn't sure if he'd imagined the slight stress placed on the word 'hard', but knowing Del, he wouldn't rule it out. One thing was obvious as he and Dale drove away from the bike shop.

There was no way on God's green earth that Taylor was going to last another four or five weeks without a visit to Atlanta. Hell no.

And no way was he going to put up with just his hand. Hell NO.

Del waited until the police car was out of sight before heading back to the office. Chaz followed him.

"Seeing as we've got no one booked in for today—in fact, no one for the rest of the week—I thought I might work on tuning up the bikes."

"Sure." Del peered at the falling rain. "We might as well make sure we're ready for after the holidays, because no one will be taking out bikes in this weather." When Chaz fell silent, Del patted his arm. "Hey, we knew winter would be like this. Wait until Spring, when they're lining up to take out our bikes and trikes. At least folks know we're here now."

He nodded. "I'll make sure the bikes are in top notch condition." Chaz paused. "Actually, I could use your help, if it's gonna be quiet. I wanna pick up my stuff tomorrow, but... I don't wanna go on my own."

Del straightened. "You got it. I'll go with you, no problem."

Chaz gave him a grateful smile. "Thanks." He left the office, passing Jon as he entered.

Jon helped himself to a coffee. "So, you gonna tell me what all that was about?"

"Huh? Oh. Chaz needs some help and—"

"I'm not talking about Chaz. I'm talking about you an' Mr. Law Enforcement."

"Don't know what you me-ean," Del sang at him.

Jon closed the office door. "Then I'll use small words. Where did you go this weekend, and did he go too? An' if he did, did he keep his gun in its holster?"

Del gasped, feigning shock. "The idea. And before you get to thinking I'm actually gonna *discuss* this with you, I will share one fact, and that will be the end of it."

"So what is your one fact?" Jon asked, sounding bored.

Del grinned. "There was shooting from both sides."

Jon gaped at him. "Then you *were* together. Wait—you're *fuckin'* him? What happened to 'there's nothing goin' on'?"

"There wasn't." Del couldn't suppress his grin. "There is now."

"DEL!"

"And before you start telling me it's not gonna work, and he's not out, and this is gonna break my heart...." He heaved a sigh. "Right now, I'm happy. I don't know how long it's gonna last, but..." He pointed toward the parking lot. "That boy makes me happy. Nothing heavy about it. No huge deal."

Jon fell silent, so silent that Del wondered what was going on. Finally, he nodded. "An' that right there is why I'm not gonna say another word. Because heaven knows, it's about fuckin' time." He gave Del a quick hug. "Even if it only lasts a couple of weeks, it'll be good to see you happy." He left the office.

Del stared into his coffee mug. He hadn't lied, not really. Taylor made him happier than he'd been for a long time. But he knew, deep down, that Jon was probably more realistic than he was. It couldn't last. Not when all Del longed to do was walk along the street, holding Taylor's hand in his.

This was LaFollette, there were no fairy godmothers and definitely no Happily Ever After, because Taylor Cox was *not* going to come out.

Chapter Twenty-One

Tuesday, December 4

Del switched off the engine of his truck and stared at the neat little house through the passenger window. There was no sign of life. A car was parked in the driveway, so someone was home.

Beside him, Chaz sat like a statue.

Del patted his knee. "It's gonna be okay. We're just gonna go in there, collect your things, and get out." He kept his voice quiet and soothing.

"I thought they wouldn't be here," Chaz muttered. "That's why I chose early to do this. Daddy would be at work, and Mama would be helping out. I can't think why one or more of them is here. I sent Daddy a text to tell him I was comin'."

"Well, sitting here wondering isn't gonna get anything done, so let's bite the bullet." He squeezed Chaz's knee. "Just one thing. You don't have to say a damn word to them if you don't want to, you hear me? You can let me do all the talking."

Chaz shuddered out a breath. "Thanks for doin' this, Del. I really do appreciate it." He unfastened his seat belt. "Well, no time like the present." He fumbled in his pocket and brought out a door key. "Guess I won't be needin' this after today."

"Hey, now don't go making assumptions."

Chaz snorted. "You didn't hear 'em the last time."

"And just because they're assholes now doesn't mean they'll stay assholes," Del reasoned. "You don't know what will happen in the future. None of us do." *But knowing sure would save on a lot of heartache.* Del plucked his keys from the ignition, unfastened his seat belt, and opened the door. Chaz followed, and together they walked up the driveway to the house.

Before they reached the door, it was flung open, and a tall man wearing jeans and a sweater stood there, his face red, his eyes wide.

"Boy, you got a nerve, showin' up here with... him." He sneered. "What makes you think we're gonna let any boyfriend of yours step one foot inside this house? Get the fuck out of here before I get my gun."

Beside him, Chaz was shaking, but Del laid a hand on his arm, before stepping forward. "Mr. Monroe, first of all, can I ask that you lower your voice? Unless you want all your neighbors knowing your business."

Mr. Monroe recoiled visibly, then darted a gaze at the houses on either side. Drapes were already twitching.

"Secondly, my name is Del Walters, and I own a bike shop up on Central. Chaz here is my employee. And if you go around spouting more of what I just heard, I'll have no choice but to sue you for slander. Because if that... crap hurts my business, then we're talking defamation, and I got all these good people here who heard every word you just said."

Mr. Monroe paled. "Say what?"

"You're a business owner, aren't ya, Mr. Monroe? You already know how public opinion can make or break a business. Well, I'd advise you to keep your... opinions to yourself." He squeezed Chaz's arm. "Now you get in there and collect what you need. If you need a hand, just holler. I'll be right here with your daddy." He gave Mr. Monroe a polite smile, but inside Del was already at boiling point. He wanted to snap the man like a twig. "There are boxes in the back of the truck if you need 'em."

Chaz nodded, then headed back to the truck to collect them.

Del eyed Mr. Monroe with distaste. "Now let's get one thing clear. You told him to get out of your house and your lives. Well, he's doing that. So you stay out of his. No phoning him to harass him, okay? You've made your feelings known. He doesn't need you. He's got people looking out for him, people who care about him."

Chaz shuffled past him, carrying the boxes in the crook of one arm, and slipped past his daddy into the house.

"An' are you one of the people who care for him?" That sneer was back.

Del slowly walked up to him. "Yes, I am. That's because I'm a decent human being who looks out for his fellow human beings." He lowered his voice. "And if you decide *not* to heed my warning, two things will happen. One, I will snap you in half, and two, I will make sure that photos of Chaz's injuries find their way into the hands of the police."

Mr. Monroe's eyes widened. "You just threatened me."

Del nodded. "And you can't prove a word of it, because unlike you, I didn't go shouting my mouth off for all and sundry to hear. So now we understand each other…" He called out, "Chaz, you need a hand? 'Cause it can't be easy, packing with a busted wrist."

His daddy flushed and looked at the ground.

"'S'okay, I got this."

"You one of them too?"

Del rolled his eyes. "Dude, you just don't know when to shut up, do ya? So you know what? I'm just gonna stop listening and wait for Chaz." And with that he strolled down the driveway, stopping at the halfway point between the house and the truck, close enough that he could hear Chaz if he yelled.

A few minutes later, Chaz appeared, struggling to carry two boxes, and Del hurried to relieve him. He deposited them in the back of the truck, where he'd laid a sheet to keep the rain out, then headed back to the house to help Chaz with the final boxes. Mr. Monroe stood there, his neck strained, his face red, but saying nothing.

When all the boxes were stowed away, Chaz walked back to his daddy, and held out his key. "Here." His daddy snatched it from Chaz's palm, as if the slightest contact with Chaz's skin was corrosive.

Without another word, Chaz turned his back on his daddy and strode down the driveway to where Del stood next to the truck. He climbed into the passenger side, and Del got behind the wheel. He switched on the engine and pulled away from the curb.

Chaz was quiet, and Del let him be. He drove through the town and pulled up in Jon's driveway.

"Jon says to take your time and put your things away. We don't expect to see you the rest of the day." Del smiled. "Jon did say something about a shopping list, however."

Chaz chuckled. "Yeah, he has a habit of going grocery shoppin' without one, then has to make one when he forgets lots of things. Tell him I'll get the groceries in. I'll even take care of dinner this evening. All he has to do is show up."

Del snickered. "Now, you *know* I'm gonna make all kinds of remarks about how domesticated this situation is." Secretly he was happy Chaz was living with Jon. The two men were good for each other.

Chaz laughed. He laid his hand atop Del's on the steering wheel. "Thanks for comin' with me."

Del smiled. "I told you—you're family now."

Chaz released his hand and got out of the truck. Del helped him carry the boxes into the house, then with one last wave of his hand, he got back in and pulled away.

As he drove toward Central Avenue, he caught sight of a police car coming from the opposite direction, and his heartbeat raced, until he saw that neither of the officers was Taylor.

Lord, I got it bad. How else could he describe the situation, when he got excited at the thought of just *seeing* Taylor?

His phone rang, and Del found a convenient place to stop. "I'm on my way, for God's sake! I'll be there in five minutes."

"Just checking it went okay." Jon sounded anxious. "Is he alright?"

"Chaz is fine. He's making you dinner tonight. Now stop worrying." Privately, he loved that Jon was looking out for Chaz.

"I was really callin' to make sure you weren't in a police cell for beatin' his daddy to a pulp."

Del huffed. "Oh ye of little faith. I was the picture of restraint."

There was a pause, then Jon snorted loudly. "Yeah, right. I'll have a coffee waitin' for ya." And with that, he disconnected.

It wasn't until a minute or two had passed, that Del realized he envied Jon. He had someone to go home to, even if it was his roommate, however temporary that situation might be. He had someone who cared enough to have a meal waiting for him at the end of a day. Jon had more than just his kitty.

The previous night had brought home to Del just how much he'd loved sharing his bed for two nights. Granted, the first night had been a case of falling asleep still clothed, but Saturday night had been something else entirely. He'd had his arms full of a naked Taylor, warm and sated, blissed out from sex, and more into cuddles than Del would have dreamed. Memories of waking in the middle of the night to go to the bathroom, and returning to the bed, only to have Taylor reach for him, hold him, and warm him with his body.

Even sweeter memories of waking with a hard-on, and a sleepy Taylor handing him a condom. Del had slipped inside him and lain there, buried in heat, his body curved around Taylor's back, his arm around Taylor's waist while he slowly rocked them, no hurry to reach the end, just enjoying the journey.

Del was no fool. He knew he couldn't have that every night.

That didn't stop him from wanting it.

He pulled into the parking lot and drove up to the workshop, where he parked. On an impulse, he scrolled to Taylor's number, then sat there, staring at it.

You can't call him. He's at work.

You can't call him. What if someone sees your name on his display?

You can't call him. Leave it until the weekend.

Del took a deep breath, then hit Call.

Taylor answered after five or six rings. "Hey." He sounded quiet.

"Is this a bad time?" Panic rose up, tightening his throat. *I shouldn't have called.*

"No, not at all. You… just caught me by surprise, that's all." A pause. "A nice surprise."

A small measure of calm trickled its way into his mind. "You sure?"

Taylor chuckled. "It's good to hear you. Is that clear enough for ya?"

Del heaved an internal sigh of relief.

"Now, is this a social call, or has someone decided to paint bible verses all over your shop window?"

Del went with honesty. "I was thinking about our weekend, and—"

"I haven't stopped thinking about our weekend," Taylor admitted in a low voice. "It was… amazing. All of it." He paused. "What were you thinking?"

"That… I didn't want to wait another few weeks to enjoy your company," Del said, pushing the words out quickly. "So… I was thinking… I know it's a weekday an' all, but…"

"Just ask me, Del," Taylor begged.

"Would you like to come to my house for dinner tonight? Whatever time your shift finishes." Silence fell. "Taylor?"

"Just dinner?"

Okay, he hadn't expected *that*. Except Del knew what lay behind the question.

"Just dinner. I'm not asking you to stay the night—or do anything else, for that matter. Just share some food, watch some TV, listen to music—whatever you want." As an afterthought, he added, "Ball's in your court. I'll go along with whatever you want."

There. No pressure. Del held his phone to his ear, conscious of Jon staring at him through the window, frowning. Del waved him off, and Jon rolled his eyes.

"Dinner sounds great," Taylor said at last. "My shift finishes at seven. I'll come straight there."

Del couldn't help it. The thought just slipped in there. *Don't ask him. Say nothing.*

Then Taylor snickered. "You know what? I won't even change out of my uniform. That'll save me some time."

Oh Lord. Words died in his throat, and blood headed south.

Another snicker. "Not that I don't trust you to keep your hands to yourself, but… I think I'll bring handcuffs."

Sweet Jesus.

Taylor sighed. "I just made things ten times worse, didn't I?"

It was all Del could do to manage one word before he finished the call.

"Duh."

Chapter Twenty-Two

"I thought you said you couldn't cook?" Taylor pushed his plate away with a contented sigh. "That was delicious."

"And *that* was catered," Del said with a smile. "Any fool can buy ready-roasted chicken, frozen mashed potatoes and frozen vegetables, then zap the hell out of it."

"Oh, I don't know about that," Taylor mused. "The veggies weren't overdone, and the mashed 'taters didn't have any cold bits in 'em. That takes skill." His eyes twinkled. "Now, here's the sixty-four-million-dollar question. Is there dessert?"

Del laughed and got up from the table. He opened the freezer door and pulled out a large tub of ice cream. "That enough for you?"

Taylor peered at the label, and beamed. "Man, you even bought my favorite flavor. How'd you know that?"

Del snorted. "Chocolate is *everybody's* favorite flavor." He set the tub down on the counter top. "Two scoops or three?"

"I'll go with two." Taylor gestured to his uniform. "Gotta make sure I can still fit in this, right?"

Del looked him up and down, and coughed, before getting on with scooping out the ice cream. "You seen that friend of yours since we last spoke about him? Jake?"

And just like that, the warmth that had spread through him during the meal dissipated. "Funny you should mention him," Taylor said softly. "I was thinkin' of callin' him, and settin' up a meeting. Just coffee. I figured it was about time we talked. I got some apologizin' to do." Because a lot had changed since they'd last talked.

Del placed a bowl in front of him. "I know part of you is dreading that conversation, so let me share something that I've learned in my lifetime so far."

"Yeah, because of course you're ancient," Taylor said, nodding. Del speared him with a look, and he chuckled. "Go on. Share your nugget of wisdom."

Del paused, a spoon in his hand, from which chocolate ice cream dripped onto the table. "Things are never as bad as you think they're gonna be."

"No, you're quite right," Taylor agreed. "Sometimes they're worse."

Del rolled his eyes. "I don't expect you to believe me, because right now you're in a hole where Jake is concerned. If you wanna see something positive happening, then first you gotta climb out of the hole, because down there? Trust me. All you'll see is black." He went back to scooping more ice cream.

Taylor helped himself to the delicious dessert. "You're right," he admitted in a low voice. "Sometimes it's easier to think negatively, because bein' positive takes more energy, and carries a greater risk of pain and heartache when life doesn't pan out the way you want it to."

Del put the ice cream back in the freezer and joined him. "Tell me about your department. What are they like, the guys you work with on a daily basis?"

For a moment, Taylor was puzzled. Then he sighed. "What you *really* wanna know is, how bad would it be if I came out to them? Could I still work with 'em or would they be assholes an' make my life hell?"

Del set down his spoon. "Firstly, I would never try and force you to come out. That'd be like issuing an ultimatum, and I don't *do* those. Secondly, assholes are a fact of life, like bills and taxes. They will forever be with us, much as we might wish they weren't. I just wanted to know about the people you work with, damn it. I wanted to know more about you!"

There was no missing the agitation in Del's voice.

Slowly, Taylor put down his spoon. "I'm sorry." Lord, he truly was. He hated that he'd misread Del's intent. "God, I hate livin' like this."

Del reached across and took his hand. "I get it, I really do. Hiding gets to feeling like there's a huge weight hanging over you, doesn't it? You're on your guard the whole time, afraid that one little thing is gonna give you away. You can't express how you really feel, say what you really think..."

Taylor nodded. "And yet... just lately I've spoken my mind, sayin' stuff I never thought I'd have the nerve to utter out loud."

"And what happened?"

Taylor thought back to the party, that conversation in the chief's man cave, his conversations with Dale. "People agreed with me," he said slowly.

Del's nod of approval was equally slow. "And because you're *not* happy living your life like this, there *will* come a day when something will happen to make you see reality is not as bad as you've feared."

Taylor stared at their joined hands. "Me bein' here, like this... are we changin' things?"

Del chuckled. "We changed things the night you kissed me and tried to climb me like a tree."

Taylor was sure his cheeks were on fire. "What I mean is, why did you want to go to Atlanta in the first place?"

"To decompress. To be myself."

Taylor snorted. "I think we both know that's a euphemism for gettin' laid."

Del laughed quietly. "Okay, you got me there. What's your point?"

"And now you've got your itch scratched... *still* wanna go to Atlanta like before? Or..." He swallowed. "Are you happy if we continue like this?" He tightened his fingers around Del's.

Del seemed to take ages to answer. "When I invited you to have dinner this evening, I'll be honest, my first thoughts were of everything we did this weekend. But then… I realized just how much I wanted to spend time with you. I meant it when I said just dinner." He coughed. "Of course, you *had* to go an' ruin it by mentioning that damn sexy uniform—and handcuffs."

Taylor leaned closer. "I left them at work." He regarded Del carefully. "You're kinda back in the closet since you came to LaFollette, aren't you?"

Del nodded. "Though I don't intend staying in there long. Just giving the locals time to get used to us before I reveal my true colors."

Taylor said nothing, although his mind was racing. *And then what happens? Will it be back to Atlanta for us?* Because he couldn't see Del being happy with clandestine dinners, and chaste coffee meet-ups. Taylor wouldn't be happy with that either. He hated the idea that he'd be the one putting Del back into a closet where he was obviously uncomfortable.

Yeah, things had changed, alright.

Once it had just been about sex. Now? He cared about Del— his feelings, his opinions, and his future.

"Ever see yourself as a role model?" Del said suddenly.

Taylor stared at him, the question catching him unawares. "Me?"

Del chuckled. "I'm not saying you should turn into a super hero overnight. I'm just saying you could be a real positive role model in this town. Worth thinking about."

Taylor leaned back, releasing Del's hand and picking up his spoon. "You want to know about my coworkers? You probably got a snapshot of this town in the thirty or so people who work there. And yeah, there are some great people. There are also a couple of assholes. Homophobic assholes at that."

Del said nothing, and Taylor had a twinge of guilt.

"Hey, I know you're not tryin' to force me out of the closet. You're just tryin' to help me make the right decision. But you nailed it. You nailed *exactly* how I feel about hidin'. You also got it right that there will probably be a moment when I'll see things ain't that bad after all." He smiled. "I'm not there yet, Del, but when I am? You'll be the first to know."

His heartbeat sped up as Del leaned in and kissed him, slow and easy, like it was something he did every day of his life. His lips were warm, his beard tickled Taylor's chin, and it was fucking *perfect*.

They parted, and Del's bright blue eyes focused on him. "I'll be here," he said simply. Then he gestured to Taylor's bowl. "Your ice cream's melting." A flicker of a grin.

Taylor hoped the cooling ice cream would work on his burning cheeks.

When the meal was over, and the dishwasher loaded, Del made them coffee and they sat on the couch. The TV sat in silence, its screen dark, and Taylor was grateful for that. He had so many thoughts buzzing through his head, he welcomed a little peace.

"I don't want you to take this the wrong way," he said at last, "but—"

"But you're not staying," Del concluded with a half-smile. "That's okay. I sort of expected it after our conversation. And I won't be asking you to stay, okay? I figure you're a grown man. You know your own mind."

Taylor tilted his head. "But you're not saying, 'stay away' either, are ya?"

Del shook his head. "You know where I live. You're welcome here, any time. And it's not like you're gonna walk in on any embarrassing moments." His eyes gleamed.

"I'm not?" There was an implication to that statement, and Taylor was happy about that.

Del grinned. "Nope. I'm saving all those up for you."

Taylor like the humorous note, but the bottom line of what Del was saying made him a little weak at the knees. *There's just me. He's tellin' me there's only gonna be me here.*

That was heady as fuck.

Just then, Taylor's phone burst into life, and he peered at the screen. "It's my momma." He frowned.

"What's the matter?"

"She wants me to run by the 24-hour drugstore. She thinks she's got the flu, and will I get her some meds."

"Your expression says it's more serious than that."

Taylor pocketed his phone. "She has really bad asthma, so flu on top of that is *not* good." He got to his feet. "I'd better go."

Del joined him. "Sure. Thanks for coming on such short notice. Maybe next time, we could try cooking something together?"

Taylor liked the sound of that. "You're on." He paused, acutely aware of what he wanted, but not wanting to give the wrong idea. Thankfully Del was as quick off the mark as ever.

"Come here," he said softly, holding his arms wide.

Taylor stepped into them without hesitation, and Del's hands were on Taylor's back and ass as he kissed him, another leisurely embrace that lit him up on the inside. Taylor cupped Del's head and deepened the kiss, wanting more, needing more.

When they finally parted, Del leaned, his forehead lightly resting against Taylor's. "Kissing you should come with a government health warning."

"Why's that?" Taylor asked quietly.

"Because you are fucking addictive." He laid one last kiss on Taylor's brow, then led him to the door. "Remember what I said. I'll be here."

Taylor gave him a smile, then stepped out into the darkness to head to his car.

He wasn't sure whether his momma's text was good timing or the worst ever.

Chapter Twenty-Three

Thursday, December 6

Taylor walked into the squad room and glanced over at the desks. It was the lunch hour, and most of them were empty. Dale was there, of course, his usual sub sandwich in front of him, and a cup of coffee.

Taylor went over to Dale's desk. "Got a sec?"

Dale put down his pen. "Sure. What's up?"

Taylor leaned against his desk. "We just got the forensics report back on the paint from Rainbow Racers."

"Great. We can add that to the search warrant. Not that we need it. We got 'em on camera."

"Wait a minute." Taylor placed the report on Dale's desk and leaned in, lowering his voice. "There are a couple of things that puzzle me." He pointed to the line about the paint itself. "This stuff doesn't come in a spray can, like the last lot. This was painted on, with a brush. An analysis of the paint surface proved that."

"So they ran out of red paint an' bought some new stuff. What's puzzlin' about that?"

Taylor placed a series of photos on the desk in front of him. "Look at the pics from the first incident. Look at the height of the letters, how neatly it was done. Now look at the second. This was painted much lower on the glass, with sloppier writing. Paint all over the place. Okay, ignore the height and the mess—what strikes you when you compare these two photos?"

Dale wiped his hands on a napkin, then picked up the two photos, his intense gaze alighting on first one, then the other, then back to the first. He frowned. "It's almost as if…" He gave them another look.

Taylor watched him, waiting for him to make the same leap he had.

Dale slowly placed the photos on the desk. "It's like they weren't perpetrated by the same person. Different lettering. Mind you, who's to say one of the others didn't do it? Even though it *was* Pete on the video."

Taylor nodded. "Exactly. I've had enough run-ins with Pete to know Pete doesn't share his fun. Yeah, you can bet it was him, while the other two watched. So how come there's a difference?" He tapped the report again. "Then I called around to check on who might have supplied this paint recently. The store that supplied the spray can had no recent sales, but another did—to a kid. I went over there with our copies of the CCTV footage, and they identified Pete Delaney."

Dale beamed. "Awesome. We got him."

Taylor laid a hand on his arm. "Wait."

Dale peered at him, his brows knitted. "Something's up. What is it?"

Taylor took a breath. "I went back to the first store, because they couldn't remember who they'd sold to? I figured the photos might jog their memory. No luck there. But…" He glanced up, checking they couldn't be overheard. "It turns out that in the meantime, he remembered something. He follows the police department on Facebook, and he was looking at a photo of several officers who'd just finished their probation periods and were now full-time." Taylor placed the publicity photo in front of Dale. In the foreground stood three officers, all smiling proudly, the chief off to the left. Taylor pointed to a figure who'd been caught in the background, an unintentional photobomb. "He says this is one of the guys who bought that brand of spray paint in that color. Seeing him there jogged the clerk's memory."

Dale stared at the photo in silence, before slowly raising his head. "Just so we're clear, you're not accusing anyone—are ya?

Because this is circumstantial."

Taylor sighed. "I'm not about to do anything with this information, but it makes you think, doesn't it?" He looked over to Mark Teagle's empty desk. "He was the one spoutin' off about fags, an' that was before the first incident. He even mentioned bible verses, and whadda ya know, Rainbow Racers received anonymous letters quoting bible verses. And he said he wanted 'em gone. So yeah, it's circumstantial, but if we can't prove Pete and his little gang were involved in the first incident…"

Dale looked a little green around the mouth. He picked up his sub, wrapped it in its paper and dropped it into his trash can. "I think I just lost my appetite."

Taylor collected all the photos and stuffed them inside the folder containing the report. "I hate the idea as much as you do, that a serving officer could do a thing like this. Regardless of how you feel about… homosexuals, this was a hateful act, and if it *was* him…"

Dale drained his coffee cup and shuddered, before dropping the paper cup into the trash. "We got no proof. No fingerprints. Nothing, beyond a store clerk recalling—a few weeks *later*, mind ya—that Mark *might* have bought the same paint."

"Agreed, but I had to tell someone."

Dale patted his arm. "I know. But right now, we're gonna pay a visit on Pete and his buddies, and bring 'em in. Want me to sort out the warrant?"

"Can we include a seizure of their clothing too? Yes, I wanna check for paint splatter, but I'd like to check their footwear for evidence linkin' them to the car vandalism."

Dale nodded. "Sounds good." He got up from his chair and put on his jacket and cap. "Off to the courthouse." He peered closely at Taylor. "Have you eaten?"

Taylor shook his head. "Not that hungry."

Dale's gaze was sympathetic. "Grab yourself a coffee, and when I get back with the warrant, we'll go bust their asses." And with that, he strode out of the room.

Taylor went over to the coffee machine and helped himself to a cup. He still felt sick to his stomach. He didn't want to believe any of it, but when he added up the evidence, and what he knew of Mark, it didn't look good.

All he wanted right then was to be with Del, to feel his strong arms around him, and to hear him whisper that 'it'll be okay, honey'. That one little word didn't make him feel weak or feminine. Far from it.

It made him feel like somebody truly cared.

Taylor waited for Dale outside the interview room, clutching the folder containing the photos and forensic reports. They had Dan and Mike in separate cells, and Pete was already in the room awaiting them.

"Want me to take the lead on this one?" Dale asked.

Taylor nodded. It wasn't that he was nervous, it was just that Pete had already proved in past altercations that he was damn perceptive. The less Taylor said, the better. "What bugs the hell out of me? Even though the damage is sure to amount to more than $500—which makes it a felony—because they got no priors, we're talkin' probation. Okay, so restitution to Kendis's car would be part of the sentence. That doesn't address the hate behind those acts."

Dale shrugged. "You never know. Get 'em in front of the right judge, and he may decide a spell in jail is warranted. You know, to send the right message."

They entered the room, and Pete grinned. He rocked back on his chair, almost to the point where he was about to fall on his ass. "Officer Cox. How's your boyfriend? See much of him these days?" Still grinning, he addressed Dale. "Did y'all know he has a boyfriend? They're so *cute*. They go bowlin'."

Dale didn't react, but sat in the chair nearest the recording equipment. Taylor joined him, placing the folder on the table. He wagged his finger. "Gotta keep up, Pete. You're behind the times."

He turned to Dale. "Apparently, in Pete's world, if you go bowlin' with a friend, that means you're in a relationship. As I pointed out at the time, what did that say about Pete and his two buddies?" He smiled at Pete, who snarled.

"Why am I here? I got nothin' to do with no graffiti, and you can't prove otherwise."

Dale cleared his throat, pressed the button, and went into the intro, identifying those present and mentioning that Pete had waived the right to have a lawyer present. Then he went for the jugular, placing the CCTV photos in front of Pete, along with the photo of their handiwork.

It was instantly obvious Pete hadn't expected actual evidence. His jaw dropped, and he fell silent. Then Dale went through the report, showing that Pete had been identified by the clerk as the one buying blue paint.

"Nothing to say?" Taylor asked at last, when Pete had sat there for a couple of minutes in silence.

"And this is not the first time your little gang has gotten creative with paint, is it?" Dale placed the photos of the first incident on the table.

Pete's reaction was instantaneous. His eyes widened and he gaped. "Hey, now, wait a minute. What are you tryin' to pull here? That has nothing to do with me."

"According to you a short while ago, none of it has anything to do with you," Dale replied, calmly. "Are you sayin' you wish to change your story?"

Pete's gaze darted from Dale to the photos, to Taylor, then back to Dale again. "I... I'm sayin' nothin'."

"Take off your sneakers." Taylor folded his arms across his chest.

Pete's eyes bulged. "Say what?"

"I said, take off your sneakers. We have a warrant to examine your clothing."

"Well, you're not gonna find any paint spatters, if that's what you're lookin' for," Pete retorted with a sneer. He kicked off his sneakers, bent down, and handed them to Dale with a smug expression. "See? No paint."

Dele held them with two fingers at arms' length as he carefully placed them in a clear evidence bag taken from within the folder. He sealed the tamper-resistant bag, then wafted the air with his hand.

"I've been sprayed by skunks that didn't smell this bad."

Taylor turned to Dale. "At least now we know to look for more footwear." He turned back to Pete. "And we're not lookin' for paint." He took the bag from Dale, turned it over, and examined the soles. Tiny slivers sparkled in the light, and he smiled. *Gotcha.*

"What the fuck are you lookin' for then? Fairy dust?" Pete's sneer was still in place.

"Glass. To be specific, specks of safety glass. You know, like the kind they use in car windshields and windows?" Taylor watched Pete's expression.

Pete blinked, then swallowed hard. "I… I don't know what you're talkin' about."

"Didn't know we have a witness who identified y'all, did ya?" Dale smiled in satisfaction. "I think their description, plus the physical evidence, should just about nail you."

Pete appeared to consider Dale's words. He shrugged. "Well, you go ahead and waste your time. If you can prove it, the court'll slap me with a fine, more 'n' likely, and I ain't got a pot to piss in, so they can whistle for it."

Taylor mimicked Pete's shrug. "Oh, I don't know. Your truck'll be worth something." That got a reaction. Pete glared at him. Taylor went for the throat. "If I were you, I'd be more concerned about your little paint job."

Pete guffawed. "Who the fuck is gonna care about that? It's not like we're talkin' lastin' damage, right? Like they say, shit wipes off."

Taylor leaned in closer. "Maybe so, but they *are* gonna care about *what* you wrote."

Dale folded his arms across his chest. "You never heard of a hate crime, boy?"

Pete stilled. "Ain't no one gonna convict me for that. Not in Tennessee."

Taylor shook his head, sighing dramatically. "Like I said, you need to keep up with the times. There's been hate crime legislation in this state since 2001."

Pete set his jaw. "I want a lawyer. I ain't sayin' nothing else till I get one."

Dale got to his feet. "An officer will escort you back to your cell, and you'll be given access to a phone to call a lawyer. We'll talk more when they get here." He motioned to Taylor to follow him out of the room. Once outside, Dale signaled to another officer to have Pete taken back to the cells, then he led Taylor into an empty interview room.

Dale closed the door and faced Taylor. "So… what was all that about?"

Taylor frowned. "Excuse me?"

"That crap Delaney came out with, about a boyfriend."

And just like that, Taylor's heartbeat changed up a gear.

"That? He's talking about a friend of mine. Hell, you've met him. Jake Greenwood, whose brother Caleb was killed in a car crash?"

Dale's furrowed brow smoothed out. "I remember. You two are friends?"

Taylor nodded. "I knew his brother." *Had an enormous crush on his brother* might have been nearer the truth, but Dale didn't need to know that. "He was goin' through a bad time, an' I gave him support. We'd go to the movies, or bowlin', which was where we ran into Pete and his gang. Course, on Pete's warped little planet, two guys can't be friends. There has to be somethin' sleazy goin' on." He rolled his eyes.

His heart was still pounding.

"What did you mean, he's behind the times?"

There was no way out of this one. "Jake's got himself a boyfriend. They've been together a couple of months, I think. The guy's not from around here, an' I don't think it's common knowledge, which is why I didn't come right out an' say it."

Dale nodded, apparently satisfied, and Taylor breathed a sigh of relief. Then Dale cocked his head to one side. "I take it you and Del Walters are friends too?" Taylor feigned puzzlement, and Dale continued. "I kinda got that impression based on the way he talks to you. Of course, it might just be his manner, but… when we were last at the bike shop, he introduced you to that trainee as Taylor Cox. Not *officer* Cox, mind you." He regarded Taylor closely. "You can see why I might have gotten the impression that you two knew each other."

Taylor fought to maintain his calm. "We met up once or twice in a coffee shop when I was on a break, and I've run into him around town. So yeah, we're not exactly strangers." He held his breath as Dale studied him a moment longer, before nodding and opening the door.

It took every ounce of effort Taylor possessed to walk out of there and not run to the nearest exit.

Fuck. Fuck. Fuck.

Chapter Twenty-Four

Taylor kept telling himself his panic was irrational, but his stupid brain wasn't listening. He had the insane idea that somewhere in his head was a hamster, caught on a wheel that was forever turning, its little paws going like fury, the same little squeak bursting from it at regular intervals.

Caught. I'm caught.

He knows. Dale knows.

Fucked. I am so fucked.

That last image was the one to break through his layers of panic, because whoever heard of a hamster saying fuck?

The interview over, Taylor had grabbed another coffee, sat at his desk, and analyzed Dale's words over and over for any sign of a threat. When it became apparent there was none, Taylor's heartbeat at long last started its slowdown from its present precarious position, and he began to breathe normally again. But as the day wore on, an idea took root in his mind, growing all the more entrenched by the end of his shift.

I can't go through this every time someone makes a comment.

How could he function if he was continually on tenterhooks, always on the lookout in case something he said or did attracted attention? And in the midst of all this febrile brain activity, he latched onto the one thing that had changed. The catalyst for all the panic and suspicion and fear.

Del.

Take Del out of the equation and everything changes. Life was fine when he wasn't doing anything that would have attracted attention. He had nothing to fear then. No chance of being spotted with a guy. No chance of being seen dancing with Del in Atlanta, close enough that—*oh my God*—Taylor had felt the heat of him. No opportunity for some random person to look out their window with a high-powered telescope and spot him kissing Del within the confines of Del's home.

Okay, now he *knew* he was getting paranoid, but it didn't mean he was on the wrong track. Distancing himself from Del would solve everything. Never mind that the sex had been *so* much better than he'd ever thought possible. Never mind that a minute didn't go by without him thinking of Del, seeing him smile, hearing that laugh, feeling those large hands on his body, comforting, soothing, or stirring the heat inside him.

I could stop it all, right now.

It wasn't as if Del had been looking for someone, right? With Taylor out of the picture, he could step out of that closet he'd temporarily decided to reside in. He could go right back to visiting Atlanta and have any number of hot guys lining up for him to fuck them.

Except that last thought… Christ, that hurt. Taylor didn't want to think about Del holding someone else. Kissing someone else.

Making love to someone else.

Then what's the alternative? Carry on as we are, and put up with this tension and fear and panic?

Taylor knew one thing. He couldn't live like that. And by the time he'd clocked out for the day, and was on his way home to his quiet, lonely little house, he'd made up his mind.

Forgetting all about Del was the right thing to do. It was for the best, for all concerned.

Even if it was going to break Taylor's heart.

Taylor had no idea what time it was, and he wasn't about to look. It didn't matter anyway. The rain was lashing down outside, and it wasn't the cozy, soothing rain that gently rocked you into the arms of sleep.

This was a *needles-hitting-glass* kind of rain, and that was fine, because Taylor's hamster was wide awake and squeaking. In spite of all the convoluted thoughts that had plagued him that afternoon, all the decision-making he'd put himself through, all the reasoning and weighing up and analyzing, his resolution had hit a brick wall.

Taylor didn't *want* it to stop.

Never mind that it was safer in his closet.

Never mind that his job was more secure.

For the first time in his life, Taylor was happy, and he did *not* want to give that up. Del made him happy. And on the subject of Del, Taylor was guilty of assuming a helluva lot. Like, he'd be happier without Taylor, which sounded egotistical, and Taylor sure as hell didn't mean it that way, but—

"Fuck this," Taylor said out loud. He was so messed up, that to quote a line from one of his favorite movies, he didn't know if he was shot, fucked, powder-burned, or snakebit. He threw back the covers, climbed out of bed, and grabbed the first items of clothing he laid his hands on, the sweats and T-shirt he'd worn that evening while lying on the couch, unable to focus on a damn thing. He studiously avoided the LED alarm clock, reasoning that if he didn't know what time it was, he couldn't feel guilty about what he was contemplating doing.

Taylor left the house by the back door, the cold rain hitting his body, and it provided enough of a stimulus to dissuade him from cycling the seven miles to Del's house. *Fuck that.* He ran back into the house, grabbed his car keys, and went to his driveway. Inside the car, shivering, he switched on the engine, pulled out onto Meadowood Circle, and headed for the highway.

There was little or no traffic, and he had the wipers going full blast to be able to see through the windshield. Christmas lights sparkled here and there, blurred by the rain. He hadn't given a thought to the holidays, but right that second? Delightful thoughts cascaded through his head of a Christmas where it *wasn't* just him and his momma, thoughts that gave him a real pang.

Driving through the memorial park in daylight was one thing—at night, with no lights overhead, the car's beams bouncing off trees or the occasional house, it was a different matter entirely, and he was relieved to reach Del's house at the end of the lane. Taylor pulled onto the driveway behind Del's truck, and switched off. The house was in total darkness, and for one lucid moment he debated turning around.

Fuck it.

Taylor got out of the car and ran toward the front door, the rain deciding that very minute to descend in an even greater deluge. He rapped on the door, not too loudly for fear of disturbing Del's neighbors, but when no light resulted, he repeated the action, only a little heavier.

From within the house, a light glowed, and Taylor shuddered, either from relief, apprehension, or the damn freezing rain. Light came on in the hallway, the door opened, and Del stood there, clutching his robe at the waist.

"What the fuck?"

Fortunately, Del didn't wait to hear Taylor's explanation. He grabbed him by the shoulder, hauled him into the house and closed the door.

Before Del could say another word, Taylor blurted out, "I don't want this to stop." Another shiver coursed through him with icy fingers.

Del stilled. "Huh?"

"You. Me. This. I don't want it to stop." Taylor's teeth chattered.

Del rolled his eyes. "You are gonna catch your death. C'mon, let's get you out of those wet clothes and dried off. Kick off those sneakers and leave 'em here." He waited until Taylor's feet were bare, then led him through the house to his bedroom, not pausing until they were standing in his warm bathroom. "Arms, up," Del instructed.

"'M not a kid," Taylor protested as Del removed his T-shirt, before tugging down his sweats.

"Sure you're not," Del said, tossing the soaking clothes into the hamper, then grabbing a thick, fluffy towel from the rail. He wrapped it around Taylor, then took a smaller one and proceeded to dry his head, before moving down his body, rubbing vigorously.

The warm towels were heaven, and Taylor submitted to Del's rough version of drying. When he stopped shivering, and his breathing was normal, he laid a hand on Del's bare chest, not missing his naked body beneath the open robe. "'S fine now."

"Okay. *Now* d'you wanna tell me again why you're—"

Taylor stopped his words with a fervent kiss, looping his arms around Del's neck. Del's hands were warm on his back, moving higher to cup his head, deepening the kiss. Noises escaped Del's lips, that echoed the hunger swelling in Taylor, and he broke the kiss, dropped the towel, and took Del by the hand, leading him to the bed.

"Need you," he said quietly, climbing onto the mattress and sliding over to give Del room. Del got in with him, pulled the heavy comforter over them both, and took Taylor in his arms.

"What do you need?" he asked softly.

Taylor didn't hesitate. He took hold of Del's wrist, and brought his hand to Taylor's lips. Taylor sucked on a couple of fingers, making sure they were wet, then dragged Del's hand lower, spreading his legs wide and pulling one knee to his chest.

In the lamplight, Del's eyes widened. His breathing hitched as he slowly sank first one, then two fingers deep into Taylor's ass. "Whatever you need, baby," Del whispered as he prepared Taylor's hole, before reaching into a drawer for lube and a condom.

Taylor closed his eyes at the first burn of penetration, then held onto Del with arms and legs as they slowly rocked together, moving as one, their kisses constant as they enjoyed each other's bodies. Taylor tried to burn it all into his memory: Del's gentle hands on his back, his chest, his dick; the way he took care of Taylor, treating him as if he were something precious; the leisurely undulation of Del's body on top of his, sliding into him, a delicious rocking that had the heat within him spiraling, spreading to every crevice and extremity; and the way their breaths mingled as they quickened their movements.

"Oh God, yes." Taylor was caught up in a wave of intense pleasure, that rolled over and through him, leaving him trembling in its wake. Del gave a low cry as he came, shuddering, and Taylor held him close, kissing him, touching him, caressing him as he too succumbed.

The condom dealt with, they lay in silence, arms entwined, until Del propped himself up on his elbow.

"What happened?" His gaze was locked on Taylor, one hand stroking his chest.

Taylor breathed more easily. "You could've said any number of things. You could've joked about me needin' a booty call. Made some remark about me not bein' able to keep away. But you didn't."

Del let out a wry chuckle. "Sweetheart, it's…" He peered at the clock beside the bed. "Two-thirty in the morning. Whatever brought you over here in the pouring rain, with little clothing, it was *nothing* as trivial as a booty call." His fingers were gentle on Taylor's forehead. "Wanna talk about it?"

Taylor shook his head. "I just wanna sleep. Here, with you."

Del became still. "You sure? You got work in the morning, right?"

"Yup. But tonight I wanna sleep in your arms, in your bed. That okay?" Taylor looked him in the eye. "I promise, I'll tell you everything tomorrow."

Del leaned over and kissed him lightly on the lips, before reaching over to switch off the lamp. "Now, where were we?"

Taylor cuddled up close, molding his body to Del's, feeling safe and warm and happy. "Right here," he whispered, closing his eyes and letting himself drift away into a deep, wonderful sleep.

Chapter Twenty-Five

Friday, December 7

Del awoke to find a note on the pillow beside his.

Sorry I had to run, but I had an early start. I'm free on Sunday, if you're around. We can talk then. Tx

He sat up in bed, dragging his fingers through his hair. It wasn't ideal, not when there had plainly been something on Taylor's mind, but he figured he could wait until Sunday.

Not really like I have any other choice. His thoughts went to Taylor. *Poor baby. He must be exhausted.* Del had been looking forward to an early morning snuggle, but he knew there'd be other times.

From outside came a burst of birdsong, and Del sat still, listening to the excited chattering. The sun was just about up, and another day beckoned.

Damn it. I do not *wanna work today.*

He wanted to lie in bed and sleep some more. Veg out on the couch and read, or listen to music, or watch soap operas. *Anything* but work. Then he smiled. *I'm the fucking boss. If I wanna take a day off, who's gonna stop me?*

Still smiling, he reached for his phone, and messaged both Jon and Chaz.

Hey. Don't expect to see me today. Gonna take it easy. I'll be in tomorrow. If we get hundreds of customers, CALL ME. LMAO

He clicked Send, then tossed aside Taylor's note, pulled the comforter over his head, and lay beneath it, listening to the birds with his arms around the pillow, drinking in Taylor's scent.

Perfect.

Dale came out of the coffee shop carrying two steaming cups and a paper bag. He got back into the patrol car and handed Taylor a cup. "There. That's what we need this mornin'.""

Taylor snickered. "You have *no* idea. I missed my early mornin' coffee, and there was no time to grab one before we had to leave." He regarded the bag with interest. "Don't tell me. Donuts." He let out another snicker.

Dale gave him a friendly whack on the arm. "Hey. Ain't nothing wrong with donuts. You can tell a lot about a man by the donut he chooses."

Taylor sipped his coffee before replying. "Oh really. An' what does your choice say about *you*?"

Dale removed a donut from the bag and grinned. "Regular cake donut. Nothin' but a hole. Plain 'n' simple. Now *you*, on the other hand…" He held out the bag, and Taylor peered inside, intrigued.

"Oh my Lord, you got me a Samoa." He jerked his head up. "Just what are you tryin' to say here?"

Dale burst out laughing. "Man, you think I don't see those desserts you try to hide in the refrigerator sometimes? We are talkin' *sweet*. So I figure any donut that's covered in caramels, toasted sweetened coconut, and melted Ghiradelli dark chocolate wafers has to have your name written all over it."

Taylor took it, laughing. "Thank you—I think." He glanced at Dale. "You seem in a good mood today."

"Zoe called last night. We had a good chat. Seems like she's lookin' forward to comin' home for the holidays. I guess that makes three of us, 'cause her momma has talked of nothin' else for days."

Taylor thought for a moment, then reasoned he had to ask. "Is she comin' alone?"

Dale frowned. "Why wouldn't she be?"

Taylor shrugged. "Well, it's the holidays. She might not wanna spend nearly a month without seein'… Fran, is it? Especially over Christmas."

Dale fell silent, warming his hands on his coffee cup. "She hasn't mentioned bringin' anyone." His frown deepened. "But… if she wanted to bring this girl home with her, all she had to do was ask. So why wouldn't she ask?"

Taylor tried to bite his tongue, but it was like fighting a losing battle. "Maybe she was afraid to," he said softly. When Dale gave a start, he sighed. "Jus'… think about it for a minute. Think about how you reacted when she came out to ya. You spoke first an' thought afterward."

"But how am I to know these things if she doesn't come right out an' ask me?" Dale seemed bewildered. "How am I supposed to know—by mind reading?"

Taylor had said way too much, and he wasn't about to worsen the situation. He drank his coffee, and took a bite out of his donut.

"Oh, come on. Say what you wanna say. I'm not gonna bite your head off."

Taylor swallowed. "Maybe… she was hopin' the idea would come from you."

Dale blinked. "Say what?"

He drew in a long breath. "Well, if it was *me* comin' home, and my folks knew I had someone, I'd kinda hope that they'd know us bein' apart was a big deal. An' sure, this Fran needs to spend time with her family too, but… maybe Zoe was hopin' you would tell her it was okay to bring Fran to meet y'all, even if it was only for a couple of days. What's a couple days in nearly a month of vacation?" He paused before delivering the last part. "And it would send her a really important message—that you wanted to get to know Fran too. This is someone who's real important to her, right?"

Dale stared into his coffee, his donut forgotten. He was so

quiet that Taylor was afraid he'd gone too far. At last he sighed. "That makes a lotta sense. I just didn't see it." He turned his head toward Taylor. "But you did. You see things so clearly. Maybe it's 'cause you're young. You know, on the same wavelength, an' all that?"

Taylor caught his breath, suddenly feeling more exposed than he'd ever felt in his life. Dale stared at him, his eyes widening briefly, his lips parted but no sound coming from them.

Then Dale sagged into his seat, his gaze locked on Taylor. "Does *your* momma know?"

Fuck, it was quiet.

Taylor cleared his throat. "Excuse me?"

Dale's smile was warm. "It's okay, son. I just got to thinkin' about things—well, about you—an' it was like I was seein' you for the first time, an' it all made sense." He tilted his head to one side. "Well… does she?"

There seemed little point in hiding now. Taylor summoned up all his courage, and took a step out into the unknown. "No sir, not yet." He attempted a smile. "In fact, there's less than a handful who do." His heart hammered, and his hands grew clammy.

"Then I'm thankful to be one of the ones you've trusted." He patted Taylor's shoulder awkwardly. "And don't you worry. I won't breathe a word to a livin' soul. Except…." His smile grew wider. "I might tell Zoe—without mentionin' your name—that you're the reason her daddy has… mellowed a little."

"I'm glad I could help," Taylor said quietly, his voice cracking.

Just then the car radio burst into life, and the bubble surrounding them was burst. Dale noted the details on his notepad and sighed. "I guess it's back to work." He collected their cups and got out of the car to deposit them in the nearest trash. Taylor placed his donut back into its paper bag and put it aside.

He wasn't hungry anyway.

As they drove toward their destination, Taylor fought to breathe evenly. He still couldn't believe he'd come out—literally—

and said it. What struck him was that Dale hadn't asked if *he* had someone special. It wasn't until they'd stopped the car and were getting out that the answer came to him.

Oh dear Lord. Dale didn't ask because he thinks he already knows. He thinks it's Del.

Then laughter bubbled out of him and for the first time that morning, he felt overcome with a lightness that made him almost dizzy.

Duh. That's because it is *Del.*

Dale gave him a quizzical look. "You okay there?"

Taylor smiled. "I'm fine." Right then he couldn't wait for the shift to be over, so he could hurry to Del's shop and share his day.

An' it's a pretty fuckin' momentous day too.

Taylor had just received his latest test results, and he couldn't wait to share those too.

Taylor switched off his car engine and got out. There were still lights on inside the bike shop, so he figured Del wasn't quite done for the day. He pushed open the glass door and entered. He spotted Chaz in the office, his head bopping along to some music that Taylor could just about hear. Then Chaz caught sight of him, and opened the office door. Tina Turner's voice poured out of the small room, and he grinned.

"Damn. I figured I had the place to myself, so I cranked up the volume." Chaz hurriedly switched off the music. "What can I do for ya?"

"I was hoping to have a word with Del—Mr. Walters—about our interview with Pete Delaney and his gang." The lie heated up Taylor's cheeks, and he snickered internally. *Pants on Fire. I was hopin' for a kiss.* True, he had intended telling Del how his meeting with Jake had gone, but that was incidental.

Kissing beat every other excuse, hands down.

"Oh. Well, he's not been here today. He'll be in tomorrow

though. Jon took the afternoon off, and I was readin' up on all the trails." His eyes sparkled. "I gotta be ready when all those new customers arrive in Spring, so I can answer their questions."

Taylor was impressed. Chaz might be young, but he was obviously ambitious and hardworking. "Del had better watch out. One of these days he might find he has competition for his job." He chuckled.

Chaz let out a happy sigh. "He was honest with me from day one. His plan is to train me up to work with Jon, so that when Del sells his half of the business an' goes back to California, the shop'll be in safe hands."

When Del sells his half... goes back to California...

Taylor suddenly found it difficult to breathe. "He's not gonna stick around then?"

Chaz shook his head. "He's only here because Jon needed help setting up the business. An' I'm only here because I know bikes, and I'm young enough to learn how to run things properly. Yeah, that was always the plan." His face grew solemn. "It must be tough livin' here, after he'd spent years on the West coast. I bet he can't wait to get back there."

Taylor's throat tightened, and his stomach rolled over. "I'd... better go," he managed to croak.

"I'll tell them you called by."

Taylor didn't wait to hear anything else Chaz might have had to say. He walked out of the shop, over to his car, and got in. His hands trembled as he fastened his seat belt, and he almost forgot to switch on the headlights. He pulled away from the shop, out of the lot, and onto the highway, his mind focused on his destination.

He never said. Not once. Not one fucking word.

By the time he reached Del's house, Taylor was shaking. He locked up the car, strode up the path to the front door and rapped on it.

Del opened the door and grinned. "Why, officer, is that a nightstick in your pocket, or are you—" His face fell. "Taylor? What's wrong?" He stood aside, and Taylor stepped into the hallway, his hands clenched into fists at his sides. "Hey." Del's voice softened. "What is it?"

"When were you gonna tell me?" Taylor gritted out.

Del's brow furrowed. "Tell you what?"

"That you're not plannin' on stayin' long in LaFollette. That as soon as the bike shop is on a payin' basis, you're gonna fuck off back to California." He took a step closer. "Well? Were you gonna get round to it eventually, or were you gonna wait until the day before, when you were all packed up?"

"It's not like that." Del's voice was quiet.

"Then Chaz is a liar?" Taylor's chest heaved.

"No... what I mean is... yes, it *was* like that, but not anymore."

"So what? You just changed your mind? Why should I believe that, when you never once said a word about *any* of this?"

"Yes, I fucking changed my mind, and yes, you should believe that, seeing as *you're* the reason I changed it in the first place!" Del's face flushed.

"Me?" Taylor swallowed hard.

"Yes, *you*, you... doofus. How in the hell could I leave, when I'm..." He drew in a deep breath. "When I'm in love with you?"

Taylor's world shuddered to a grinding halt.

Chapter Twenty-Six

Del sighed. "That wasn't exactly how I imagined saying those words." He'd envisioned much more intimate surroundings, and definitely when both of them were wearing a whole lot less. But his declaration seemed to have robbed Taylor of his anger. His hands hung limply by his sides, and he gazed at Del with such wide eyes that Del couldn't help but smile. "What? Is it such a surprise to learn I love you?" He caressed Taylor's cheek. "And that's why I didn't say a word about leaving. Sure, that had been my plan in the beginning. I couldn't wait to get out of this town. Then you rode up on that bike, and suddenly life didn't look so bad after all." He sighed again. "I thought we'd have fun, that's all. Except you turned out to be so much more."

Taylor leaned into him, and Del put his arm around Taylor's waist. "The other day? When I was in such a state? I was convinced I was about to be outed, and the only way I could see forward, to prevent that from happenin', was to step away and put a stop to all this." He laid his hand on Del's broad chest. "Except... I couldn't. That was why I came chargin' over here in the pourin' rain, to tell you that I wasn't gonna give you up. That... I couldn't." Then Taylor smiled, and Lord, it was like the sun came out. "I guess I wouldn't have done that, if I didn't love you too."

Relief poured through him. "Well, that's a load off my mind."

Taylor chuckled. "What—the Big, Bad Bear was nervous? You thought I might not love ya?"

Del brought his forehead to touch Taylor's. "Even bears need reassurance sometimes," he said softly. "Especially when it was the first time he was truly in danger of losing his heart." Taylor gave a start, and Del raised his chin and looked him in the eye. "Swear to God, sweetheart. There's never been anyone like you. I don't know what it is about you, but… you found a way in, where no one's been before. And it didn't matter that I kept telling myself it wasn't gonna work… Something inside me just wasn't listening."

"D'you think you could tell yourself to kiss me?" Taylor's eyes shone in the lamplight.

Like Del was capable of ignoring *that*.

He cupped Taylor's head and fused their mouths in a not-so-gentle kiss, one that lit a fire inside him, sending heat barreling through him, a white-hot need that came out of nowhere. Taylor's body was pressed against his, and through the thin fabric of his sweats, Del became aware of various… protrusions.

"What in the hell have you got in your pockets?" he murmured against Taylor's lips.

Taylor snickered. "You really wanna know?" He slid his hand into a side pocket on his jacket, and removed a pair of handcuffs. "In fact… that gives me an idea." Taylor straightened and took a couple of steps back. "I got some business to settle with you."

Gone was the hesitancy, the trepidation, and in their place were words laced with steel. Taylor's eyes gleamed as he reached into an inner pocket, removed a folded sheet of paper and handed it to Del.

He opened it slowly, frowning in confusion at first as he scanned its contents. Then it hit him.

He was looking at Taylor's latest medical report.

Hoo boy.

When he glanced up at Taylor, Del found him grinning. "Now, the name of *this* procedure is 'I've shown you mine, now you show me yours.'"

"My last test was a week ago. The results are in my bedroom. Want to come with me and help me find 'em?" he asked playfully.

To his surprise, Taylor shook his head. "Just go get 'em, an' bring 'em back here."

Del stilled for a moment, then gave a nod and went past Taylor into his bedroom. Whatever Taylor had planned obviously didn't include a bed.

That was enough to send a frisson of anticipation skating down his spine.

"And bring the lube while you're at it," Taylor hollered.

That sent even more of a shiver through him.

Del brought the results and the bottle of lube back into the hallway, to find Taylor standing by the dining table, regarding it with a thoughtful expression. As Del approached, Taylor gestured to the table. "Put them down."

Del complied, his heartbeat racing. Taylor in uniform, in full-on officer mode, was more than he'd expected. Del couldn't recall the last time he'd been so aroused.

Taylor flicked his head toward the table. "Now. Hands on the table, and assume the position." He narrowed his gaze. "Spread 'em.'"

Holy shit. Del's cock poked the soft fabric of his sweats, jutting out like a fucking iceberg. He placed his palms flat on the table and bent over, his feet a short distance apart, his heart pounding.

Taylor was behind him in an instant. "Seems like what we have here is a failure to communicate. I said spread 'em, boy." He kicked at the inside of Del's ankles, until Del had his legs wide apart. "Better. Now... do you know your Bearanda rights?"

"What the fuck?" Del laughed.

"Apparently not. Then I'd better go over them for you." That steel edge in Taylor's voice hadn't dissipated. Del caught his breath as Taylor roughly dragged his sweats down over his ass to his knees. Taylor rubbed the edge of his hand through Del's crack, and he stifled a moan as Taylor brushed over his hole.

"You have the right to get your ass prepped." Then Taylor pulled apart Del's cheeks and dove right in, flicking Del's hole with his tongue.

"Holy fucking Christ!" Del shuddered as Taylor licked and probed and sucked. Del closed his eyes and surrendered to the delicious sensations that Taylor's tongue engendered.

Taylor stopped, and Del wanted to scream at him to *get the fuck back there.* "You have the right to have your ass eaten until you're screamin' my name." And before Del could respond, he dove right back in there, only this time he worked on the tight muscle, loosening Del up, sending waves of pleasure surging through him, until Del couldn't keep still. He pushed back, rocking his ass to get more of that tongue dancing over his hole.

"C'mon, baby. Fuck me."

Taylor came to an abrupt halt, and a firm hand pushed Del's chest to the table's surface. He let out a wry chuckle. "You have the right to remain silent while being fucked. If you cannot remain silent, a gag will be selected for you." Taylor reached down to Del's cock, which hung against the edge of the table. He pulled gently on it, then cupped Del's balls and squeezed them. Del gasped as Taylor's warm, wet mouth enclosed first one, then the other, his tongue dragging over the sac.

Del wanted to make a noise, any kind of noise, to let Taylor know how *fucking amazing* it felt. Then two slick fingers slowly slid deep into his ass, and he gripped the far edge of the table. "Aw fuck, it's been a while."

Taylor reached under his T-shirt and stroked Del's back, the motion gentle and soothing, before moving lower to caress his ass, while those fingers kept up that delicious friction as they slid in and out of his hole.

Then Del caught the sound of a zipper being lowered, and he shivered.

"You have the right to take my bare cock," Taylor whispered, and then there was slick hardness, and heat, and *fuck*, he didn't remember Taylor's shaft being that thick. Del gripped the table edge even tighter, hyper aware of Taylor's dick inching its way into him, stretching him, filling him…

It felt too damn good.

"Taylor." Del turned his head to one side. "Not gonna last long." Then he felt the brush of fabric against his thighs, the cool metal of the zipper against his skin, and Taylor was all the way inside him.

Fuck, he wished he could see the picture they made. Del, his sweats around his knees, stretched wide, Taylor fully clothed in a uniform, with only his cock bare as it slid in and out…

Then Taylor picked up speed, and Del forgot about everything but the solid shaft that was making him cry out, making him sweat, pushing him relentlessly toward a finish line that he did not want to cross.

"You have… the right to… shoot your load… only when I say so…" Taylor ground out between thrusts, his body slamming into Del's, smacking his cock against the table's edge.

"Then say the word, because I'm fucking close," Del hissed, doing his best to push back onto Taylor's rigid dick, his movements erratic, his T-shirt sliding over the table's surface.

Taylor's clothed body covered Del's back, as Taylor kissed the back of his neck. Del was conscious of Taylor's cock throbbing inside him, and he squeezed the shaft with his internal muscles. "Aw fuck." Taylor dug his fingers into Del's shoulders, his breath rapid and staccato. "You have… the right… to get your ass filled."

Those words brought home to him the one thing that marked Taylor as something rare and special. Del had never made the choice before, and as Taylor's warmth filled him, he closed his eyes and focused on the sensations; Taylor's weight on him: the exquisite pleasure as he came all over the floor: and the sound of their mingled breaths as they stood there together, bereft of energy.

"And if I choose to waive my rights?" Del said, turning his head once more, seeking Taylor's lips.

Taylor snickered. "That's when I get to use the handcuffs." Then their mouths met in another lingering kiss.

Del wasn't ready to move just then anyway. Maybe when his legs stopped wobbling.

"Taylor."

"Hmm?" He didn't want to move. He was warm and comfortable, Del's chest against his back, Del's lips laying soft kisses over his neck and shoulders.

Del chuckled. "We do have to think about dinner at some point."

Taylor sighed and rolled over to lie on his side. "So if we wanna get this right..." He'd been lying there, thinking about this.

"This?"

"Us. A relationship." He trailed his fingers through the mat of hair that covered Del's chest. "You said once that you had twenty years on me. Okay then. Tell me what you've learned in those twenty years. Share your wisdom. Because I don't wanna mess this up."

Del snorted. "It's one thing to know what you *should* be doing. It's quite another to put it into practice."

Taylor leaned across and kissed him. "Go on. Del's rules for making it work."

Del pulled Taylor to him, and hooked his thigh over Taylor's. "Okay then. Number one is communication. If something bothers you, come right out and say it. Chances are, what you think of as a huge problem can be cleared up in one conversation."

"Makes sense."

"Number two is be honest." Then Del sighed. "You know what? There isn't a series of rules, just common-sense things that should be obvious. Like trusting one another. Respecting one another. Being able to make compromises. Giving each other space."

"Can I ask you something? If all these things help to make a relationship work, then how come you've..." Taylor broke off. He couldn't ask because it would come out all wrong.

"How come I've been single up till now?" Del wrapped his

arms around Taylor and drew him closer. "That's easy. *Both* parties need to work at it. I seem to have had relationships where I was the one doing all the work. It takes two, simple as that." He kissed Taylor's forehead. "I mean, look at us. We know this isn't gonna be easy. I swore I'd never be in this situation again, but hey, here I am, back in the closet with you."

"Yeah, about that…." Taylor sighed. "I… kinda came out today."

Del stilled. "You did? Why didn't you tell me?"

Taylor snorted. "Because we were a little busy doin' other things?"

"And? Who did you talk to? How did it go?" He related the conversation with Dale, and Del's face glowed. "That's awesome."

Taylor was less impressed. "It was… okay. I had a feeling it would be, just 'cause I know Dale. But as for the other guys I work with? There are some who won't be so acceptin'. And a smaller number who'll be downright mean."

Del's expression grew thoughtful. "But what if—"

Taylor's phone rang, shuddering its way across the nightstand. He picked it up and frowned at the screen. "I don't recognize this number." It was getting on for eight o'clock. Curiosity got the better of him and he pressed Accept.

"Hi, am I talkin' to Taylor Cox?" It was a woman's voice.

"Yes, ma'am."

"This is Laurie Michaels. I'm callin' from the LaFollette Medical Center. Your momma has just been admitted, and—"

"What?" Panic seized him. "I'm on my way." He disconnected the call, his heart racing, then scanned the room for his uniform.

"Taylor? What's wrong?"

"Momma. She's been taken to the Medical Center." Taylor launched himself off the bed and squirmed into his pants.

Del was at his side in a heartbeat. "Okay. Calm down. Did they say what's wrong with her?"

"I didn't give 'em the chance." Taylor looked around wildly.

"Where's my shirt?"

Del picked it up off the floor. "Here. You get dressed, and I'll take you."

"You don't have to do that," Taylor protested, trying to get his arms to go through the sleeves.

Del grabbed hold of his shoulders, and forced him to be still. "Breathe, baby. It's gonna be okay. When did you last see her?"

"A couple of days ago. She's still gettin' over the flu, but she seemed okay. Still wheezin' a lot, but that's normal."

"Alright then." Del helped him into the shirt. "I'm gonna take you there, because I do *not* want you driving in *your* state of mind. Okay?" He locked gazes with Taylor, who took a long breath.

"Okay," he said, nodding. "And... thank you."

Del kissed him. "Just remember. You're not on your own now." He smiled. "You've got me, and I've got your back."

It was probably the most comforting thing Del could have said.

As they left the house to drive to the Medical Center, Taylor realized that in the space of a few hours, everything had changed. He wasn't alone anymore, and someone loved him.

He did *not* want to screw this up.

Chapter Twenty-Seven

Taylor thanked the receptionist and walked over to where Del was leaning against a faux stone wall. "Well, I've got her room number, and she said they'll tell me more when I get to talk to her doctor."

"Then let's go." Del walked at his side through the lobby and along the hallway. "And remember, stay relaxed. You don't want her to think you're panicking."

"But I *am* panicking," Taylor remonstrated.

Del sighed. "And that won't help her, okay? Trust me, I've been in your shoes."

It was then Taylor remembered Del's momma had died of lung cancer. *Yeah, I guess he has.*

They found the room, and nearby was a nurses station. A middle-aged nurse with a kind face glanced up as they approached. "Hi, can I help you?"

"I'm here to see my momma, Ruth Cox."

She smiled. "Hey. We spoke on the phone. I'm Laurie Michaels."

"How is she?"

Laurie's eyes were compassionate. "She said you'd worry. She was all for not tellin' you." Laurie got up from her chair and walked around to them. "The doctor saw her half an hour ago, and he's given her something to help her sleep. She's gonna be with us for a few days, till we know she's breathin' easier and her oxygen levels are stable. She'll probably be home in four days or so." She led them to the door. "I'll just see if she's awake. If not, it might be better if you come back tomorrow." She bit her lip. "I didn't really get the chance to tell you much over the phone."

Taylor knew his face was flushed. "Yeah, I'm sorry about that."

Laurie patted his arm. "You're here now." She gave an inquiring glance in Del's direction, but said nothing. She pushed open the door and peered around it. Laurie withdrew, smiling. "Okay, she's awake, but seeing as it's getting late, and visiting time is about to end, maybe it's best if you don't stay too long."

Taylor nodded, then waited until she was heading back to her desk.

"Want me to wait out here?" Del asked.

It took Taylor less than a heartbeat to answer that one. "Nope. You're comin' in too." He pushed open the door and stepped into the warm room, Del close behind him.

His momma lay in the bed, almost sitting up, four or five pillows supporting her upper body and head. There was a monitor beside the bed, from which came a cable that attached to a gray clip on her middle finger. The TV on the wall was on, but the sound was real low, and she was staring at the screen, a breathing mask over the lower half of her face.

"Hey lady," Taylor said softly.

She jerked her head in his direction and smiled briefly, before her face fell. She pulled the mask aside. "They called ya, didn't they? I told 'em not to." Then she caught sight of Del, and she frowned. "I don't believe we've met."

"Momma, this is Del Walters." It was all the introduction Taylor could come up with for the moment.

Momma gave a polite nod in Del's direction. "Mr. Walters." She flashed Taylor a quizzical look. "And why exactly is Mr. Walters here?" She replaced the mask.

I should've known she wouldn't let it go at that.

Taylor took a deep breath, grabbed Del's hand, and led him over to the bed. Momma watched their approach with slightly widened eyes, her gaze flickering down to their joined hands.

"Momma, you remember you said that when I was in high school, no girl was ever good enough to bring home to meet you?"

She nodded, her brow furrowed.

"Well, I figured out why," Taylor said simply, meeting her gaze head-on. He held onto Del's hand and gave it a squeeze.

Her lips parted, and she let out a soft sigh, before sagging against the pillows, and pulling the mask away from her face. "Well, that explains a lot."

Taylor stared at her, taken aback by her lack of reaction. *What the hell?* Beside him, Del was clearly doing his best not to smile. *What was that he said about it never being as bad as you think it's gonna be?*

After a moment, she peered at Taylor. "So, you and Del.... Is this a recent thing?"

"Yes, ma'am."

She sighed. "Well, I'm not gonna say... you've chosen a difficult row to hoe... because that implies you... had a choice in the first place... and I never did hold with those morons who say it's a choice." She rolled her eyes. "Why in the world would... anyone choose that path who didn't have to?"

Okay, this was so far from what he'd expected that Taylor felt like he'd suddenly been dropped into the center of an alternate universe. *I never knew she thought that way. What planet have I been livin' on?*

Momma narrowed her gaze. "You gonna be marchin' in any... parades?"

From the corner of his eye, Taylor caught the twitch of Del's lips.

"No, Momma."

He caught Del's muttered, "*Day*-um!" Momma giggled, and Taylor blinked in surprise.

Momma opened her eyes wide. "What? I was hopin'... I'd get to go shoppin'... for a rainbow dress an' bonnet." Her eyes twinkled as she put the mask back in place.

Okay, Taylor wasn't sure he could take any more surprises.

"Momma? *Rainbows*?"

She snorted. "I'm old, not stupid. *And* I watch Ellen." Slowly, she pulled aside the mask and spoke carefully, taking her time. "Sweetheart, I love you with my whole heart, and that means all of you. If this is what you want, then I'm going to support you in any way I can." Her gaze drifted to Del. "And whoever you choose to be with." She held out her hand to Del. "Come sit here." She patted the bed.

His head in a spin, Taylor let go of his hand, and Del went around to the far side of the bed. He perched on the mattress. "How are you feeling, ma'am?"

She shrugged after taking a few mouthfuls of oxygen. "I'm mendin'." She gave Taylor a hard stare. "And you can stop… starin' at me like I'm about to… drop off the twig… 'S just pneumonia, for God's sake."

Taylor was only just recovering his composure. He stepped closer and stroked her hair back off her face. "And pneumonia for someone of your age, who suffers from asthma, *and* who's just had the flu… that ain't no walk in the park."

She rolled her eyes heavenward, before regarding Del with interest. "My, you're a big man. You got a job?"

He smiled. "Yes, ma'am. I own half of a bike shop here in LaFollette. My brother owns the other half."

Her eyes lit up. "So… you got a business *and* family here." The mask snapped back into place, but Taylor doubted it would stay there long. It didn't hide her satisfied smile either.

"Ma'am? I think you need to rest."

She blinked. "'M not tired." Her eyes told a different story, however.

Taylor leaned over and kissed her forehead. "I'll be back tomorrow." She narrowed her gaze yet again, and he chuckled. "And I'll make sure Del comes too."

Del lifted her hand to his lips and kissed the back of her hand. "You sleep now, y'hear?"

She gave him a drowsy smile. "Taylor, looks like you found

yourself a good one." Then her eyes closed, her breathing changed, and her face relaxed as she slipped into sleep.

Taylor stood by the side of the bed, gazing down at her. Del got up and joined him. "Well? Did that go like you expected?"

Taylor felt like he was in a daze. "It was like… she already knew."

"Mommas have a sixth sense, I guess. But it looks to me like you got nothing to worry about there."

"Wasn't my momma I was worried about. Although I never imagined she'd be so… acceptin'." He was still reeling from it all.

"And that was what I wanted to talk to you about, before they called about your mom." Del reached down and clasped Taylor's hand. "Would you feel differently about coming out to your coworkers, if you knew you had backing?"

Taylor opened his mouth, but Momma stirred. "Let's go someplace where we can talk," he suggested.

Del's stomach grumbled. "And eat. We missed dinner."

Taylor snickered. "I thought you *were* the dinner. That *was* you, all spread out over the dining table?" Then his belly gave a rumble, and Del chuckled. "Okay," Taylor agreed. "Food first. But then we talk, alright?" He let go of Del's hand and walked toward the door.

"Fine." Del lowered his voice. "You didn't make any stipulations as to *where* we talked, now, did ya?"

Taylor shook his head as they walked through the hallway. *He is going to be trouble.* And Taylor couldn't wait.

Del poured the coffee, then brought the two mugs over to where they were sitting at the table. He peered at it. "Never gonna be able to look at this table in the same way again."

"You won't even bat an eyelid," Taylor assured him. His eyes twinkled. "You'll be too busy thinking about that time on the observation deck, or in the shower, or on the staircase, or—"

Del snorted. "You weren't kidding when you said you had a list."

Taylor had other things on his mind just then. "Now tell me what you meant by backing."

Del sipped his coffee. "I'd have thought it was obvious. If the chief of police is behind you, people are less likely to step out of line. And you've said yourself, on more than one occasion, that he's okay." Del cocked his head. "You said you had a feeling about Dale. What does your gut tell you about the chief?"

Taylor fell silent for a moment, mentally going over every conversation he'd had with Chief Tillerson. "I guess... I get a good feeling."

Del nodded slowly. "Well okay then. That's your next move. You need to sit down with the chief and be straight with him." His lips twitched. "You know what I mean."

Taylor shook his head. "There's something else I'd need to do first." When Del gave him an inquiring glance, Taylor smiled. "Talk to Denise. I'm about to blow the cover on our 'relationship'," he said, hooking his fingers into air quotes. "She needs to be ready if he asks questions." He glanced at the clock. "And right now, it's Friday night, which means the chief and Mrs. Chief are watching a movie, and she's on her phone, trying to make it look like she isn't."

Del chuckled. "I guess you should know her by now, right?"

Taylor pulled out his phone and composed a text. *Got time to talk?* Within less than a minute his phone rang.

"Now, there's a dumb question." He caught the soft *snick* of a door closing. "Are you alright?"

"I'm fine. Actually?" Taylor gazed across the table at Del. "I'm better 'n' fine. I'm just callin' to give you a heads up."

"Uh oh. That doesn't sound so good."

"Well, once I talk to your daddy, I don't think I'll be invited to any more suppers."

There was silence for a moment. "Oh Lord. You're gonna tell him. Why now?"

"I thought it might be wise, before he got to hear about me being seen with my... partner." God, the look in Del's eyes when Taylor said that word. A wave of heat rushed through him, leaving him weak.

"Your... Taylor Cox, have you got a boyfriend?" He couldn't miss the glee in her voice. "Well, I'll be. That's awesome news. I'm real happy for you. Less happy about my own circumstances, but hey, I'm a big girl."

That did it. If there was *anything* Taylor could do to improve Denise's situation, he was going to do it. "Thank you. For being so understanding. And... for not sharing."

"Wasn't my business to share. But you know what? Once it's common knowledge, and people have picked themselves up off the floor and started with the stupid remarks, I'll be there for you." Another pause. "You know this ain't gonna be easy, right? Not everyone is like my daddy."

Taylor sighed. "I know. But as long as I got people like your daddy, you, my momma, and a few others I could mention, I'll be okay." He hoped. "I'll say good night. I'll talk to him on Monday."

"Good luck."

When he'd finished the call, Taylor was conscious of Del's gaze.

"You missed someone out when you listed all those folks who'll have your back. I didn't hear my name."

Taylor smiled. "That's because I took your name as read. Presumptuous, I know, but I kinda assumed the guy who loves me would have my back."

"And your front, and every goddamn inch of you." Del got to his feet. "And now I'm gonna take all your delicious inches to my bed, where I'm gonna kiss every one of them. For starters, at least." He held out his hand and Taylor took it.

"Who's driving?"

Del snorted as he led him into the bedroom. "After the pounding you gave my ass? It sure ain't you."

Taylor had no problem with that whatsoever.

Chapter Twenty-Eight

Saturday, December 8

"I'm goin' in search of coffee. Want one?"

Taylor smiled. "Sure." He waited until Del had left the room, then turned to his momma. "Okay, out with it."

"Out with what?" Momma gave him an innocent glance that didn't fool him for a second.

Taylor rolled his eyes. "Never play poker, Momma. One look at your face when we walked in this morning told me you've got questions. Okay… ask 'em. Because I'm assumin' they're about Del, an' what's goin' on."

She worried her bottom lip with her teeth. "Like I said yesterday, I got no problem with you bein' gay, sweetheart. Honest to God. In fact, it's a relief, if you want the truth. But Del? Okay, he was a surprise."

Taylor said nothing, but waited for the rest.

"How… how old is he?"

"Forty-six," Taylor replied promptly. "An' before you ask, that don't bother me at all. In fact, it's kinda perfect."

Her eyes widened. "He's almost my age."

"Well, ain't it a good thing that you're not the one datin' him? It'd be all over town that my momma was a cougar." He grinned, but her brow was still furrowed. Taylor sighed. "Please don't worry about this, because I sure don't, and I'm the one in this relationship, right?"

"That was gonna be my second question. Is it… serious?"

Taylor fell silent for a moment, debating how to answer her.

He took her hand and stroked it. "I love him, Momma. So much that if anything happened and we had to part? I think it would break me."

Her mouth opened, and she stared at him. "Oh my. Guess that answers my question."

"Momma, I don't expect you to love him the way I do, not right away. But he's a good man. All I ask is that you talk to him. Make an effort to get to know him. Can you do that for me?"

She nodded. "Course I can. The fact that you brought him to see me says a helluva lot. I've waited all these years to meet someone who mattered to you. Guess I can't complain when they finally come along." Her lips twitched. "Even if he looks like he wrestles grizzlies on the weekend."

Taylor snorted. "Not bad, Momma. He's what you'd call a bear in gay circles. And the way he looks is what first got me to notice him."

"How could you miss him?" she murmured, as the door opened and Del walked in, carrying two cups of coffee. He glanced from Taylor to his momma with an inquiring glance.

"Have I missed something?"

Taylor patted the bed. "Come sit here, and tell my momma all about San Francisco. I'm sure she'd find it fascinatin'."

Del arched his eyebrows. "*All* about San Francisco?"

Taylor chuckled. "Yeah, well, you might wanna leave out a few details." Like Folsom, for one. He wasn't sure his momma was liberal enough to cope with that.

Del parked the truck in front of the bike shop, after first dropping off Taylor to pick up his car to do some grocery shopping for their weekend. Shopping for two had a nice, domestic feel to it that Del really liked.

I could get used to this.

He entered the shop and found Jon and Chaz in the office,

deep in conversation as they studied maps of bike trails. "Now, *that's* what I like to see."

Jon jerked his head up. "And what's that? Us plannin' our next season while you stay at home and put your feet up?" He grinned. "Not that I'm complainin'. I guess I'll have to get used to it, once it's just my name above the door."

Shit. Well, Del had come in for a reason, right? "Yeah, about that... We need to talk."

Chaz bit his lip. "Shall I make myself scarce?"

"Nope, because this concerns you too." Del went over to the coffee machine and helped himself to a cup. "I hope this doesn't come as too much of a shock, but... I won't be moving back to California."

Jon gaped. "For real?"

Del nodded. "And as for selling you my half of the business, well, I won't rule that out completely right now. If it gets to the point where we're making a profit, and you feel comfortable running the shop, then yeah, I may sell my half and look into starting up a business of my own."

"Here... in LaFollette." Jon frowned. "I don't get it. What's changed?"

Del smiled. "More than I could've imagined." Behind him, the door opened, and he turned to see a familiar face. "Hey. Good to see you." He walked out of the office and over to where Kendis Sesay stood, looking a little nervous.

"Hey. I just wanted to thank you for all you did, and to tell you what the police have said."

"They've identified the guys who trashed your car, haven't they?" Del said with a smile.

Kendis stared at him. "How'd you know that?"

"Let's just say I have my sources."

In the office doorway, Jon snorted loudly, and Chaz snickered. Kendis blinked, then took a step back.

Del wasn't having that. "Kendis, let me introduce you to my brother, Jon, who isn't *really* an asshole," he said, giving Jon a hard stare, "and our trainee gofer, Chaz. Guys, this is Kendis Sesay, who apparently is a fantastic basketball player."

"He is." Chaz flushed. "I saw you play. You're awesome." He cleared his throat. "Okay, that was embarrassing." Kendis suddenly took an interest in his own boots.

Del thought they were adorable. He chuckled. "Have the police said what's happening?"

"They're gonna charge 'em with vandalism. Seems they're facing other charges too, and the cops think they'll get six months at most. *But* what they did say was, I'd probably get my car repairs paid for." He smiled. "Which is great, because *I* sure as hell can't afford 'em." His expression grew more solemn. "It'd be better if I could hold on to a job for more than a couple of months."

Del frowned. Kendis struck him as someone who'd have a good work ethic. "What's been the problem?"

Kendis shrugged. "Fucked if I know." He bit his lip. "Sorry. That just slipped out. Anyhow, I get taken on for all these jobs, for a trial period. I work my ass off, and then at the end, they all say, thanks but no thanks, and I'm outta there." His jaw set. "I guess my face doesn't fit."

"That sucks." Chaz's face was like thunder.

"It is what it is." Kendis sighed resignedly. "I just know that if this goes on, my mom won't stay here. Not if we can't make ends meet." He held out his hand to Del. "But thank you for proving this town isn't completely made up of assholes." Del shook it warmly.

"And about my reaction," Jon piped up. "It was just funny, 'cause Del has a friend who's—"

"A cop. Sure, I met him. Nice guy. And I figured that was what you meant." Kendis gave Jon a polite smile. "'S okay. I didn't take offense." He flicked a glance in Chaz's direction. "Good to meet you."

"Yeah. Likewise."

Kendis gave Del a nod, then walked out of the shop.

"Poor kid. He's got it tough." Del wasn't about to share his suspicions with Jon that Kendis was gay. At that moment his phone pinged, and he peered at the screen.

Shopping done. On my way back to your place.

Del smiled. "Okay, I'm outta here. I'm sure you can cope without me."

Jon rolled his eyes. "We'll get by. Now go home and leave us minions to plan how to start the next season with a bang."

Del laughed, and left them to it.

He had to go deal with a hot cop and a load of groceries. Then he'd deal with any *other* loads the hot cop might have for him.

⚬ ⚬ ⚬

"I could get used to this," Taylor murmured.

Del chuckled, wiping a soapy hand across Taylor's chest. "I'll be honest. When I first saw this house, all I could think of was how good a hot bath would feel at the end of a long day. I certainly wasn't thinking about this." His head was supported by a rolled towel, and Taylor's head rested against his shoulder. There was plenty of room for the two of them, especially when Taylor sat with his back to Del.

This was just... bliss.

They'd bought a Christmas tree for Del's place that afternoon, which they decorated together, and Del had talked about every piece that he'd hung from its boughs. So many memories. After Momma had died, he and Jon had shared the Christmas decorations between them, and there were bits and pieces that he'd bought over the years.

Guess it's time to make new memories. Del smiled to himself. They needed to buy a new ornament for the tree, something that was just *them*.

"Knew there was something I meant to tell you," Taylor said, covering Del's hand with his own. "I finally met up with Jake."

"Great. How did it go?"

He sighed. "I made my peace. I apologized for messing up. I guess we're okay again."

Del was glad. Life was too short to be falling out with friends. "Good. You need all the friends you can get in this life. You gonna go back to meeting up for bowling and coffee?"

"Not right now. I think he has his hands full." He fell silent for a moment, and Del wasn't sure if he was still awake. "You ever fucked in a tub before?" Taylor asked suddenly.

That pushed aside any more thoughts of Christmas trees or friends. "Once or twice."

Taylor sat up and carefully swiveled on his ass to face Del. "Really? And how did you do it?"

Del snickered. "Carefully. You get overexcited and you're liable to cause a tidal wave." He cocked his head to one side. "Why'd you ask?"

"Oh, I was just thinkin'."

Fuck. That got Del thinking too. He pointed to the far end of the tub. "Sit there, on the edge."

Taylor grinned. He stood up, walked to the end and turned, sat down, leaned back on his hands—and spread his legs wide. "What—like this?"

Del laughed quietly as he moved into position. "Boy, do you have a perpetual boner or something? I swear, you're always hard."

"Can you blame me? I mean, look what's in front of me." Taylor pulled on his erect shaft. "I just close my eyes and picture you, that fur on your chest, that gray beard, those eyes, that firm belly… and that amazing cock—and I could drill through fucking concrete with this dick."

"You missed something."

"What?"

"My mouth," Del whispered as he bent over to slide his lips down Taylor's luscious cock. The tremor that rippled through Taylor's body was immensely gratifying, as was the way Taylor lifted his ass up, rising to meet Del's mouth as he swallowed Taylor's dick to the root.

"Oh fuck," Taylor said weakly.

"That's what we're doing," Del said as he took a breath.

"No, I mean, oh fuck, I can hear someone in your house."

Del chuckled. "All houses make noises." Then he paused and listened.

Fuck. There was someone in his house.

Del lurched out of the tub, just as the door opened, and—

"Oh my fucking God, where's the eye bleach when you need it?"

Del got a fleeting glance of Jon's wide-eyed stare and open mouth, before the door swung shut. *What the fuck?* He reached for a towel. "Better get out of there," he told Taylor. "I'll go deal with our Peeping Tom."

He wrapped a towel around his hips, secured it, and left the bathroom. Jon was sitting on the edge of the bed, his head in his hands.

Del walked up to him and stood in front of him, his hands on his hips. "That's it. I want my key back."

Without even raising his head, Jon fumbled in his jacket pocket and held out the key. "Take it, take it."

Del grabbed it and tossed it onto the bed. "Okay. How about you tell me what you're doing here? They have these wonderful things called phones nowadays. They're great for lots of things, like, oh, I don't know—*calling* people before you come barging into their house."

"I just wanted to talk to you about what you said earlier," Jon protested. "I wanted to know what changed your mind." He shuddered. "I guess I know now." He raised his head as Taylor came into the bedroom, wearing only a towel. "Hey. I'm guessing this wasn't an official call."

Del sighed. "Well, I *was* gonna tell you, just... not like this." He gestured to Taylor to approach, then put his arm around Taylor's waist. "Jon, meet my partner, Taylor."

Jon gaped. "Your... Shit, for real?"

Del smiled. "As real as it gets."

Jon's face lit up. "Aw, that's great!" He launched himself to his feet, stuck out his hand, then withdrew it quickly. "Hey, can we do this when you guys have got some clothes on?"

Del laughed. "Are you sure you're my brother?" He waved his hand toward the living area. "Go pour us a glass of wine, or whatever you wanna drink. We'll join you when we're dressed."

Jon gave him the thumbs up, and left the room in a hurry.

Taylor put his hand to his chest. "My heartbeat is nearly back to normal. And can I just say? Your brother's timing sucks—pun intended. I was enjoying that."

"We could always finish what we started," Del said, licking his lips.

"And you could wait until I'm gone, how's *that* for a better idea?" Jon shouted from the other side of the door. "*Jesus*, guys...."

Del looked at Taylor, and they both burst into laughter. Del kissed him on the mouth. "Later. Let's go introduce my brother to the man who stole my heart."

Taylor gazed at him with what looked like awe. "You are amazing. One minute, you're smackin' your lips, thinking about suckin' me off, and the next, the sweetest words are coming out of that same mouth."

"I like to keep you on your toes," Del said with a wink. "And you did, you know."

"Did what?"

"Steal my heart."

Taylor smiled. "Don't worry. I'm gonna take real good care of it."

Del didn't doubt that for a second.

Chapter Twenty-Nine

Monday, December 10

As he stepped through the door of the police department, what was foremost in Taylor's mind was not his upcoming conversation, but the last forty-eight hours, spent in Del's company.

I could get used to that.

The highlight had to be buying a Christmas tree and decorating it. Although he loved the idea, Taylor's initial reaction to Del's request to accompany him on his shopping trip to locate one, had been to refuse. Who knew whose eyes would be on them? Then he'd reasoned that once Monday had come and gone, there would be no need to hide any longer, and was one shopping trip really gonna matter in the vast scheme of things? When Del had given him a quizzical glance, Taylor finally made up his mind.

Fuck it.

They'd intended on spending an hour at the Medical Center, but Momma had had other ideas. In spite of her concerns about the age difference, she'd done as Taylor asked and made an effort to get to know Del. That translated as having a ton of questions for him, which he answered with good grace. Taylor reckoned Del had gotten himself a new fan, especially when she learned about his work with several charities in San Francisco. The images on his phone of Del, posing with the Sisters of Perpetual Indulgence, had caused her eyebrows to virtually disappear into her hairline.

It had given Taylor an insight into Del too. He'd always known instinctively that Del was a good man. It was good to have his instincts proved correct.

Saturday evening had been memorable, for all the wrong reasons. He guessed Jon wouldn't arrive unannounced in the future. Man, he wanted to forget that moment.

"Mornin'," Dale greeted him from across the squad room. "How's your momma? I heard you took Saturday off 'cause she's in the hospital." He gestured to the coffee machine. "Want one?"

"Please." Taylor glanced around the room. Lieutenant Purdy was in deep conversation with Brian, Ethan was already pounding away at his keyboard, and Mark was leaning back on his chair, a cup in his hand, laughing and joking with Terry.

Business as usual, only it didn't feel that way for some reason.

I'm just nervous, is all.

It wasn't as if he was going to stand in the middle of the squad room and make a declaration, for Christ's sake. Nothing that melodramatic.

Taylor walked over to Dale and waited as he filled two paper cups with coffee. "The chief in yet?" Taylor had left a voicemail message with the chief's secretary.

"He's in a meeting with the Campbell County prosecuting attorney. Shouldn't be long now. They had an early start." He grinned. "What the chief refers to as a power breakfast." He handed Taylor a cup. "How's your momma?"

"She's got pneumonia, and they're keeping her in till everything is stable. But she's getting back to her usual self. I pity the poor nurses." He took a sip of coffee. "I know we're out on patrol later, but I'm hoping to see the chief ASAP."

Dale stilled. "I see." He cast a glance around the room before continuing. "You sure?"

Taylor nodded. "I figure it's about time he knows," he said in a low voice. "And it's not like word isn't gonna get around, right? 'S only a matter of time."

Dale regarded him steadily. "You've made up your mind, I see. Well, you're a good man. This don't change nothin', not to my mind." He glanced in Mark's direction. "Can't speak for others, of course. But it would be better for some folks if they kept their thoughts to themselves."

"Taylor?"

He straightened and turned. The chief stood in the doorway, beckoning. "Bring your coffee."

Taylor was aware of Dale's reassuring pat on his back as he walked over to the chief, cup in hand. Chief Tillerson led him into his office and closed the door. He gestured to the chair facing his desk.

"Got a message that you wanted to see me. Now you know, leave a message like that, and I get to thinking there's a problem somewhere." He sat in his high-backed chair, his elbows on the arms, fingers laced. "So suppose you tell me what the problem is."

"'S not exactly a problem, although... I guess... it could be." Now that he was there, Taylor wanted to puke.

The chief arched his eyebrows. "How about you take a drink of coffee, then start at the beginning."

Taylor did as instructed. "Sir, remember at your party, remarks were made about Del Walters—from Rainbow Racers— being gay?"

The chief grimaced. "Don't remind me. That was my fool of a brother-in-law, Cal."

Taylor shifted in his seat. "Well, sir, the rumors are true. Del is gay. And... the reason I know this is because... I'm... in a relationship with him." His heart hammered.

Chief Tillerson blinked. Blinked again. Then he narrowed his gaze. "Does my daughter know? About you, I mean."

In spite of his anxiety, Taylor liked that the chief's first concerns had been for Denise. "Yes, sir. Don't you worry. This isn't gonna break her heart, I can assure you of that."

The chief's face fell. "I gotta tell ya, I'm disappointed. Not that you're... *you* know... but because I'd gotten used to the idea that you and she might... tie the knot one day. That you might end up as family."

Taylor sighed. "I'd have liked that too, sir. But…" When the idea struck him, he couldn't hold it in. "Sir, you could bring home a *line* of guys for supper, and I don't think any of 'em would make an impression on her."

Chief Tillerson became very still. "Are you telling me my daughter is a…lesbian? Not that that would be wrong, y'understand," he added quickly. "It's just that my ticker can only take so many surprises in one day."

Taylor smiled. "No, sir. She's not a lesbian. She just doesn't want a husband right now. She wants… other things."

The chief leaned forward, his clasped hands on the desk. "Hell, you've gotten this far, you might as well tell me. What does my Denise want, that *you* know about and *I* don't?"

Aw fuck. Taylor took a deep breath. "She wants to study," he said softly. "That's what she's always wanted."

The chief regarded him with a pained expression. "Oh my. She did tell me. And I wasn't listening. I was too busy thinking of myself." He cleared his throat. "I can see some long conversations in my future. God, it would've been easier if she'd just been a lesbian." Taylor blinked at that, but the chief plowed ahead. "Right now, let's talk about you." The chief speared him with an intense look. "What you've told me about your… relationship doesn't have to go any further. But to be honest, I'm not completely sure why you're telling me in the first place. This is none of my business." He frowned. "You're not doing this to… unburden yourself, are ya? Because that's what therapists are for."

Taylor shook his head. "I'm telling you because… I'm not hiding anymore. And that bein' the case, you're about to gain… an openly gay police officer." His heart quaked just saying the words, but he knew it was the right thing to do.

The chief said nothing for a moment. Then he narrowed his gaze. "You're not exactly the first gay cop in Tennessee, y'know."

"I know, sir. I worked with a gay officer in Nashville. It was partly seeing how he was received by his fellow officers that gave me the courage to take this step. And seeing the impact he had within the community."

The chief leaned back, stroking his chin. "Really."

Taylor was thankful for the conversation with Del where they'd discussed what tack he was to take with the chief. 'Police chiefs are basically politicians,' Del had reminded him. 'They'll do anything to look good.'

"First and foremost, sir, I believe it's the best policy to be honest with people. After all, everyone's gonna know eventually, especially in a town this size."

"And that includes your fellow officers," the chief remarked. "The people who work with you. Not that they should have any issues working with you. You've saved their asses enough times in the past." He snickered. "If you'll excuse the pun."

Taylor bit back his chuckle. "Sir, I'm hoping that once they see my sexuality isn't a problem for those in authority here, they just won't think about it. After all, what they want is to work with an officer who cares about the job, someone who'll have their backs in a crisis, someone they can turn to… and who just happens to be gay." Then Taylor played his pair of Aces. "Of course, in these days of diversity, it'll look good for *you*, having an openly gay officer in your department. Not to mention having an officer to liaise with the LGBT community here in LaFollette."

Another blink. "We have an LGBT community?" He snickered. "I'm jokin'."

Taylor wasn't so sure. "I'm not the only gay cop in the state, sir, but I am *definitely* not the only gay guy in LaFollette. If those in the LGBT community choose to keep their heads down, then what does that say about our town? And is that what you *want* said about our town?" *And God bless Del for coming up with all this.*

The chief leaned forward again, elbows on the desk, his fingers steepled. "You've obviously considered this carefully. And although you make a lot of good points, I think the main one that mustn't be overlooked is that by… coming out, you're giving yourself the possibility to be happy. To be yourself. I think you're right to focus on that." He coughed. "Did you want to say something in the squad room?"

Taylor shook his head. "I think I'll just deal with the questions as they arise. As long as I have your backing...."

The chief's gaze intensified. "We already take a dim view of those officers who use hateful language. You can bet we'll be even tougher if that language is aimed at one of our own." He came out from behind the desk and patted Taylor on the back. "Don't you worry none. We've got your back."

Taylor thanked him. As he got to the door, he turned. "I'll look forward to introducing you to Del next summer." When the chief appeared puzzled by this, Taylor grinned. "At the annual summer police department BBQ. We all get to bring our significant others and our families, right? Well, I'll be bringing Del." And with that, he left the chief's office.

He walked back to the squad room, chuckling to himself. *Del is gonna cause quite a stir.*

Del pulled his truck into the driveway and smiled. Taylor's car was already there, Taylor behind the wheel, asleep. Del couldn't resist. He gave a short blast on the horn, and Taylor jumped. He glared at Del as he approached.

"I just closed my eyes for a moment." He got out of the car.

Del chuckled. "Sorry. Why didn't you go inside?"

Taylor arched his eyebrows. "How? By breaking in? There are laws against that, y'know."

Del rolled his eyes. "The back door is open. I always leave it open."

Taylor shook his head. "Uh-uh. I locked it this morning before we left. You can't go around leaving doors unlocked." He wagged a finger. "You and I need to have a conversation about basic security."

Del stepped past him, opened the front door and switched on the lights. "If you're gonna be a bossy boyfriend, we may have to call it quits now."

Taylor followed him in, closed the door, walked up to him, locked his arms around Del's neck, and pulled him into a kiss. In an instant, Del was holding him, fully invested in the kiss.

"Maybe it's time to give you a key," he murmured against Taylor's lips.

"Mm-hmm." Taylor didn't pause for an instant.

"I mean, I got Jon's key, right?"

Taylor's soft moan of approval had Del diving back in for more, stifling his own groans when Taylor kissed his neck. "Aw fuck, yeah." On impulse, he hoisted Taylor into his arms and carried him toward the bedroom.

"What you got in mind?" Taylor wrapped his legs around Del's hips and held on tight.

"You, me, in a bed. For as long as we want."

Taylor buried his face in Del's neck. "Shower first, fuck later."

Del paused. "Fuck in shower, then in bed."

"Good enough."

Talking would come later, when they were sated and cozy, limbs entwined beneath the covers.

It was good to have routines.

Epilogue

Monday, December 24 - Christmas Eve

Del shoved the bread rolls into the top oven, then checked on the roast. Ruth had come over that afternoon to talk him through it, and it smelled amazing. The vegetables were ready in a warming dish, and the potatoes made his mouth water, a wonderful blend of garlic and rosemary.

Then he took a last glance at the living area, the lights on the tree twinkling, some gifts already heaped under it. He'd lit a couple of candles on the coffee table, and they'd given the room a romantic feel.

Now all I need is one sexy cop, and I'm done.

He hurried into the bedroom where he stripped off and dove into the shower. Taylor wouldn't be long, and Del couldn't wait to hear his news. He stood under the jets, letting the hot water soak away his aches.

If this is how forty-seven feels, I'm dreading fifty.

His birthday three days previously had been a source of amusement for Taylor, who'd joked that for a whole week, Del got to be the *even older* man. The gap would close up again between Christmas and New Year's, and Del meant to get in a lot of teasing, about how Taylor was almost thirty, and how ancient that was.

What he loved most was that Taylor didn't give a shit about the age difference. He hadn't since the day they met. Ruth was still on the fence about that, but Del was gonna wear her down. Like Taylor said, it didn't matter if she thought it weird. She wasn't the one living with Del.

And that was another thing Del loved, how Taylor just rolled with things. It didn't matter that they'd only known each other two months. When Del asked him to move in, Taylor hadn't hesitated. He hadn't balked at the idea that Del loved him after knowing him for only five or six weeks, just liked he'd accepted that he loved Del.

He's fucking perfect for me.

If there was one thing Del had needed to adjust to, it was Taylor's… appetite. Because the wind could simply change direction, and that boy was horny.

But hell, keeping up with him was a whole lotta fun.

"Ooh, nice."

Del turned to find Taylor standing in the bathroom doorway, leaning against the frame as he slowly disrobed, leaving his uniform in a heap on the tiled floor.

Del laughed. "Uh-uh. You are *not* getting in here. I wanted a quick shower before you showed up. Dinner's almost ready."

"I can do quick," Taylor said with a gleam in his eye as he unfastened his pants and slowly pushed them down to the floor. He straightened after removing them, and his cock sprang up, ready for action as always, looking so goddamn gorgeous that Del wavered in his resolve for a moment. Taylor grinned. "Yeah. I can see how you're dying to get out of here." He walked slowly toward the shower cubicle, pulling on his thick dick. "Got room for me in there?"

"Nope. Uh-uh. No way." Except Del knew he'd already lost.

Taylor opened the door, stepped into the steamy enclosure, closed the door, then leaned in to kiss Del with such focus that it made Del forget for a moment about dinner.

"Welcome home," he murmured, before taking Taylor's mouth in a far from gentle kiss. He caught his breath when Taylor wrapped his fingers around Del's shaft and gave it a good tug.

"Did you mention dinner? I'm starving." And before Del could respond, Taylor squatted down in front of him and engulfed his cock in wet heat, his head bobbing enthusiastically as he sucked him deep.

Like Del could stand still for that.

He grabbed Taylor's head and held it steady while he fucked that wonderful mouth, sliding in and out, picking up speed. "Play with yourself," he ground out, "because if you don't come when I do, you'll have to wait until later."

Taylor moaned around his dick, his hand stroking his own cock, getting faster and faster, keeping pace with Del's thrusts. Del shuddered as he shot his load down Taylor's throat. "Well... you said... you were hungry..."

Taylor's throat worked as he swallowed, and Del put his hand there to feel it. Then Taylor rolled his eyes heavenward, and Del's feet and lower legs were covered in spunk.

When he was done, Del made Taylor suck on his dick to get every last drop, then hauled him up by his pits and kissed him, sharing the taste. From the kitchen came a loud ping, and Del grinned. "And there's your entree." He spun Taylor around, and landed a satisfying smack on his ass, that made it jiggle.

"I wanted a shower too," Taylor protested, but Del knew better.

"You wanted to poke the bear. Well, you got what you came for. So now you get to put out dinner, and I get to wash your come off me."

Taylor reluctantly got out of the shower, but Del wasn't fooled. By the time he reached the bathroom door, that ass was already wiggling.

Later, Del told himself. He had plans for that ass, which included a newly acquired, soft fur rug, a heap of pillows, and a room lit only by the lights from the Christmas tree.

"That was delicious," Taylor said with a sigh, pushing away his plate.

"You can thank your mom. She helped."

He raised his eyebrows. "Cool." He reached for his wine glass and took another mouthful of Merlot. He was as full as tick on a hound dog, and the dinner had been the cherry of top of a very satisfying day. "How did the Community Business Owners meeting go?"

"Not bad. We've only lost two members since word got out. And if they don't want to associate with a gay guy, that's their choice. We certainly won't miss 'em."

"I am so proud of you," Taylor said in a low voice. "The way you're pulling all these people together…"

"Never mind me—I'm waiting to hear about *your* day." Del leaned back, his arms folded. "You can't say I haven't been patient. The number of times I wanted to call you today, to find out how things were going…"

Taylor let out a contented sigh. "He's gone."

Del threw his crimson napkin into the air with a whoop. "Hallelujah! Did he go quietly?"

Taylor snorted. "Hell no." The day had been the culmination of two weeks of verbal abuse and snarky comments, but thank God, it was over.

"So tell me. What happened?"

"I had no idea anything was going down. The first I knew of it was when word got around that Mark was transferring to another precinct."

"About fucking time, bye Felicia, and don't bother to write a postcard," Del said with a growl.

Taylor reached across the table and covered Del's hand with his own. "Have I told you how awesome you've been these last two weeks?"

"Was that when I threatened to smash Mark Teagle into a pulp? Or when I wanted to hang him up by his balls?"

Taylor curled his fingers around Del's. "It was when you told me this wouldn't last, that we'd get through it, and every goddamn night you held me while I tried to sleep." He'd relied on Del so much, and Del had been there for him, his own personal bear-shaped rock.

"Love you," Del said softly. "We knew it wouldn't be plain sailing, right? Because since you came out and word got around, we've got assholes crawling out of the woodwork, just dyin' to make their views known."

There had been a few people who'd decided to share their views on social media, and Taylor had taken to avoiding certain platforms. It was bad enough that he knew they were out there—he didn't need to read their garbage too.

"Now, are you gonna tell me what happened, or do I have to spank it out of you?"

Taylor chuckled. "Like that would be a hardship—for either of us. Anyhow, I got the whole story from Dale at the end of my shift. Seems like the chief hauled Mark over the coals again, only this time he told him he had two choices. Either they were gonna bring him before a tribunal for all the shit-stirring he'd been doing, or… he got a transfer. The thing is, the chief didn't want a tribunal, 'cause that made it look like he couldn't control his department, not after all the warnings Mark had received. What he really wanted was Mark outta there. Only, Mark didn't wanna go."

"Of course not," Del mused. "And he'd know the chief didn't wanna proceed."

"The way Dale tells it, he asked the chief for five minutes with Mark—alone."

Del widened his eyes. "Oh really."

Taylor nodded. "Dale took Mark into an interview room, told him to put in for a transfer—or Dale would make sure the chief got to see certain evidence reports about locally acquired spray paint."

Del's jaw dropped. "He *blackmailed* him?"

"Yup. Although at first Mark was trying to bluff it out, but Dale out bluffed him. Something about finding the paper Mark had printed those anonymous letters on, in Mark's locker. He must've been close to the mark—pun intended—because when Dale was done, Mark went into the chief's office and put in for a transfer."

Del let out a long breath. "Well, thank God for that. Which

precinct gets his delightful company?"

Taylor bit back a smile. "Nashville."

Del stared at him for a moment, then guffawed. "There *is* justice after all."

"Yup. I see a lot of re-education in his future. Which is apparently what the Nashville chief of police said when they agreed to take him, according to Dale." He finished his wine. "And that's not all. Mrs. Tillerson and Denise came by this morning, delivering bottles of wine and little gifts to everyone. Denise and I had a chat." Taylor beamed. "Her parents have been talking about her going back to school in the fall. She's so excited. I don't think she stopped smiling the whole time she was there."

"Sounds like you said the right thing to the chief, then."

It seemed to Taylor that he must've said the right thing to Dale too. That afternoon, Dale had taken Taylor aside and told him that they were having a visitor for New Year's. That was all he'd needed to say for Taylor to have a smile on his face the rest of his shift.

He sighed. "I don't think there's any way to top today."

"Oh, I think I can manage that." Del leaned in close. "Your momma isn't coming here this evening. She's gonna join us tomorrow instead, when Jon and Chaz come here. So tonight, it's just you and me."

"So, what are we gonna do? Discuss plans to bring in more business next year? Develop strategies to put Rainbow Racers on the map?" Taylor was enjoying himself. Poking the bear was a whole heap of fun, and it usually came to a sticky end.

Del's eyes gleamed. "Tempting as those might be, I have a few suggestions of my own." He got up and slowly walked around to stand behind Taylor's chair, his hands on Taylor's shoulders as he bent down to nuzzle Taylor's neck.

A familiar shiver trickled down Taylor's spine, and he fought to keep his voice even. "Such as?" Taylor had a pretty good idea he knew what they were, and that nakedness and lube would be in there somewhere.

Strong arms encircled him, and Del's breath tickled his ear. "Figuring out how to show you all the ways I love you, but I'm not sure we have enough time for that."

And that moment right there was when Taylor melted into his arms.

"We got time, honey. Lots of time."

The End

A message from KC

Thank you for purchasing this book, and I hope you enjoyed it. As soon as I'd created the character of Taylor Cox in Truth & Betrayal, I knew I wanted to tell his story.

All I needed was a bear.

Enter Del Walters, who really does remind me of Kristofer Weston, on the cover. I am very grateful to him that he agreed to do this.

I've already been asked if there are any more Southern Boys stories to come. One more, I think. Chaz will be in there. So will Kendis. And a third familiar character, who is discovering all kinds of things about himself...

As always, I ask you to consider leaving a review on Amazon / BookBub. Your reviews help keep books visible, and it doesn't matter whether you write a couple of lines, or an essay. All I ask is that you're honest.

Thanks again. See you in the next book!

KCWell

TITLES by K.C. Wells
Learning to Love
Michael & Sean
Evan & Daniel
Josh & Chris
Final Exam

Sensual Bonds
A Bond of Three
Le lien des Trois
A Bond of Truth

Merrychurch Mysteries
Truth will Out
Au nom de la verite

Love, Unexpected
Debt
Dette
Il Debito
Schuld
Burden

Dreamspun Desires
The Senator's Secret
Le secret du Senateur
Der Verlobte des Senators
Out of the Shadows
My Fair Brady

Love Lessons Learned
First
Prime Volte
Waiting for You
Step by Step

Pas à Pas
Schritt für Schritt
Un passo alla volta
Bromantically Yours
BFF
BFF Best Friends Forever (Italian Version)
Gerstern, Jetzt und Auf Ewig

Collars & Cuffs
An Unlocked Heart
Trusting Thomas
Someone to Keep Me
(K.C. Wells & Parker Williams)
A Dance with Domination
Damian's Discipline
(K.C. Wells & Parker Williams)
Make Me Soar
Dom of Ages
(K.C. Wells & Parker Williams)
Endings and Beginnings
(K.C. Wells & Parker Williams)

Un Coeur Déverrouillé
Croire en Thomas
Te Protéger
Valse

Herz Ohne Fesseln
Vertauen in Thomas

Secrets – with Parker Williams
Before You Break
An Unlocked Mind
Threepeat

Avant que tu te brises

Personal
Making it Personal
Personal Changes
More than Personal
Personal Secrets
Strictly Personal
Personal Challenges

Une Affaire Personnelle
Changements Personnels
Plus Personnel
Secrets Personnels
Strictement Personnel
Defis Personnels

Una Questione Personale
Cambiamenti Personali
Piú che personale
Segreti Personali
Strettamente personale
Sfide personali

Es wird persönlich
Persönliche Veränderungen
Mehr als Persönliche
Persönliche Geheimnisse
Streng Persönlich
Persönliche Herausforderungen

Confetti, Cake & Confessions
Confetti, Coriandoli e Confessioni

Connections
Connexion

Saving Jason
Per Salvare Jason
Jasons Befreiung
A Christmas Promise
The Law of Miracles

Island Tales
Waiting for a Prince
September's Tide
Submitting to the Darkness

Le Maree di Settembre
In Attesa di un Principe
Piegarsi alle tenebre

Lightning Tales
Teach Me
Trust Me
See Me
Love Me

Unverhoffte Liebesgeschichten
Lehre Mich
Vertrau Mir
Sieh Mich
Liebe Mich

Il Professore
Fidati di me

A Material World
Lace
Satin
Silk
Denim

Spitze
Satin
Seide
Jeans

Pizzo
Satin
Seta

Double or Nothing
Back from the Edge
Switching it up
Scambio di ruoli

Anthologies

Fifty Gays of Shade
Winning Will's Heart

About the author

K.C. Wells started writing in 2012, although the idea of writing a novel had been in her head since she was a child. But after reading that first gay romance in 2009, she was hooked.
She now writes full time, and the line of men in her head, clamouring to tell their story, is getting longer and longer. If the frequent visits by plot bunnies are anything to go by, that's not about to change anytime soon.

If you want to follow her exploits, you can sign up for her monthly newsletter: http://eepurl.com/cNKHlT

You can stalk – er, find – her in the following places:
Facebook: **https://www.facebook.com/KCWellsWorld**

https://www.facebook.com/kcwells.WildWickedWonderful/
Goodreads:
https://www.goodreads.com/author/show/6576876.K_C_Wells
Instagram: **https://www.instagram.com/k.c.wells/**
Twitter: **https://twitter.com/K_C_Wells**
Blog: **http://kcwellsworld.blogspot.co.uk/**
Website: **http://www.kcwellsworld.com/**

Alter Egos

Writing gay erotica as Tantalus

For those who like their stories intensely erotic, featuring hot men and even hotter sex....
Who don't mind breaking the odd taboo now and again....
Who want to read something that adds a little heat to their fantasies....
...there's Tantalus.
Because we all need a little tantalizing.
Tantalus is the hotter, more risqué alter ego of K.C. Wells
Amazon page:
https://www.amazon.com/Tantalus/e/B01IN33IZO

Playing with Fire (Damon & Pete)
A series of (so far) five short gay erotic stories:
Summer Heat
After
Consequences
Limits
Fractures

Pete's Treat

(Hopefully) coming in 2020, the first Tantalus novel in a new series, Leather & Kink

Learning the Notes

Steven Torland is about to reach his fiftieth birthday, and to
celebrate the occasion, his publicist decides it's time someone wrote
a biography of the famous composer and musician. When writer
Kyle Mann is approached with the idea, he's flattered and leaps at
the chance. It will be his first biography. The idea of spending six
months getting to know Steven and researching his history excites
him, but there is the added frisson that Steven is sexy as hell. Kyle
has always had a thing for older men, and it's no secret that Steven is
gay. In his heart Kyle knows it's just a fantasy, but he can still
dream, right?

It doesn't take Steven long to realize he wants Kyle in his bed, and
Steven usually gets what he wants. But Kyle proves to be more than
a convenient fuck. There's something about him that leads Steven to
think maybe it's time to let Kyle see the real Steven Torland, the one
who is no stranger to the leather community of San Francisco.
Steven aims to take things nice and slow, because he doesn't want
this one to get away. He wants it all – a lover in his life and a boy in
his bed – and he wants to see just how far he can push Kyle, and
what Kyle is prepared to do to please him.
Kyle has no idea how much his life is about to change....

Writing MF romance as Kathryn Greenway

Kathryn Greenway lives on the Isle of Wight, off the southern coast
of the UK, in a typical English village where there are few secrets,
and everyone knows everyone else.

She writes romance in different genres, and under different pen
names, but her goal is always the same - to reach that Happily Ever
After.

Pulled by a Dream is Kathryn's debut novel, although in a whole
other life, she is K.C. Wells, a bestselling author of gay romance.

26295131R00151

Printed in Great Britain
by Amazon